Also available in the STORM series:

STORM: The Infinity Code

STORM: The Ghost Machine

STORM
The Black Sphere

by E. L. Young

DIAL BOOKS FOR YOUNG READERS

DIAL BOOKS FOR YOUNG READERS
A division of Penguin Young Readers Group
Published by The Penguin Group • Penguin Group (USA) Inc., 375 Hudson Street, New York, NY 10014, U.S.A. • Penguin Group (Canada), 90 Eglinton Avenue East, Suite 700, Toronto, Ontario, Canada M4P 2Y3 (a division of Pearson Penguin Canada Inc.) • Penguin Books Ltd, 80 Strand, London WC2R 0RL, England • Penguin Ireland, 25 St. Stephen's Green, Dublin 2, Ireland (a division of Penguin Books Ltd) • Penguin Group (Australia), 250 Camberwell Road, Camberwell, Victoria 3124, Australia (a division of Pearson Australia Group Pty Ltd) Penguin Books India Pvt Ltd, 11 Community Centre, Panchsheel Park, New Delhi - 110 017, India • Penguin Group (NZ), 67 Apollo Drive, Rosedale, North Shore 0632, New Zealand (a division of Pearson New Zealand Ltd) • Penguin Books (South Africa) (Pty) Ltd, 24 Sturdee Avenue, Rosebank, Johannesburg 2196, South Africa • Penguin Books Ltd, Registered Offices: 80 Strand, London WC2R 0RL, England

First published in the United States 2009
by Dial Books for Young Readers

Published in Great Britain 2008
by Macmillan Children's Books

Text copyright © 2008 by Emma Young
Pictures copyright © 2008 by Spencer Wilson

Printed in the U.S.A.
10 9 8 7 6 5 4 3 2 1

Library of Congress Cataloging-in-Publication Data
Young, E. L.
STORM : the Black Sphere / by E.L. Young.
p. cm.
Summary: The teenaged geniuses of STORM, a secret organization dedicated to eliminating the world's misery through science and technology, head to the Swiss Alps seeking the last of six scientists whose Project FIREball is of interest to MI6, the CIA, and an unknown assasin.
ISBN 978-0-8037-3268-1
[1. Secret societies—Fiction. 2. Scientists—Fiction. 3.Inventors—Fiction. 4. Spies—Fiction. 5. Adventure and adventurers—Fiction. 6. Alps, Swiss (Switzerland)—Fiction. 7. Switzerland—Fiction.] I. Title. II. Title: Black Sphere.
PZ7.Y8547Sqb 2009
[Fic]—dc22
2008023923

For James

Prologue

David Wickett thought his blown-out tire was bad luck.

He was late. And now he had to jack up the car and replace the damaged wheel. No one stopped to offer help. He was high in the Alps. Tourists in sports coupes were zigzagging around the spectacular corners, grinning in their expensive sunglasses. From here, he had a postcard view across a deep valley dotted with wildflowers.

But Wickett's mind wasn't on the view. It wasn't even on the tire. Hanging on a titanium chain around his neck was a locket-shaped miniature hard drive. On that locket was a document so secret and so important, he'd been forced to spend the past eight months in almost total isolation while he'd worked on it.

It had been the same for the others. There were six of them. Scientists from four different countries. All at the top of their field. All working on the same "impossible" problem.

And now Wickett had *succeeded*. Even beyond his own hopes.

Those pension-minded establishment types who had claimed it was inconceivable—they'd be the ones with egg on their faces.

About as likely to happen as an invasion by synchronized-swimming aliens, one French expert had quipped, to great merriment at an international conference.

Wickett's cheeks had burned. *Bring on the little green men,* he thought now.

Wickett had called the urgent meeting for one o'clock. "Assembly Point Zebra," he had whispered down the secure line to his colleagues, his pulse rushing.

At last, Wickett threw the jack into the trunk and leaped back into the driver's seat. Sweat dripped down his neck. His hands shaking, he pushed the gearshift into drive and shot forward. The road snaked violently. Wickett slung the car around the dangerous bends, his foot jerking between the accelerator and the brake.

Through the next village, he said to himself as he recalled the map. *Right at the church, up the mountain . . . Breathe. Breathe!*

And there it was.

At least, there were the fir trees that partially concealed it. Wickett recognized their outline from the photograph in his security dossier. The disused farmhouse. Assembly Point Zebra.

Wickett urged the car up to the top of the steep mountain road, the engine straining. He crawled to a halt. Cautiously, he stepped onto the dry grass and scanned the scene. He was late, but he still had to observe protocol.

Make sure no one sees you together. If you meet, no one must be watching.

Through the drooping branches of the firs, Wickett could just make out the whitewashed wall and the lopsided door of the farmhouse. To the east, two red cars were parked in a field. Pike's and Khan's. A black motorcycle. It belonged to Gide. A bicycle was leaning against the front step. Pope's. Bailey lived near Khan. He must have caught a ride.

Wickett's colleagues were extremely punctual. They insisted on precision in everything. They would be inside, waiting. *Tapping their fingers.*

Wickett ran his eyes over the ragged line of the trees and the rocky mountainside. He could see no one. Protocol had been observed. He could go in. Then his thoughts blanked.

A horrendous noise pummeled his eardrums. *Something* came shooting through the air, slamming into the sapling beside him, splitting the bark. The crack made him jump. At the same instant, a sudden force struck him in the chest, shoving him backward. Wickett thudded down hard on his back, his head banging on the ground. His vision flickered. Orange. Black. He coughed. His lungs felt thick.

Wickett raised his head—and stared.

The farmhouse had been obliterated. All he could see was a mass of dust and broken wood. Splinters were still falling through the sky. He looked up at the sapling. A ragged chunk of split pine—it looked like a piece of *floorboard*—was jutting from the trembling trunk.

Wickett's brain felt like mud.

The farmhouse had *exploded.* Could it really be . . . It had to be . . . An accident? *A bomb.*

But the others! They must have been inside.

Wickett registered motion. A figure.

A man.

He was running from behind the rubble of the farmhouse to the scrubby path that led farther up the mountain. It was

Bailey! Unmistakable curly blond hair gleamed in the sun. Bailey was all right!

Wickett took a deep breath. He was about to call out—when Bailey stopped. He lifted his hand. He was holding a *gun*. Wickett's eyes tracked, following Bailey's aim. He gasped. A circular black object, about the size of a dinner plate, was zinging through the air, right toward Bailey.

Wickett rubbed his head. The fall had jolted him. He was even seeing UFOs.

But what he saw next was even more astonishing.

Two events. They happened simultaneously. Bailey let off a bullet, and at precisely that moment a red beam shot out from the *thing*. It connected with Bailey's chest. Wickett saw blood suddenly rush from Bailey's rib cage. He smelled burning skin. Bailey staggered, his face deathly white. Then he fell. But his bullet had already arrived. The UFO was blasting apart, tiny fragments flying like black confetti.

Bailey wasn't moving. He was lying facedown on the grass.

Wickett staggered up. His car door was still open. He stumbled in.

His arms felt like lead. With a clenched hand, he turned the key and threw the gearshift into reverse. He swung the car in a wild semicircle, slamming his foot down.

At seventy miles per hour, the Nissan jolted down the mountain and onto the main road. It picked up speed. Ninety. One hundred. Wickett didn't dare to look in the rearview mirror. He drove with his eyes fixed and staring dead ahead. Two thoughts searing his stunned mind:

My colleagues are dead. Someone has killed them.

And: *If that tire hadn't blown, I'd be dead too.*

London. 8:22 P.M.

The black cab swerved. Will Knight was thrown against the window. A pedestrian in shorts had stumbled into the road. He held up a hand apologetically.

"Open your eyes, mate!" the cabbie yelled.

But Will smiled. London in summer, and the city was walking on air. People swarmed over the sidewalks with cardboard cups of coffee. Water-swigging tourists brandished cameras out of open-topped buses. Will drank it all in. He'd spent the past three days in rural Oxfordshire, and he'd missed the city.

As the cab swerved onto Seymour Street, Will checked his watch. He was late, but only by ten minutes. He should still have plenty of time. The driver flicked on the radio, and Will glanced again at his backpack.

It was still there, on the seat beside him. *Of course.* But he couldn't help that trace of anxiety. Maybe it was just anticipation, he told himself, knowing what was inside that bag—and what he was about to do. As he turned back to the window, his pocket vibrated. A text.

Where r u? r u here?

Will could hear Gaia's impatience. In his mind he could see her. Bright brown eyes flashing.

He texted back: *In cab. Nearly there.*

As the taxi crossed Tottenham Court Road, Will's brain tuned in to the voice of the radio presenter.

"And now we're about to go to Jenny Lake, who is at Bushell House, which is playing host today to a conference on computer security—and a very special guest: Walter Dillane, the Vice President of the United States.

"Vice President Dillane is in London for this week's International Energy Summit. He's putting in a brief appearance at the IT conference today to make a speech on global Internet access. However, it's his controversial views on the *environment* that are getting most people talking. In fact, green groups are expected to turn out later today to stage a demonstration in support of Dillane's calls for firm international targets for phasing out fossil fuels like oil and coal."

The cabbie turned the volume down. He glanced back at Will, a gleam in his eye. "So, you're a greenie, are you?" And he nodded at the backpack. "Is that placards you've got in your bag?"

Will swallowed a smile. "Something like that," he said.

A black T-shirt. Jeans. Curly brown hair, pulled back.

Will spotted her from across the road. Gaia was standing under an oak tree near the front steps of Bushell House, hands plunged in her pockets. Will hitched the backpack higher on his shoulder. He made for the tree. "Gaia!"

She turned.

As he reached her, she said, "Finally!"

Her eyes *were* flashing. But it was hard to tell if she was annoyed or pleased. Both, he decided.

It had been a week since they'd seen each other—at one of the regular STORM meetings in Andrew's basement in Bloomsbury, central London. Andrew had dreamed up the "official" Tuesday night update sessions after a particularly eventful Easter in Venice. But they weren't really necessary. Andrew, Will, and Gaia spent most of their time out of school in one another's company anyway. It had been that way since Christmas, since the first STORM mission to St. Petersburg.

Sometimes, though, Will headed out to Oxfordshire, to work at Sutton Hall, the headquarters of STASIS, the Science and Technology Arm of the Secret Intelligence Service, also known as MI6. Shute Barrington, the STASIS director, had become a colleague in Russia. In Venice, Will had saved his life. Every few months, Barrington invited Will to Sutton Hall to help him hone his skills as an inventor. Now Will was back in London to put a few new devices to the test.

"So you've got the kit?" Gaia asked.

"Yeah."

"And Barrington *knows*?"

"Barrington's gone fishing."

Gaia flashed him a look of total disbelief.

"That's what it says on his door."

"Yeah, well, last time he was supposed to be on holiday—"

"I know, but apparently he really is fishing." Will started to dig into his backpack, looking for a blue pencil case. "I hear he's promised to bring back enough salmon to keep STASIS fed for a month."

She raised an eyebrow. "What's he going to do—dredge the rivers?"

"I guess he'll have something more high-tech in mind.

Cloning, maybe." Will smiled. Carefully now, he opened up the pencil case. Inside was an asthma inhaler. At least, it *looked* like an asthma inhaler. Will slipped it into his pocket. Then he pulled a gray canvas bag from the backpack and slung it over his shoulder.

In his pocket he had a map of Bushell House. It was a printout of a page he'd downloaded that morning, showing the layout of the conference center and the entrances and exits. The front doors were marked EXIT ONLY in black, for everyone but Vice President Dillane, Will guessed. Regular delegates were instructed to use a gate at the back. He had to go around the block. It wasn't far.

He held out his backpack to Gaia. "Can you look after this? I'll see you back here." He started to head off.

Gaia called: "Don't you want me to wish you luck?"

Will glanced back. Smiled. "If I need luck, I'm in trouble."

Malet Street, London WC1

The single occupant of the Mercedes Pullman limousine tapped a manicured finger against her phone. She connected to the Internet. In moments, she brought up the website for the *IVth Annual Conference on Information Technology Security.*

Some of the unclassified presentations were being streamed live. Right now, a pale fourteen-year-old boy wearing frameless glasses and a black suit over a black T-shirt bearing the slogan *Soft Wear* was standing at the podium in Hall C, waving his right hand animatedly. With his other hand, he pushed the glasses back up the bridge of his nose.

"And so, I have demonstrated that it is indeed possible to hack into a printer and thereby *steal* documents that have recently been printed. The security implications are of course enormous. Now, I will move on to potential methods for protection."

"Printers . . ." she murmured. "Surprisingly low-tech." She flicked open the cover of the black folder on the seat beside her. The report was on top.

She had found it late the previous night, posted on the website of an Italian girl named Cristina della Corte.

STORM

(Acronym, but I do not know for what). They seem to think they are a secret organization. Based in London.

Will Knight, 14. Inventor of devices. Arrogant but daring. His mother is an astrophysicist. His father was a field officer for MI6, now deceased.

Andrew Minkel, 14, has made millions from software. Funds STORM. Is a computer genius, I think. Though very willing to use underhanded methods. Wears T-shirts with molecules on them. Father is a psychiatrist. Mother's occupation unknown.

Gaia Carella, 14. I do not know her specialty. Languages? She thinks it is explosives. Allegedly, she has a photographic memory. Rebellious and demanding. I know nothing of her family.

December. STORM went to St. Petersburg, where apparently they successfully stopped the testing of a revolutionary new weapon. They met someone called Shute Barrington, allegedly a director of science and technology at SIS, also known as MI6.

April. I invited STORM to Venice, after an intriguing theft at my palace. They did not respond at once. So I went undercover. I found a secret cult. I found "ghosts." We followed the trail to an island. And we prevented an attack that threatened the security of the world . . .

Abigail Pope slipped the report back into the folder.

She turned to the screen of her phone. *Andrew Minkel, 14, has made millions from software,* was still talking about printers.

"Stevens." Her voice was small but commanding. Polished English. Cut-glass. "Could you check in, please? Where are you?"

A rangy man in a dark blue suit touched his ear. He was making his way toward the front steps of Bushell House. His colleague was already outside the front gate, watching the street. Exactly as planned. Into the microphone woven into the lapel of his jacket, he murmured, "We are in position, Ms. Pope."

Will kept his head down. He was itching to run but forced himself to walk.

Attention was the last thing he wanted. The presence of the U.S. vice president meant security cameras would be covering the streets around Bushell House. Automated computer systems and caffeine-enhanced surveillance officers would be checking the live footage, looking out for unusual actions or behavior. Those officers would belong not to MI5, the British home security service, but to the CIA.

In the cafeteria, STASIS HQ, the previous morning, Will had been eating toast and had caught scraps of a conversation between two techies talking in low voices at the table behind him. One of them had mentioned Vice President Dillane's

6

attendance at an international conference on computer security in London. It was the conference Andrew had told him about. Andrew had been invited to speak and was ecstatic.

"The U.S. VP is going, so the CIA are insisting on leading security," the first techie had said. "The Firm is furious."

The Firm. A nickname for Britain's MI5.

"Can you really blame our American friends? After Grosvenor Street."

"Are you telling me the CIA has never made a mistake?"

Will had turned and asked them what was going on. In an irritated whisper, the first techie had explained. "The visit by the U.S. vice president to London—the CIA are going to run the security. Usually, it would be led by Five."

That made sense, Will thought. MI5 handled security and intelligence within the UK. But then the CIA—like MI6—was responsible for threats from foreign countries— which for the CIA, in this case, meant England.

"But Five have made a few stuff-ups recently," the other had put in. "Like when the CIA told them they were going after a wanted man at an address in Grosvenor Street, and someone at Five leaked that intel, and the man got away. So now the Americans are *insisting.* It's not as though we really have any choice. They're taking the lead at the Energy Summit and this computer conference."

That was when Will had hatched his plan. He had new kit to test. Where better than *here*—and *now*?

Keeping his head down, Will edged around a parked bus, which was disgorging a stream of conference delegates.

Security passes dangled on red cords around their necks. He dodged a souvenir stand bristling with Union Jack flags and postcards. And he stopped. His plan had been to get in and to get close to the VP. But what if . . .

A smile crept across his face. Will grabbed a shiny postcard of Big Ben, framed in a border of red, white, and blue. He handed over fifty pence and slipped it into his pocket.

Ahead, Will could make out the black wrought iron gates of the rear entrance. They were standing open. Four British police officers were on guard outside, there to deal with trouble rather than to check security passes, Will guessed. The CIA operatives had to be inside the gates.

To Will's right, a line of chattering delegates had formed against the wall. He slipped behind two men with black shirts and ponytails and pushed a hand into his pocket—double-checking the inhaler was still there. And he remembered what Gaia had said.

The basement, two months ago. She'd run down the steps, holding a journal and talking about an oxytocin nasal spray.

Andrew had looked up from his laptop. "Oxy-what?"

"Oxytocin. It's a chemical. A hormone. It helps mothers bond with their babies. There's been an experiment—if you spray it in people's faces they react."

"If you sprayed anything in *anyone's* face, they'd react."

"No, they become more trusting," Gaia said impatiently. "It looks like oxytocin helps you trust other people. What if we could use this? Maybe not just oxytocin. If there are other hormones or other chemicals—if we could make a spray that would make people believe what we said and do what we wanted?"

"Like a *mind control* spray?" Will said.

"Sort of—but *scientific* mind control."

"I read the other day about a parasite that hijacks the part of a rat's brain that makes it fear cats," Andrew had said. "This parasite lives in a rat but it can only complete its life cycle if the rat that it's living in is eaten by a cat. So the parasite brainwashes its rat into liking the smell of cat urine—so it's more likely to be eaten. If that's possible, maybe you really could brainwash a person."

Gaia had raised an eyebrow. "Where exactly did you read about that?"

"The Proceedings of the National Academy of Sciences, if you really want to know. Are you doubting its accuracy, Gaia?"

Will had discussed the mind-control idea with Barrington, who'd liked the sound of it. The next day, two STASIS techies had been assigned to the job. They'd scoured the scientific literature and tested different combinations of hormones and chemicals, looking for a fast-acting formula that would render someone relaxed and trusting. Six weeks later, it was ready. There was only one problem: How to spray someone so that they didn't notice—and weren't alarmed?

Now as Will inched along the wall toward the black gates, he reached into his pocket and touched his solution. The modified asthma inhaler. Its cartridge contained the formula, but if he pressed the gray button, it didn't spurt chemicals into his mouth. Instead, minute pores in the plastic casing would blast a fine spray in the opposite direction—into the face of anyone standing in front of him. The prototype cartridge contained enough to dose two people.

Barrington had set a deadline for delivery of the device, and Will had gone to Sutton Hall earlier that week partly to make the final modifications. The deadline had passed yesterday. And Barrington was *fishing*. What was Will supposed to do? Wait around for Barrington to come back? Then he'd seen the other device just lying on the lab table, crying out to be tested.

"Come on, ladies and gents. Get your passes ready for inspection."

Will reached the gates. One of the policemen was waving the delegates on. Will stayed close behind the two young men, following them through. Ahead, he could see a courtyard. At the far end, steel and glass doors opened into the modern conference center attached to the back of Bushell House.

Will was separated from that conference center by thirty feet of flagstones and eight bulky men standing by plastic inspection tables, wearing close-fitting black suits. *CIA.*

The ponytailed delegates were at the first desk. The officer scrutinized the photographs on their passes, then ran a wireless scanner across a barcode on the front. Everyone registered for the conference must have been allotted their own code, Will guessed. The CIA officers were verifying that the people turning up were on the official list of attendees— and were who they claimed to be.

Along the courtyard, another officer called out, "Next!"

Will swallowed hard. He felt his heartbeat kick up a notch. As his legs moved, he forced himself to meet the officer's eyes. They were black. Blank. The man was in his mid-twenties. He was blinking in the sunlight.

The officer said, pleasantly enough, "You IT hotshots get younger and younger. May I see your pass?"

For a moment, Will was afraid his hand wouldn't move. Then he pretended to cough, and he pulled the inhaler from his pocket. He put it to his mouth and pressed the button down firmly, then he gasped, pretending to breathe the chemicals hard into his lungs.

As Will lowered the inhaler, he smiled apologetically, his eyes fixed on the officer's face. "Sorry," he said. "Asthma."

"Yeah, I guessed."

The man blinked again. Sudden confusion seemed to flash over his face. Or was it just the sunlight?

"Your pass?" he said.

Will nodded. "Yeah, unfortunately my dad went through in front of me, and he has my pass. He forgot to give it to me. He's just gone in—"

The man frowned. In his mind, Will could hear the voice of Thor, one of the techies assigned to the project. At the last briefing, he'd said: *We've been working on improving the speed of action. Of course, ultimately we'd like an immediate response when sprayed, but in the short term we'll have to settle for something slightly less.*

Exactly how much less, Will wondered now.

"You're telling me your dad has your pass?" the officer said.

"Yeah. Look, it's okay to let me in." Will smiled. Behind him, he could hear the low voices of the delegates still waiting to show their passes. The line had been moving smoothly.

If this man didn't let Will through very soon, surely his colleagues would notice.

"It's all right," Will said in a low voice. "Really. My pass is inside. You can let me through."

For a long moment, the officer didn't respond. Will felt sweat on his palms. Maybe he should try again—

"Ah. Well, I need to see inside your bag."

Will forced himself not to break the man's gaze. "Yeah," he said. "Of course." He slipped the canvas bag from his shoulder and opened it up. The officer peered in.

"Okay, that's fine."

What did he mean, exactly? The bag was fine? *Everything* was fine?

Then the officer looked over to the line at the gates. He called, "Next!"

For a split second, sheer surprise made Will freeze. Of course, this was what he'd hoped for. But now he could hardly believe it! Before the man had a chance to change his mind, Will strode through the courtyard, a grin busting out across his face. Maybe there was a chance that in *ordinary* circumstances, an *ordinary* guard would have bought his story and let him through anyway. But in *these* circumstances? No way. The spray had worked.

Now Will clasped the canvas bag against his body.

Stage one of his plan was down.

Stage two to go.

2

Will headed into the foyer and told himself to stay calm. The spray had performed brilliantly. But he couldn't let himself get carried away.

Against the wall, he noticed a table piled with thick abstracts, summaries of the presentations being made at the conference. Will grabbed one. He held the book against his chest, hoping it would conceal the fact that he didn't have a pass. And he watched the commotion. Ahead was a long, bright corridor. People were hurrying, shouting out, waving papers. Men and women in suits and old sweaters. Neat crew cuts and ragged beards.

Focus, Will told himself.

There were six auditoriums. The map showed him exactly where he needed to be.

Will veered left, on a beeline for Hall A. He stayed close to the wall as he made his way through the crowd, his head down, until he spotted a tall pair of beechwood doors on his right. They were closed. Two men in dark suits were standing guard outside. He wasn't too late. Inside Hall A, Vice President Dillane had to still be making his speech.

Quickly, Will pulled the postcard from his pocket. He glanced around and noticed a gray-haired man in jeans standing a few feet away, writing something in a notebook.

"Excuse me. Could I borrow a pen?"

The man looked up and nodded. "Sure." He pulled one from his pocket and handed it to Will.

So the CIA was insisting on taking control of security for the VP's visit, were they? He scribbled on the back of the postcard: *Hope you're enjoying your trip. Regards, MI5.*

As Will returned the pen, the beechwood doors of Hall A were flung open and people started filing out. Will stayed back, watching. He heard an American voice from inside: "Clear the route, ladies and gentlemen. Please stay back. There is to be no physical contact, unless authorized."

A moment later, three men and a woman in black suits with matching earpieces emerged and started to fan out. They created a buffer zone against the crowd. Into this space walked a tall man with silver hair, a Roman nose, and bushy eyebrows. Will recognized him at once. Walter Dillane.

Behind Dillane were three more officers, busily scanning the corridor. The entourage turned to head toward the atrium, and the main exit.

Now! Will thought. *If you're going to do it, do it now!*

Holding his breath, he pulled the canvas bag from his shoulder and dropped the abstract book inside. Then he felt for the sheath. He pushed his arm into it, right up to the elbow. Will made a fist, bracing his thumb and his knuckles against the end of the rigid tube to stop it from slipping off.

Keeping his back to the wall, Will eased his arm out of the bag and angled it up behind him. Then, with his other hand, which held the postcard, he reached behind his back. He loosened his right fist slightly, so he could take the card and pull it up inside the sheath.

The vice president was walking slowly, smiling at the world in general. Will couldn't wait any longer. He edged behind two CIA officers, to Dillane's left flank. Keeping his upper arm hard against his side, Will suddenly reached out from the elbow. And he stared. *At nothing.*

Where his forearm should be, he saw only the pattern of the carpet. Will got his hand as close to Dillane's jacket pocket as he dared. And he slipped the postcard in! Excitement rushed. He'd done it! But no one had seen him. As far as Dillane's security detail was concerned, no one had touched their man.

The glove had worked.

Barrington had been working on it for six months. It was made from a meta-material—a tough fabric with fibers just a few hundred nanometers across—the wavelengths of visible light. Light striking the tubelike "glove" was pushed around it, so the material itself appeared invisible.

So far, this was all Barrington had made. One glove.

The problem with the meta-material was that, as yet, Barrington hadn't been able to create a flexible version. It had to be rigid. In theory, you could still use the material to become completely invisible, but only if you wore an armorlike setup of invisible components. The glove was the first step.

His heart racing, Will slipped the glove back into its bag. He pulled out the abstract book and held it against his chest as he veered into the corridor. A voice called out.

"Young man!"

Will froze.

Very slowly, he started to turn. The CIA officers were

reassembling in a semicircle behind Walter Dillane. The man's brilliant gray eyes were fixed on Will.

Will couldn't believe it. Dillane *had* noticed. He was about to be arrested, he—

Suddenly, Dillane cracked a toothy smile. He stepped toward Will, extending his hand, and he said: "It's great to see youth here at this conference. Tell me, what's your specialty?"

For a moment, Will blanked. The jovial face of the Vice President of the United States seemed surreal. Still clutching the book to his chest, Will took Dillane's hand. His own hand was damp, he knew, but Dillane didn't seem to notice. Suddenly the shock passed, and Will's brain kicked back in.

"My specialty is secure systems penetration," he said.

Will wiped the sweat from his face. The grin could stay there.

First the inhaler. Then the glove. *Both* had worked.

The VP and his entourage had moved on. Will was in the corridor that led to the atrium—and the exit. He should head straight for it, he knew. But to his left was a green sign marked with the words *Halls C, D, and E.* He had to do it. He couldn't miss a chance to see Andrew onstage.

Will headed along another passageway, up three steps and through two more beechwood doors. Hall C. In the semi-darkness, he made out a lecture theater half-filled with thirty or so people.

". . . and that concludes my presentation. Are there any questions?"

There was a round of applause, and then a murmur. People looked around the room expectantly. But Will's eyes were fixed on that podium, on the small, skinny fourteen-year-old boy with the pale face and the new glasses.

Will knew what he should do: Stay back and keep quiet.

But he suddenly remembered Cristina's report and her verdicts on each of them. He couldn't resist. "Just a comment," he called out, "to echo the opinion of the Italian, er, *expert,* Cristina della Corte, I think you are a true computer genius."

A couple of people clapped in agreement. Onstage, Andrew flushed. His blue eyes blinked. He knew that voice! But he'd had no idea Will was coming to the conference. Registration had closed weeks ago—how had Will managed it? And why hadn't he told him?

With one hand, Andrew pushed his glasses back along his nose. With the other, he acknowledged the contribution from the floor. Andrew lowered his mouth to the microphone and cleared his throat. He smiled.

"Thank you, Mister . . . ? If there are no questions, perhaps you and I could talk further *outside*?"

"What are you doing in here?" Andrew asked. "How did you even get in?"

Outside Hall C, delegates milling around them, Will pulled the inhaler from his pocket. "*It works*," he said.

"The . . . the *hormones*?" Andrew stared. "Are you serious? What happened?"

"I sprayed one of the guys checking badges outside. I told him it was okay to let me in. Then I used the invisibility glove to slip a postcard into Walter Dillane's pocket."

Andrew looked incredulous. "You really are insane. I don't need my father's psychiatry qualifications to tell you that." He shook his head. "I can't believe Barrington let you take those things away with you! When did you get back to London? No wait, you can tell me everything somewhere away from *here*." Andrew took Will's arm and propelled him rapidly along the corridor, toward the exit. "If they spot you without a pass, you'll be in serious trouble."

The central atrium was dead ahead. At the far side, to

the left of the grand doors, Dillane was still surrounded by his protection officers. But they had formed a channel to allow delegates to approach, one by one. The VP seemed to be signing copies of the conference program.

Will and Andrew walked out onto the front steps of Bushell House. Will held up a hand to shield his eyes from the sunshine.

Gaia had already seen them. She was making her way around the growing pack of journalists. She looked anxious.

Andrew's astonishment returned. "Gaia!" he exclaimed. "What are you doing here? You knew Will was coming? You didn't think to *warn* me?"

"Sorry," she said, handing Will his backpack. "They *worked?*"

He nodded.

"*Really?*"

"Even without you wishing me luck." He grinned, and Gaia smiled back.

Andrew watched them closely. There was something new in their expressions, he decided. He'd seen it a couple of times recently. It gave him the impression they had temporarily forgotten he was there.

"Can I see the glove now?" Gaia asked.

"I have to get back," Andrew said loudly. "I've really only got time for a cup of coffee. Let's find a café. Will can show us both the glove—and he can tell us exactly what happened."

Will's gaze flickered. Out of the corner of his eye, he'd seen movement. A man with a black mustache in a dark suit. Touching his ear.

Will watched as, with the faintest of gestures, the man pointed toward Will, and then to another man, standing at the far side of the steps, dressed identically. At once, they started to move.

Will tensed. *CIA?* They had to be. There must have been security cameras in the conference center. *Someone had noticed he didn't have a pass.* And he had all sorts of kit with him! Just the sort of stuff the CIA would love to get their hands on . . .

"Andrew," Will started, *"I have to go—"*

Will started to dash down the steps, but the man with the mustache suddenly stepped into his path. Will tried to swerve, but the man was fast. Will slammed sideways right into his chest. He staggered. He dropped his backpack. Quickly, he slung it back onto his shoulder. Before he could start yelling, the man grabbed his arm and said: "Will Knight. Andrew Minkel. Gaia Carella. You're coming with me."

"*Who are you?*" Gaia's voice was strangled. The man's powerful fingers dug into her neck. He'd forced her down the steps of Bushell House and now he was almost pushing her down the street. She kicked out at his legs. "You can't just grab people! *Police!*"

Now the other hand suddenly clamped over her mouth. "There's no need for that, miss."

The man's accent was English. Not CIA. Were they *MI5*?

"Yeah, there is!" Will hissed from behind. The accomplice was holding him and Andrew, a beefy hand around each of their necks. "Those are journalists back there!" Will shouted. "They'll have it all on camera!"

But their abductors continued to stride toward a black limousine parked in the shade.

When they reached the car, Gaia's captor held her close and opened the door. He bent down. Said something Will couldn't hear. Then he nodded and straightened.

"Ms. Pope asks that you join her in the car," he said.

Will glared, anger boiling. "And who is *Ms. Pope?*"

From the interior came a cut-glass voice. "I'm so sorry about all this, but if you come inside, I can explain everything."

A *girl's* voice.

The two men suddenly let go. Will stumbled forward. Gaia rubbed her neck. Glancing uncertainly at Andrew, Will put a hand on the open door and peered inside.

Settled back on the beige leather seat was a thin girl of about their age. Blond, bobbed hair framed a serious face. She held out a delicate manicured hand.

"Will Knight," she said. Small blue eyes brightened. "My name is Abigail Pope. I'm extremely glad to meet you."

For a few moments, no one spoke.

Will, Gaia, and Andrew sat side by side on the limo's rear-facing bench seat, staring at the girl named Abigail Pope. She was studying their faces. Outside, her two goons paced by the car.

Will's brain raced. Whoever this girl was, she wasn't CIA and she wasn't MI5. So what *did* he know about her? The limo and the hired help suggested she was rich. Her face gave little away. If anything she looked somehow sad *and* pleased. Clearly she wanted something. But what? Instinctively, Will clasped the backpack to his chest.

"So, are you going to tell us why we're here," he said, "or are we supposed to guess?"

His voice seemed to shock Abigail back into the immediate present. She nodded slightly. "I'm sorry. Yes, I know you'll be wondering who I am. And why I asked those men to collect you from the meeting. I hope they weren't rough. I asked them to talk pleasantly, but I don't think they're that sort . . ."

Will's expression remained defiant. Neither Gaia nor Andrew responded. Abigail bit her pale lip.

"I didn't realize you'd all be here," she said. "This is a real bonus. I was hoping to find you, Andrew, and to talk to you, then to ask you to talk to your team."

Andrew's rare anger melted slightly. She seemed sincere. And she was being polite. *Your team.* Yes, it *was* his team.

Perhaps Abigail sensed Andrew would be an easier touch than himself or Gaia, Will thought, because she focused her steady gaze on the blue eyes behind those frameless glasses. "I went to your house earlier this morning and your mother told me you were at the conference. I couldn't risk missing you. I had to find you as soon as possible. So I asked those men to intercept you. They work for my father. He's a banker. He does business all over the world, not always in the nicest parts. Those men are skilled in protection—"

"And abduction?" Gaia interrupted. She was looking at Andrew. His *mother*? Gaia had been at the house two days ago and, as usual, there had been no sign of either of Andrew's parents. They seemed to spend most of their time abroad on field trips, researching traditional psychiatric practices.

Abigail switched her gaze to Gaia. "If you're wondering, I found out about you through the report by the Italian girl Cristina della Corte."

Will tensed. In his mind, he could still see Andrew's face, red and indignant, as he'd shown them the "report" on her website. It had been three months ago.

Cristina had wanted to leave Italy, to join STORM in London. They had discussed her proposition but decided they worked well together now, as a *three*-person team. It seemed Cristina hadn't liked rejection.

"So," Will said, "for the last time, why are we here?"

To his surprise, a tear suddenly rolled down Abigail's cheek. She brushed at it, and she reached for the folder on the seat beside her. Discarding Cristina's report, Abigail picked up a photograph. She held it out.

Will took one quick look and turned away.

The man was on a mortuary slab. His skin was blackened. A huge gash slashed through his cheek. The top of his head was caved in.

"This man's name is Edmund Pope. He was my uncle. He died yesterday in an explosion at a farmhouse near Interlaken in Switzerland. At least four other people died with him. The police are saying it was an accident."

Andrew looked at her warily. The gruesome image was making him feel nauseous. And he could guess what was coming. "But you think differently?"

"Edmund Pope was a great scientist. One of the world's top physicists. He'd been at Cambridge University for twenty-four years and then, six months ago, he told us he was leaving to work on a project in Switzerland. He wouldn't tell us what it was. He said it was secret.

"Three weeks ago, he came to visit us in London. He was afraid. I heard him talking to my mother. He said he didn't trust anyone. I heard him say, *If anything happens to me, it will be because of InVesta.*"

"InVesta, the *arms* company?" Gaia glanced at Will. She couldn't help being interested.

"Not just arms," Abigail said. "Energy, security . . ."

"And the secret project?" Will said.

"I don't know. It was *secret.* I don't know what he was

involved in. He didn't even tell my mother. But it was serious. And now he's dead."

Andrew adjusted his glasses. "Abigail, this sounds like a matter for the police."

"Whom my uncle couldn't trust. Who are saying this was an *accident*."

"Coincidences happen," Gaia said. "Just because your uncle was afraid doesn't mean he wasn't killed in an accident."

"And if it wasn't a coincidence?" Abigail asked. "If he *was* killed by InVesta because of this project? Companies like InVesta don't get a bad reputation for no reason."

Will was thinking. In April, stories about InVesta had been plastered all over the Internet. The company had been slated for a controversial new weapons deal with India. Then news blogs had alleged that InVesta's energy division had used political contacts in Europe and the US to gag scientists trying to reveal startling new data on global warming.

But even if that were true, ordering a scientist to be silent was a long way from killing one.

"Why are you telling us all this?" Gaia asked.

There was a pause. At last, Abigail said, "My uncle said he trusted no one. Not even the police. I don't know who else to go to. I thought perhaps . . ." She trailed off.

But her meaning was pretty obvious. She wanted STORM to help.

Edmund Pope sounded like a classic paranoia case, Will thought. A brilliant scientist too involved in his own work, wrapped up in some project that he came to believe was the be-all and end-all of everything, seeing threats around every corner.

Andrew was thinking much the same thing. His psychiatrist father would waste little time in making his diagnosis. Except for one fact: Edmund Pope was actually dead. So it might be argued that his paranoia was justified.

"What do your parents think?" Andrew asked.

"My mother is very upset," Abigail said. "But she would prefer to believe the police report."

"You mean she doesn't think anything sinister happened," Gaia said.

"Perhaps she would rather not," Abigail said stiffly. "It would make life easier in some ways, wouldn't it?" She switched her focus back to Andrew. "My father is in Kazakhstan. He says I should do what I think is best. I think it would be best if you could help." Sensing that she might be losing her grip on the situation, Abigail pressed on quickly. "I have a file for each of you," she said, patting the folder beside her. "It contains everything I know. Money is not a problem. You could have use of a car and a private jet. Whatever hourly rate you charge—"

Andrew blushed. "We don't charge—"

Will touched his arm. "He means, we don't usually charge—"

"No," Andrew said. "I mean—"

"We need to talk," Will interrupted. "The three of us. Alone."

Abigail nodded. "Of course." She didn't move.

Will reached past Gaia, opened the door.

Twenty seconds later, they were standing together in the sunshine. Will looked at Gaia. "What do you think?"

"I think he probably died in an accident, and she can't

accept it. She's looking for *reasons*." Her gaze was steady. And Will met it. Gaia's mother had died in a car crash. Will's father was dead, killed on active duty in eastern China only nine months ago. "Andrew?" he asked.

"I think that if we do agree to help, we can't charge her!"

"Why not?"

"Will, I'm a multimillionaire! I have money for STORM. When have you ever needed to spend anything—"

"But if she wants to pay, I don't see why we shouldn't take it."

"So you think we should agree to look into it?" Gaia said. She sounded surprised.

"Why not?" Will said. "It sounds interesting. If we find nothing, we haven't lost anything. Barrington's away. I haven't got anything better to do. Have you?"

Andrew thought for a moment. He had the conference. But this girl was clearly in distress. "No."

"Gaia?"

She scowled at the ground. Then she shrugged.

Will nodded.

"But if we do this," Andrew said quickly, "we are *not* charging her."

Will got back into the car first, followed by Andrew, then Gaia. Abigail Pope looked at them hopefully.

"We can't promise anything. But we'll do what we can," Will said. With a glance at Andrew, he added, "And we don't charge."

Relief washed over Abigail's pale features. "So I presume you'd like to start with InVesta? Their European headquarters are in Theobald's Road. It isn't far. And they're hosting summer workshops for school groups all week. It's part of the Energy Expo. I saw the ad when I was looking at their website last night. I'm sure it wouldn't be difficult for you to get in."

"It might be better to start with their computer network," Andrew said. "I could try to hack it. See if I could find anything on your uncle."

Will looked at Andrew. He was still riding high from his success at getting into the conference. "We can always try the network if we don't find anything in the HQ."

"I don't know, Will—"

"Come on, where's your sense of adventure?"

Andrew sighed. He rolled his eyes. "Gaia?"

She shrugged. Nodded.

Will smiled. "All right," he said to Abigail. "We'll see what we can do."

Gaia grabbed the files and headed out of the limo. She was glad to be back out in the sunshine. As Will and Andrew joined her, they heard Abigail's voice: "One last thing."

Raising an eyebrow, Will turned back. Abigail was poking her head out of the car.

"Cristina della Corte said you have links with MI6. Is that true?"

Slowly, Will nodded.

"When he was in London, my uncle said it wasn't only the police he didn't trust. He said he trusted no one. Not even MI6. I'd ask you not to talk to them—unless you feel you really have to. Agreed?"

Will hesitated. The conspiracy theory seemed to be getting more complicated.

"All right."

Abigail gave a tight smile. "And I forgot to give you this— my card."

Andrew reached out. Took it.

"My mobile phone number is on there. I have access to a private plane, cars, chauffeurs—if you need anything, let me know. And please keep me up to date."

Andrew nodded.

Abigail fixed him with her sincere gaze. "Thank you," she said. "And good luck."

David Wickett shivered.

Through cracks in the rotting wood of the hut, he could see a turquoise glimmer. The lake.

Twenty minutes ago, after a sleepless night in a cowshed, he had arrived here at the hut, where he had picnicked barely two weeks ago in very different spirits. Then, he'd felt the need for a change of scene for his thinking. And how dramatically it had paid off!

Wickett raked a trembling hand through his hair. So far, he reflected, he had acted almost entirely according to protocol. After finalizing his Method, he had saved it on a memory stick. Then he had wiped the hard drive on his laptop. He had summoned his colleagues to Assembly Point Zebra—and he had watched it explode!

Now what should he do?

The dossier had been clear.

In the event of discovery of any threat to the group, contact your task officer.

His group was *dead*. Was that a threat? No! It was significantly worse. Should he really call his task officer, whom he had never even met?

Someone, in fact, had been calling repeatedly. Wickett's mobile phone had been going off half the night. Whoever it was, they'd appeared as *Number withheld* and they hadn't left a single message. Wickett had been too afraid to answer.

He now glanced anxiously at his dusty surroundings.

They looked much as he remembered. Shafts of bright sunlight sliced through the gaps in the ancient roof. They illuminated a broken shovel. A moldy blue tarpaulin. The rusting remains of some kind of agricultural implement. And a wooden trapdoor. Two weeks ago, Wickett, exploring, had discovered that the trapdoor led to a small cellar. He could only guess at the cellar's original purpose. But it was an ideal hiding place.

Now he dragged the tarpaulin over the trapdoor. Then he slipped underneath, into the warm space.

He sat down. It was dark. And very quiet. He listened to his own breathing. A nervous hand crept to his neck—and the precious high-tech locket. His heart felt feeble. It was pulsing like a jellyfish.

Then Wickett made a decision. He *would* call his task officer. But first, he dialed a familiar number. He waited. She'd be there. She had to be!

At last, he heard: "Ja?" His housekeeper.

"Greta!" he whispered. "Thank God. Has anyone been to the house?"

"Anyone? Who do you mean?"

"*Anyone.* I mean since yesterday at lunchtime, has anyone been to the house?"

"Yesterday afternoon, a few hours after you left, the pest control officers came. I wrote you a note. It is on the kitchen table."

"I didn't go home last night, Greta. I didn't read your note! What pest control officers? What did they want?"

"They said there has been a termite outbreak. They needed to check all the houses in the area. They were very thorough. They left the rooms in a mess!"

There was a long pause. Those were no pest control officers. David Wickett knew that much.

"Did they search outside? Did they look in the woodpile?"

"No." Greta knew why Wickett asked the question, but she was afraid to admit it. This was a man who liked his secrets kept. "Are you all right? Where are you?"

Another long pause. Wickett didn't want to tell her. But he was afraid. And he wanted someone to know where he was—especially if things went wrong. At last, Wickett said, "I'm at the hut—the one I picnicked at. I told you. You remember? I'm in some trouble, Greta. But I'm going to try to sort it out. I will call you again at eight o'clock tonight. If you don't hear from me by then, call the police."

"The police!"

"Only if you don't hear from me. And tell no one else I called you. Tell no one anything. Carry on as normal. You understand? You promise?"

"All—all right. Yes. I promise."

Wickett ended the call. Then, before he had a chance to try his task officer, the mobile phone rang. Again, the screen said *Number withheld*. Perhaps this was the task officer. Perhaps he *should* answer.

Wickett pressed the phone to his ear.

"David Wickett? Listen very carefully. *If you do not do exactly as I say, or if you go public with your findings, two thousand people will be dead.*"

6

The Junction Pool, River Tweed, Scotland

Shute Barrington tied his fly and cast the line. It settled on the rippling surface of the water.

Barrington was three days into one week's vacation. It had been forced upon him by C, the chief of MI6, who had checked Barrington's records and found he had taken only two days off in twelve years.

High above, a kestrel circled. Barrington tried to concentrate on the peace of the scene.

The breeze in the oak leaves. The sunshine on the ripples.

He sighed.

It was very beautiful.

And extremely dull.

A moment later, the peace was broken by an electronic ring tone.

Barrington's mobile phone was beside him, on the grass. Instantly, he squinted at the screen. The caller ID read _Charlie Spicer_. His deputy. Barrington snatched up the phone. But it wouldn't do to let Spicer know he was glad to be disturbed.

"Spicer, I'm right in the middle of playing a particularly juicy-looking twenty-pounder. This had better be good."

"You've heard about what happened in Switzerland, sir? The explosion at the farmhouse, and the dead scientists?"

Barrington might have been on vacation, but that didn't mean he couldn't access the main STASIS computer network. He'd read all there was to read. Which wasn't exactly much.

"Yeah, Spicer, I heard. And I heard the project was classified *Alpha*."

"Yes, that's right. I'm calling because C is asking for tech support for the field officers on the ground."

"Which you, as acting director while I am *on holiday*, are of course providing."

"Yes, but sir, they want us to deploy the Eagle."

Barrington screwed his eyes shut. C had requested an update on the Eagle only the previous week. "How badly do they seem to want it?"

"They're demanding it, sir. We did promise it would be ready last month."

"And it is ready." *Just about*, he thought.

"But I can't find the remote or the display screen, sir. They were on the bench in Lab 12 but now—"

"They're here," Barrington said.

"You took them with you?"

"No, Spicer, they followed me up here like little puppies. Of course I took them with me! There were a few software kinks. I wanted to make sure I'd ironed them all out."

There was a pause. "Sir, you didn't by any chance take up that new transmitter with you too, did you?"

Barrington was about to ask, *What transmitter?* Then he remembered. Spicer had given it to him in the corridor the previous week. It was designed to work with a new laptop Spicer had been building. Barrington had thrust it into his jacket pocket.

"Ah, maybe," he said. "Do you need it urgently?"

"No, it's all right, sir. If it was in your office, I'd get it, but it can wait. What do you want me to tell C about the Eagle? Shall I send a courier?"

Barrington thought for a moment. "No. I can control the Eagle from here."

"I'll have to set up a live relay to Operations Control. Then they can see what's happening."

"I understand that, Spicer."

"And the software kinks—you don't mean—"

Barrington had to interrupt. If he didn't, Spicer would have the chance to finish the question, and Barrington would have to lie. "Hold on Spicer, I'm losing her! She's a beauty! I'll call you back."

Barrington flipped his phone shut and surveyed the glittering water. His face was grim.

The Eagle should work.

He had only one concern.

One small concern.

It'll be all right, Barrington told himself.

7

"There's not much here," Gaia said.

They were walking down Southampton Row, toward InVesta's European headquarters. Will was leading the way. Gaia was leafing through Abigail's file, Andrew peering over her shoulder.

"Some stuff on InVesta," Gaia continued. "The CEO's a guy called Saxon Webb, based in New York. The European president is Sir Evelyn Hughes. He's based in the London office. There are photos. Then there's a biography of her uncle. Including the names of the schools he went to. Which I'm sure will be *extremely* useful," she added, rolling her eyes. Then she paused. "In Cambridge, he was working in electrochemistry."

"I don't see how that could be of any particular interest to a company like InVesta," Andrew said.

"Or the Swiss police. Or MI6," Gaia said. She raised an eyebrow—and almost collided with Will.

He was walking slowly, unwrapping a package that he'd received that morning at Sutton Hall. It had been posted in Russia—by his grandmother, he guessed—and then his mother had forwarded it from their home in London.

Will had stuffed it into his backpack, meaning to open it on the train. But then he'd been busy thinking about the inhaler and the glove and the U.S. vice president, and he'd forgotten about it—until now.

Inside the brown wrapping, Will found a cigar box and a letter. In fact, the box wasn't from his grandmother, but from her new fiancé, Vanya, who had helped STORM in St. Petersburg.

Dear Will,

I trust you will have heard the news. The church is booked. You are to be my step-grandson. What joy!

Will smiled. He could hear the teasing in *What joy!* His mother had told him about the engagement two weeks ago. She'd also decided it was time to reveal that Vanya himself had been a spy, with thirty years' service in the KGB. And, it seemed, he hadn't left his old life behind completely. When Will had called his grandmother to congratulate her, Vanya had answered the phone. He was about to leave for Bonn, he'd said, to chair a three-day meeting of an *international association of retired spies.*

Will read on:

And so, since you will be family, your grandmother tells me that I must tell you that if you should ever get into any difficulty anywhere in the world—and she means ever and she means anywhere—you must call me and I will help. I know people, Will. I know people all over. People like me, you make a lot of friends who owe you their lives, and you make a lot of enemies. Naturally, I would put you in touch with my friends.

In the meantime, please accept this token. I anticipate that you will find them useful. Operating instructions are inside the box.

"Love" (I believe it is convention to sign family letters so),

Vanya

Intrigued, Will studied the outside of the box. He noticed a series of tiny holes in the lid. Holes had also been drilled into the base, to which a small plastic packet was taped. There were two possible reasons for the holes, he decided: Either the contents needed air to circulate to stop them from going moldy—or the contents were alive. Will flicked open the metal clasp. It was the latter.

Will stared in disgust. Contained behind plastic seals over each half of the box were what looked like cockroaches. Flat brown wing cases and waving antennae, as long as the bodies. The insects scuttled over one another. A folded sheet of paper almost fell out of the box.

Will opened it up. He scanned Vanya's writing.

They *were* cockroaches. *Blattella germanica.* The German cockroach.

In fact, they were bugs in every sense of the word.

Will read Vanya's instructions:

Each casing incorporates a miniature audio receiving device. This was inserted while the roaches were in the egg and has become part of the exoskeleton.

Taped to the bottom of the cigar box is a pheromone stick. It is covered in female attractant chemicals. After deploying a roach, you can recall it using this stick.

To listen to the audio transmitted by a bug, slot the little gadget over your ear. It is contained with the pheromone stick, and it is waterproof. It transmits through the skull. Each of the twelve roaches is numbered on the underside. Check the number, then set the earpiece to pick up from the relevant roach.

See? I am not so slack on the inventions! A worthy grandfather? Enjoy!

Will felt his eyes drawn back to the box's grisly interior. Each brown insect was about half an inch long, with two long feelers and three pairs of hairy, spindly legs. The bellies looked jointed. They were gruesome.

Will remembered a biology class in which the teacher had told them that the roach's nervous system was spread through the insect's body. So even if you cut off its head, it would survive—until it died from thirst. Or from being stomped on, Will thought as he snapped the box shut.

Gaia's voice was suddenly loud in his ear.

"What have you got there?"

They were at the corner of Theobald's Road. Andrew was double-checking the address on his smart phone. Gaia had closed Abigail's file. Will pushed the box back inside his backpack. "Trust me," he said. "You don't want to know."

Gaia's eyes narrowed.

"*Trust me,*" Will said.

"It's not far," Andrew said. "It should just be up on the left."

"*Will,*" Gaia said, annoyed at the brush-off.

"Later," he said. "I'll show you later."

Because Andrew was pointing. "Actually, there it is."

One block up, on the left-hand side. The building was imposing. Ten stories, with a black glass skin.

As they got closer, Andrew saw that *InVesta Corporation* was written in square steel letters across the façade. Maybe he should have tried harder to convince Will to start with the computer network. After all, if InVesta *was* involved in the deaths of five scientists, should they really be trying to investigate in person? Had his judgment been affected by the sight of a girl in distress? "You know, I think it really would

be better if I tried to get into their computer systems first."
Andrew looked at Gaia, hoping for support.

But Will was already at the revolving door. Gaia watched two older kids in school uniforms slip in past him. The workshop would mean there should be plenty of kids inside to provide cover.

"We're here now," she said. "We might as well take a look." She glanced back at Andrew. "We'll probably be escorted around the building by security anyway. I doubt there'll even be any way for us to get into trouble. Come on."

Andrew shook his head. "In my experience," he said as he followed her, "where there's a Will, there's a way."

The revolving door opened into an airy foyer. Almost everything was white, from the polished marble floor to the ceramic pots holding tall fan palms—even the two elevators, on the left, and the corridor that stretched behind a marble reception desk. A neat woman in a white suit was sitting at the desk, talking to a gray-haired visitor in a light suit. "Eighth floor, sir. Go on up."

As the man headed for the elevators, she turned to Will, Andrew, and Gaia. "You're here for the workshop? You're a bit late, but go on in. The welcome video has just started. It's in there."

She pointed across the foyer to an open door. Beside it was another. Closed.

"Thanks," Will said. He led the way, hearing his sneakers squeak on the marble.

Through the door, they found a small lecture theater. Kids aged from about ten to sixteen were sitting in rows of white, molded plastic seats, their eyes fixed on a large screen. Will, Andrew, and Gaia kept their backs to the wall.

On the screen, images of grinning men striking oil were replaced with a close-up of a bald middle-aged man with a thick neck and a tanned, pug face. Prominent ice-blue eyes flashed in a corporate smile. It was obvious this man was powerful, Will thought. He oozed self-confidence.

"I do hope you enjoyed that introduction to InVesta Corp. My name is Saxon Webb, and I'm the CEO. The head honcho, you might say."

Webb's accent sounded mid-Atlantic, Will thought. It was difficult to tell if he was British but had spent a lot of time in the United States, or vice versa.

"Now, I'm sure you're all going to get something valuable from our workshops. The second one will look at our research into new ways of generating renewable energy. But first we're going to take a look at some of the claims made about climate change, and ask: Is the science really right?"

Beside Will, Gaia whispered, "Let me guess—he thinks burning fossil fuels has nothing whatever to do with global warming. Typical."

But Will didn't respond. Out of the corner of his eye, he'd seen movement in the lobby. Will peered through the gap in the door. A brown-haired man in a dark suit was hurrying toward the marble desk.

He listened hard and heard the receptionist say, "The meeting is in the boardroom on the eighth floor, sir. Sir Evelyn is expecting you."

Sir Evelyn Hughes. European president of InVesta.

Will turned back to Gaia and Andrew. "Someone else

has just turned up for a meeting on the eighth floor," he whispered. "It's with Evelyn Hughes."

Andrew glanced at Gaia. "What exactly are you thinking?"

"If Hughes is in that meeting, it means he's not in his office," Will said quickly. "You and Gaia see if you can get in there. I'll try to listen in on the meeting."

Andrew's eyes opened wide. "*How?* You can't just walk in!"

Will tapped his pocket. "I've had some unexpected help from Russia."

"You really are going to have to show us," Gaia said.

"Actually, I can't wait," Will whispered truthfully. "*Later.*"

Gaia took a deep breath. In her mind, she could still see the grim picture of Edmund Pope's dead body. "But I don't see how we could get up to the eighth floor," she said. "The receptionist will see us."

Will glanced back into the foyer. The two elevators faced the reception desk. True—it would be hard to slip in unnoticed. But now Will saw that the door next to the lecture theater was marked in small stenciled letters: *Stairs.*

On the screen, Webb was wrapping up. "So, I'll hand you over to my staff, who will take excellent care of you. Enjoy your day. And farewell."

Ten seconds later, three InVesta employees stood up at the rear of the theater.

Two minutes later, they led sixty children out, past the receptionist, toward the white corridor.

Using the kids for cover, Will, Andrew, and Gaia made straight for the stairs.

Floor 8.

The words were painted on the back of the heavy fire door.

Cautiously, Will pushed it open.

Andrew and Gaia were in the stairwell behind him. They peered out.

Charcoal carpet covered the floor. On the white walls were black-and-white photographs of smiling African children, with what looked like wind farms in the background, gleaming in the sun.

Methodically, Will scanned the walls and ceiling. He couldn't actually see any cameras, but that didn't mean there weren't any. At least, the bug-spotter in his watch was telling him there were no hidden mikes.

Very slowly, Will stepped into the corridor. To the right, at the far end, a black-tinted glass door stood ajar. A plaque on the wall beside it said *Sir Evelyn Hughes*. Will glanced back at Andrew and Gaia and jabbed a finger toward it.

"There'll be an assistant," Andrew whispered. "It's not as though we'll be able to just walk right into his office!"

"Do what you can," Will whispered back. "If we get caught, they'll just think we're nosy workshop kids. What's the worst that could happen?"

Andrew shot Will a look that suggested he could imagine worse than a slap on the wrist. But he nodded.

Will's gaze shot to the other end of the corridor. Halfway along, he saw another door, black-tinted and frosted. *Boardroom* was written beside it in chrome.

"I'm going to try to listen in on the meeting. Meet me back here," Will whispered. He hitched the backpack higher up his shoulder.

Gaia glanced at it. "You don't have the tooth phones in there, do you?"

Will shook his head. His tooth phones—tiny receivers and radio transmitters designed to be slotted over a molar, to allow covert communication—were back at Sutton Hall, being upgraded. "I'll see you back here in ten minutes." Will started off.

Gaia took in Andrew's worried expression. She could guess what he was thinking: *This is foolish*. But she'd expected nothing less. She *knew* what Will was thinking: *The risk is worth it*. It always was, to him.

Gaia led the way. She walked slowly, keeping her steps light. And she peered into what had to be the assistant's office. She made out the edge of a wooden desk, apparently unoccupied. Three sets of metal filing cabinets. Two ferns in white pots. Another door, presumably into Hughes's own office. A leather sofa, angled toward the desk. And a printer.

"What can you see?" Andrew whispered behind her.

Gaia held a finger to her lips. Inside, someone was moving. A gray-haired woman in a black skirt and high heels. She had been hidden, behind the door. Now she strode past Gaia's narrow field of view and went into the far office.

Gaia turned instantly to Andrew and grasped his arm. She whispered: *"Now."*

Will felt exposed. Which he was, here in the corridor. He had to work fast.

Quickly, he pulled Vanya's box from his backpack. He tore off the packet taped to the bottom and ripped it open. Inside he found a clear case, containing a slender swizzle stick and the wireless earpiece. On the side of the earpiece was a numbered dial. First he had to choose a roach, and check its number. Then he had to turn the dial to match.

Will forced himself to look. Behind their plastic seals, the insects were climbing all over one another. Their shiny brown wing cases and the probing antennae were repulsive. Will started to feel itchy. They're just *tools*, he told himself.

Why couldn't Vanya have picked something attractive, like a ladybug? But he knew the answer. Cockroaches hate light. Release one and it would instantly seek out the nearest, darkest hiding place—which made them perfect for covert audio surveillance.

Squinting so he didn't have to see the insect too clearly, Will reached in and grabbed one by the wing case. It curled in his fingers, its legs waving frantically. Will saw the number seven marked on its belly and dropped it at the bottom of the boardroom door. He watched it race in.

Andrew took a deep breath. Held it.
Stay calm, he told himself. *Stay calm.*
Easier said than done when he was crouching behind a leather sofa with Gaia's knee digging into his ribs. Barely

three feet away, Hughes's assistant was tapping at her keyboard. She'd returned just as he and Gaia had slipped down out of sight.

Behind Hughes's assistant was the printer. Andrew had registered the model as he'd dashed past. Not all printers were hackable—but this one was. Behind it was a door to what seemed to be a mini-kitchen. Andrew had caught a glimpse of a toaster and a kettle.

Very slowly now, Andrew exhaled. His palms were sweating, his fingers slipping against the plastic casing of his smart phone. He'd used the device to give his lecture earlier that morning, and it was loaded not only with his presentation, but also the printer hacker.

Andrew glanced up at Gaia.

She nodded reassuringly. Or as reassuringly as she could, given their present circumstances.

It's fine, Andrew told himself. *Pretend you're at home. Take your time . . .*

He started up the software and concentrated.

Beside him, Gaia watched closely. After a few moments, lines of code suddenly ran across the screen, and then she saw a logo:

InVesta

Then:

Minutes of the meeting of July 12 . . .

Behind the sofa, Gaia grinned. They were in.

Outside the boardroom, Will put a finger to his ear. His blood was rushing, making it even more difficult for him to hear the quiet voices. He had no idea how many people were inside. But at least one was angry. Another was defensive. Will caught only snatches.

". . . in pursuit now."

". . . how could it happen? Mr. Webb has been . . ."

". . . from the Sphere. Don't you think . . . ?"

Will frowned. Was the insect moving around? Or was Vanya's hardware acting up?

". . . in Interlaken right now."

Will tensed.

Interlaken.

That was where Abigail Pope said her uncle had been killed—at least, she'd said *near* Interlaken.

Coincidence?

Really?

Then one voice rang clear. "I will check the latest. I seem to have left my BlackBerry in my office. I'll be right back."

Evelyn Hughes. It had to be.

Will darted. Dashing across the corridor, he slammed his shoulder hard against the fire door. He slipped through, into the stairwell, then pushed it shut. Just in time. Through a tiny gap, he could see the shadow of someone striding past.

Heading for his office.

Heading for Andrew and Gaia.

. . . to clarify, health and safety requires all staff to be instructed in one topic each week on a rotational basis, each topic to be repeated every six months.

Suggestions for new emergency access explanations follow guidelines established . . .

Andrew sighed noiselessly. So far, the hack had revealed

directives on lifting heavy objects in the workplace, on stretching exercises and body posture, on the legality of hiring and firing temporary assistants, on recycling office waste—and absolutely nothing of any interest.

Two more minutes, he thought. Then *somehow* they'd sneak out of the office, meet up with Will and do this *properly*—that is, they would try to gain access to the InVesta network from the safety of home.

Suddenly, Andrew stiffened. He almost cried out. Gaia had seen it too.

On the screen of his smart phone, a new document was starting.

A printout of an e-mail.

> **From:** Black Sphere
> **Subject:** URGENT: Project FIREball, reference Interlaken
> **Sent:** 07/15 14:02 PM

Yesterday afternoon! Andrew quickly read on:

> Gerard Bailey—deceased.
> Marcel Gide—deceased.
> Johannes Pike—deceased.
> Edmund Pope—deceased.
> Azra Khan—deceased.
> David Wickett—under pursuit.
> Wickett's last known address: Blaustrasse 14, Kleinkirchen.
> Confirmed?

Andrew's blue eyes stared urgently at Gaia. *Edmund Pope. Deceased.* This had to be the team of scientists. Was this the project they'd been working on? Project FIREball? Could Abigail Pope really be right—InVesta *was* involved? And this man, David Wickett, he'd escaped? He was still alive?

Andrew's head jerked. The door to the assistant's office had been pushed open. Around the edge of the sofa, he could see a pair of legs in blue pinstriped trousers.

"I'm looking for my BlackBerry," a male voice said. "And we could do with some coffee.

"Your BlackBerry's here, Sir Evelyn," the assistant said. "And I'll bring the coffee right through."

Andrew squinted around the sofa as Evelyn Hughes left, BlackBerry presumably in hand. His assistant got up. She passed the printer and went into the kitchen.

From his crouch, Andrew could easily see the kettle, the toaster, and the fridge. More importantly, he could see the woman's face. Which meant that if she looked around, *she* could see *him*.

Gaia squeezed his arm hard. Twice. Andrew understood. Hughes's assistant opened a cupboard and peered up, probably looking for coffee, and Andrew slipped out around the sofa.

They were in luck—the corridor was clear. Andrew led the way back along it. He slammed open the door to the stairs—and slammed right into Will, who had been standing behind it. Will waited for Gaia to dash through, then he shoved it back, hard.

"What did you do that for?" Will whispered.

"Why are you standing there?" Andrew asked.

"You could have been anyone! I was hiding."

"*Listen,*" Gaia said. "We found something from the printer—a document. Edmund Pope's name was on it."

Will nodded, rubbing a bashed shoulder. "They were talking about Interlaken," he said in a low voice. His bug was still in the boardroom, he realized. But he wasn't about to rush in with his pheromone stick. He still had eleven roaches. One insect wasn't a huge loss. "Let's get out of here," he said. "We'll talk about this somewhere safer."

"By all means!" Andrew whispered.

Will took the concrete steps as fast as he dared, using the metal rail to help him swing around the corners. At the ground floor, he hesitated before opening the door. He could hear Gaia and Andrew, puffing slightly behind him.

Will glimpsed something moving. He glanced up—right into the lens of a security camera. He swore under his breath. "I think we've just been spotted," he said, jerking his head toward the camera. "We have to hurry. But don't run."

Will pushed the door open a crack. He could just make out the receptionist. She was on the telephone. Her gaze was fixed down.

Will slipped quickly out of the stairwell, followed by Gaia, then Andrew.

Casually now, they started to cross the lobby. As they passed the marble desk, the receptionist put down the phone and glanced up. She looked surprised. "Have you broken for refreshments already?"

Will nodded, still walking quickly. "Yeah. And unfortunately we have to leave early. But it was great." He added meaningfully: "We learned a lot."

"*Hey!*"

A shout from behind. Will's head shot around. A security guard in a baseball cap and blue uniform emerged from one of the elevators. He was holding a walkie-talkie.

"You three! Stop!"

"Go!" Will urged. *"Run."*

His feet skidding on the polished marble floor, Will made straight for the emergency exit beside the revolving door and pushed it hard. As the door swung open, an alarm went off. The siren rang through his head. "Don't turn around," Will called. "Don't stop!"

He ran out to the sidewalk. Ahead were three lanes of traffic. Directly opposite, a brightly colored hop-on, hop-off tour bus was preparing to pull away from the curb.

"The bus!" Will yelled. He grabbed Gaia's arm and started to weave through the traffic.

A guy in a red Ferrari hit the horn and yelled, "Watch out!"

From behind came more shouts. "Hey! Hey! *Stop!*" The guard. Then the sound of tires screeching on asphalt.

But they were across the street. Still gripping Gaia's arm, Will rounded the bus and knocked hard on the doors. Andrew ran up behind. Will forced himself to smile. They *had* to get on.

The driver looked a little puzzled, but he released the doors.

"We're just leaving, kids. Hurry up and take a seat. If you haven't got a ticket you can buy one from George." He jerked his head in the direction of a skinny teenager who was selling tickets as he made his way along the aisle.

Then the driver closed the doors and pulled into the inside lane.

Breathing hard, Will reached for the pole that ran up alongside the stairs to the open top deck. He raced up and peered over the edge at the street. The security guard was in the road, looking around wildly. He hadn't seen them get on the bus!

Will turned. Grinned.

Gaia shook her head and sat down hard. Behind her, twenty or so tourists paid them absolutely no attention.

Andrew took a seat next to Gaia. He ran a hand across his damp forehead. "That guard saw us."

"Saw us on the stairs," Will said as he sat down across the aisle from Andrew. "I didn't see any other cameras."

"If he saw us going down, he must have seen us go up," Gaia said. She gripped the rail. The bus turned sharply around a corner, heading south, toward the Thames.

"If he was paying full attention to his monitors," Will said. "And if he'd been paying attention, do you think he'd have left us to explore the eighth floor?"

"So you don't think he knows what we were doing?" Andrew asked.

Will shrugged. Exhilaration was pounding through his veins. "It really doesn't matter. *We got out.* So tell me what you found."

Andrew pulled out his smart phone. "I got this from the printer," he said, resisting the temptation to sound triumphant.

As Will read the e-mail, his expression turned black. "Project FIREball," he said, almost to himself. "That has to be it. So InVesta *is* involved. And this David Wickett—he's escaped." Will scanned the From line again. "The Black Sphere . . ." He frowned. "I heard something . . ."

The list of names was running through his brain, leaving mysteries in its tracks. Five people. All deceased. "Someone mentioned a sphere," Will said at last. "And they were talking about Saxon Webb, InVesta's CEO. And Interlaken. They didn't sound happy."

"But just because InVesta knows about the project, it doesn't mean they actually killed the scientists," Gaia said. "It says Wickett is under pursuit, but it doesn't actually say *by them*."

"Tickets, please!"

The conductor was staggering up the stairs. Andrew hardly looked at him. Just plunged his hand into his pocket and brought out a wad of cash.

When George had passed on, Andrew blinked at Will. The sun was glaring through his glasses. It was turning into a hot morning. "So what now?"

Will glanced over the side of the bus. It was slowing. Ahead was a brightly colored stop.

They had to find David Wickett, he decided. Wickett could tell them about the project, and about Edmund Pope. *If* no one else had gotten to him first. Which was a huge *if*.

They could work out what was going on with InVesta later.

The bus's brakes screeched. "We'll get out here," Will said. "Meet me at my house in half an hour. Andrew, can you call Abigail? Tell her we'll be needing that plane."

Gaia's eyes widened. "We're going to *Switzerland*?"

Will smiled. "Where else?"

"Will, I want to find out what's happening here too, but five scientists have *died*," Andrew said. "They were working on a secret project. I imagine Barrington would know about it. Or he'd be able to find out. Perhaps he could tell us all about this Project FIREball, and we wouldn't actually need to go anywhere."

Gaia headed for the stairwell. She could still feel the adrenaline coursing through her body—it was getting addictive. "We did tell Abigail we wouldn't go to MI6 . . ."

"And at the moment we don't have much," Will said. "If we go to Barrington, he'll ask a lot of questions and he doesn't have to tell us anything. MI6 will be looking for Wickett. They'll have to be."

"So we're competing with MI6 to find him, and find out the truth?" Andrew said. "Don't you think that's a tough ask?"

"Tough asks," Will said as he swung himself down after Gaia. "I thought that's what STORM was all about."

9

The house was silent.

The peace seemed strange after the blaring London traffic.

Will ran upstairs, thoughts speeding. *Interlaken. Project FIREball. David Wickett. Under pursuit . . .*

He dropped his backpack onto the bed and threw in his passport and toothbrush.

There wasn't much else to add. Most of his devices were back at Sutton Hall. The new stuff, which he'd been working on with some of the STASIS techies, was already in the backpack—plus the roaches.

Will rummaged around for the canvas bag. He knew he should leave the invisibility glove behind. If Barrington found out he'd taken it, he'd be in serious trouble.

But Barrington was away, *fishing*. No one else would even notice it was gone. Not for a few days, anyway. Will was about to put the bag back. But he stopped. The drawstring was untied—and he could *see* something.

He yanked the canvas bag open, and stared. The top end of the glove had been crushed. The damage stopped the fabric from working. It was no longer invisible! It must have happened in the collision with Abigail's henchman, he thought, jaw clenched.

Will cursed. The glove was useless. There was no point taking it to Switzerland. Even worse, what was he going to tell Barrington?

He'd think of something. He'd have to. Hurriedly, Will stashed the canvas bag on a shelf in his closet. He zipped his backpack. A moment later he heard footsteps on the landing.

Gaia.

After they'd gotten off the bus, Andrew had called Sean, his driver, to pick him up. Will and Gaia had found a cab. Gaia's apartment was on the way to Will's house. She'd said she'd only be five minutes. Will had offered to wait outside. She'd shrugged. Said he might as well come up.

It was the first time Will had ever been inside her apartment.

She'd left him on a small blue sofa in the living room, listening to the traffic rumbling past on Charlotte Street. On the wall, he'd seen a framed print of Padua in Italy, Gaia's father's birthplace. Then he'd noticed a photograph on a dusty table beside the TV.

Her dad, Will had guessed. Red-eyed by a camera flash in what seemed to be an Italian restaurant. A small girl beside him, laughing. Pink dress. Bright brown eyes. Dark hair.

Gaia didn't get along well with her father. They hadn't gotten along even before her mother had died, she'd told him. Will remembered the basement at Andrew's house, six weeks earlier, when Gaia had turned up on edge. She and her dad had just had a fight. He was still drinking. Even now—when the doctors had told him to stop.

At Easter, he'd been admitted to the hospital. It was

cancer. Will and Andrew had gone with her to see him. The doctors couldn't be sure how long he would last. And *still* he kept drinking. He didn't care if he died. And so he didn't care about her.

But what about *then*, Will wondered, looking at the picture. Had her father cared then? Had her mother been behind the camera?

But then Gaia had appeared at the door, a backpack in her hand, a small black bag slung across her chest. She saw him looking at the picture and fixed her eyes on him. *"Let's go."*

Now, in Bloomsbury, Gaia stood in the doorway of Will's bedroom. She was carrying a brown rat. Her gaze ran over the plain walls, and the desk, with its piles of books and magazines, and the cricket ball that Will's father had given to him the Christmas before he'd died. And she finally asked him the question she'd been carrying around all day.

"So," she said. "Did you meet with David Allott?"

Will looked up, surprised.

He had first met David Allott, an MI6 officer, in Italy. Afterward, Allott had sent him a cryptic text. *There are things I should tell you about your father's death . . .* Meetings had been set up. Allott had pulled out of every one. Urgent business, he'd said.

Then Barrington had told Will that Allott would be at Sutton Hall this week.

"The Democratic Republic of Congo," Charlie Spicer had told Will apologetically, after Will had asked him to check the MI6 assignment files. "He was called away on Tuesday. Looks like it was very sudden. But I didn't tell you any of that."

Now Will looked at Gaia. "He wasn't there. He had to go to Congo."

Gaia nodded. Waited. Will didn't seem to want to say anything else.

Maybe she shouldn't have mentioned it. Will was touchy about his father. And she could hardly blame him. She was even touchier about hers.

Ratty's ears twitched. "Is he coming with us?" she asked, stroking the fur between his ears.

Will held his hand out for the animal. Gently, Gaia passed him over, and Will patted his brown fur. As presents from Vanya went, the rat was *significantly* better than the cockroaches. He had been surgically altered so that he could be remote-controlled. The electrodes were implanted. A miniature video camera and a mike could be attached to a head strap. Ratty could be their eyes and their ears.

Could be. But not this time.

Sticking out at a sharp angle from the animal's body was a tiny splint. Ratty had broken his leg, and it had been Will's fault. Nine days ago, Will had let Ratty out of his cage without the foot pads that let the rat scale even the smoothest of walls. Ratty had immediately attempted a vertical climb, and fallen.

"He might still be useful," Gaia said quietly.

Will understood what she meant. Ratty was part of the team. But he had a broken leg. It wouldn't be fair.

"Not this time." He checked his watch. Andrew would be here any minute. Will slipped the rat onto his shoulder and picked up his bag. He hesitated.

Perhaps he could still ask Gaia about the photograph.

His eyes flicked to her face. She was looking at him intently. Perhaps he could talk to her about Allott. They had other things to think about. Dead scientists. Secret projects. But he *wanted* to talk to Gaia. And he wanted her to talk to him. He took a deep breath—

Suddenly, the jangling of an old-fashioned doorbell filled the house.

"That'll be Andrew," she said. She smiled faintly, and Will wasn't sure why. Gaia turned and headed downstairs. He let out the breath he'd been holding and followed.

He ran into the kitchen and put Ratty back in his cage. The rat's beady eyes blinked up at him. Will glanced along the hallway. Gaia was opening the front door. "Yeah," he whispered to Ratty, "I know." Then he scribbled a note to his mother.

Going to stay with Andrew for a few days. Big project.

With Andrew—well, that part was true. Will wasn't sure what else to add. So he put down the pen. He could hear Andrew's voice, loud in the hall. "Come on! I told Abigail we'd be at the airport in half an hour. We'd better hurry!"

10

"What are you doing, man? Speak to me!"

On the banks of the River Tweed, Shute Barrington was tense. The Eagle had arrived in Switzerland, and right at that moment was being unpacked from its transfer crate by an MI6 *field officer*. They might know how to take out an opponent with their little finger, but when it came to technology, Barrington fumed, they were about as gentle as a blind rhinoceros.

"We're just lifting it out."

"Watch the wings!" Barrington shouted into his phone. "Be careful of her beak!"

The voice came back exasperated: "If it's that delicate, is it really going to be much use?"

Barrington flushed. "Of course it damn well is!" He refrained from adding: *Be careful of her beak for* your *safety, not hers.*

There was a pause. Then the voice said, "Right. She's out on the ground. What now?"

"Now you stand back!"

Barrington wedged the phone between his ear and his shoulder. He picked up the control pad, with its touch screen and joystick. First, he activated the central systems. Then, very slowly, he used the joystick to spread the Eagle's wings.

Ten seconds later, the bird left the ground—and she soared. On a handheld monitor, Barrington could see green fields. A hut. Two cows. He brushed the touch pad and patted it twice. Then he stroked it again. Instantly, one of the cows reared onto the screen. Barrington could even count the strands of grass dangling from its pink mouth.

The field officer said: "It's in the air."

"Yeah," Barrington said tetchily. "I can see that."

"I've got the surveillance coordinates here. You're meant to be responsible for monitoring a zone that stretches—"

"*Yes,*" Barrington interrupted. "I know."

Another pause. "So now what?"

"Now *I* run a full systems test and put the Eagle to work. And *you* go back to bludgeoning people with your bare hands."

"Right," the officer said tightly. *"You're welcome. Great working with you."* He cut the connection.

On the riverbank, Barrington gritted his teeth. He let the phone drop to the ground and concentrated on the images from his Eagle.

She was no ordinary bird.

Her body was made from carbon fiber—strong and light. The wings, each a foot and a half across, were fashioned from a plastic-metal composite. Apply electricity to this material, and it changes shape. Remove the electric field, and it returns to its original state. Get the engineering right—and Barrington had—and you could create flapping wings. Barrington himself had covered them with artificial, flame-retardant feathers.

The Eagle's eyes were equally cutting-edge. They could

move independently of each other. The left acted as the lens for either a low-light camera or a high-resolution digital daytime setup, both mounted inside her slender belly. The right eye concealed an infrared camera for use at night.

To control the Eagle, Barrington had only to manipulate his joystick. He did this now, checking the results on his monitor. The bird responded instantly. She soared to an altitude of three hundred feet and hovered.

Barrington started to perform a full systems check.

"Wings, check," he murmured to himself as the built-in sensors reported flapping. "Cameras, check."

"Beak—*Beak* . . ."

Barrington cursed. This was the best bit! He'd thought he'd fixed the bugs in the software. So why wasn't the damn beak working?

Barrington shook his head. He should never have gone on vacation, he thought. He should have finished work on the Eagle. And right now, he should be trying to find out exactly what was going on in Switzerland. The project was *Alpha*-classified. Even he, the head of STASIS, wasn't allowed to know about it. Just what could be so important—and so secret?

11

"I think," Andrew said, "I would like one of these."

The Gulfstream G550 jet was tearing across the runway at London's City Airport. Abigail Pope had been as good as her word.

As the twin-engine plane took off, Will surveyed the cabin's sleek interior. Fourteen cream-colored leather seats were arranged in facing pairs, separated by polished walnut tables. Across the aisle was a cabinet filled with cans of soda, sandwiches, and chocolate.

It was the first time Will had been on a private jet—if you didn't count his father's old Cessna. And you couldn't, really. Not when you were in a fancy cabin like this.

Andrew and Gaia were sitting opposite him. Gaia was still in her jeans and black T-shirt. Andrew had changed out of his suit. He wore his khaki outdoor trousers, with their multiple zip pockets, and a T-shirt bearing the logo *Open Sourcery*. It was a pun on the brilliance of open-source software, he'd tried to explain, which was created by contributions of code from volunteers working anywhere in the world, rather than by employees of an individual company.

"Uh-huh," Gaia said, raising an eyebrow. "I *see*."

Now, for the first time that day, Will started to relax. STORM. In a private jet. On their way to Switzerland. On the trail of a secret project and a missing scientist. Will smiled to himself. Cristina della Corte could add *that* to her report.

"We will shortly be reaching our cruising altitude of forty thousand feet," came the crisp voice from the cockpit. "I'll alert you just before our descent into Interlaken."

Andrew unfastened his seat belt and stretched. He smiled at his surroundings. "You know, I *am* missing an interesting presentation on firewall updates. But I guess that's just one of the sacrifices I have to make to be a member of STORM."

"If we're talking about sacrifices," Will said, "we need to find out how and why those scientists died." He dug out his smart phone and connected to the plane's local network.

"What are you looking for?" Gaia asked.

"Abigail's file wasn't really much use. I'm looking for anything that could tell us what those scientists were working on."

He'd meant what he'd said on the bus about Barrington. *If* STORM wanted to chase down the truth about Project FIREball, they needed information to bargain with. If they went to him with nothing, Barrington would simply tell them to back off. He'd have to.

Will looked at Andrew. "Do you want to give the InVesta network another try?"

Andrew shook his head. While they'd been waiting to board the jet, Andrew had tried to access InVesta's computer systems. But the security had been exceptional—as might be expected from a global company with hugely valuable commercial secrets to protect—and Andrew had gotten nowhere.

"I'm not saying it's totally unhackable," he said now, "but I don't have the tools to do it, and I don't know anyone who does.

At least no one who wouldn't take weeks to get anywhere."

"Good thing we went to the HQ in person, then," Will said, pulling up the Wikipedia entry on InVesta.

InVesta is a multi-national oil and arms company with headquarters in New York and London. Among the largest private sector energy corporations in the world.

Recent developments

In 2007, the Fortune Global 500 list of companies ranked InVesta third in the world for turnover. Sales in the energy division were at US$198 billion. Sales in the arms division stood at US$17 billion.

Eighty-eight percent of InVesta's energy income comes from oil, natural gas, and petroleum. The company runs oil exploration ventures in the North Sea, Alaska, and the former Soviet Union.

Image

InVesta's name has been tarnished by a number of allegations of environmental contamination and undue political influence. In 2006, the company was fined US$7.5 million for leaks from oil wells in Alaska. It has also been alleged that InVesta used political contacts to gag three scientists with new data on global warming.

The arms division has also been hit by claims of corruption. In 2005, an international watchdog alleged that InVesta Arms had offered substantial bribes to influential figures in twelve nations in Africa in order to secure landmine sales worth US$600 million.

Present

InVesta has increased funding for its research and development centers in Europe. The company is believed to be developing a new form of solar panel, and shifting to a more high-tech focus for the arms division.

Then there was a list of links to other sites and articles.

None of the information really stood out, Will thought. And while the entry said that InVesta was ramping up its funding for research and development, it didn't mention any projects related to electrochemistry—or anything, in fact, that linked the company with the dead scientists.

Next, Will did a search for journal papers by Edmund Pope.

The search brought up 134 hits. Will scanned the list of titles.

Electrodeposition of gallium onto vitreous carbon.

Activity of gold toward methylamine electro-oxidation.

Andrew and Gaia had been watching him. "Anything yet?" Andrew asked.

Will read out the next title.

"Response of surface modeling and optimization to study the influence of deposition parameters on the electrodepositing of Cu-Zn alloys in citrate medium."

Andrew looked blank. "I have absolutely no idea what that means."

Will glanced at Gaia.

"I understand the gist. I don't know *everything* about chemistry."

"Then, no," Will said. "So far, nothing useful. Read the Wikipedia entry if you like, but it doesn't tell us much."

While Andrew took Will's smart phone, Gaia's gaze flicked across the cabin to their small pile of luggage. Her small red backpack, Andrew's neat leather satchel. Will's black backpack. "Maybe now you can show us what you've brought," she said.

Will looked at her. "You already know about the inhaler. I'm calling it Brain Sprain."

"Right, but what else do you have? How did you listen in on the meeting?"

"You *really* want to know?"

"*Yes.*"

And he *did* want to show them. It just always made him feel strange, showing anyone—even Andrew and Gaia—his devices. He put so much time and effort, and so much of himself, into them.

Will hesitated, then went to his backpack and opened it up. He'd shoved Vanya's present on top. Underneath was the pencil case with the modified asthma inhaler. The other stuff was at the bottom.

From a plastic bag, he pulled a black, stretchy, long-sleeved top. Will pushed his right arm into the sleeve. He rooted around in the refreshments cabinet until he found a fork, which he held out to Gaia. "Stab me with this."

"*What?*"

"Stab me."

She looked at him like he was crazy. "In the arm?"

"Yeah."

Gaia looked unconvinced, but she took the fork.

"You mean you've never wanted to hit him?" Andrew said. "Now's your chance."

Gaia looked at Will. "If I stab you with this, it *will* hurt."

"Just do it," Will said softly.

Shaking her head doubtfully, she lifted her arm, and she brought the fork down with just enough force that Will would think she'd tried.

And she stared. The fork had hit something *hard.*

Will smiled. "The fabric's made from seven thin layers

of Kevlar. Some of the layers are impregnated with a liquid made up of particles of silicon dioxide in a mix of ethylene glycol and ethanol. Normally, the liquid acts like a lubricant, so if you're walking around in the armor, it's flexible and you can move easily. But if there's an impact, the fabric becomes hard, like a shield. I tried it with an ice pick. It still works. I had suits made up. There's one for each of us. You wear them under your clothes."

Will tossed a top and a pair of leggings into Andrew's lap. Warily, Andrew held up the leggings.

"Don't tell me," Will said. "They're not your color."

"No, it's fine," Andrew said quickly. "I'm sure they'll be very useful . . . I presume they have a name?"

In fact, Will had been trying to think of a decent name for the invention. Then he remembered the logo on Andrew's T-shirt at the IT conference, *Soft Wear.* "Hard Wear," he said, smiling.

Gaia smiled too. "Have you got anything else in there for us?"

Will pulled out a transparent plastic box and lifted the lid. Coiled inside was a slender metallic tendril. "This is Eye Spy. It's prehensile," Will said. "The arm can extend twelve inches. At the end, there's a cutting tool and a bug-eyed lens."

Still holding on to his leggings, Andrew came closer to inspect. "It reminds me of Grabber," he said, referring to one of Will's earlier inventions.

"It's based on Grabber's tentacle," Will said. "But there's a diamond cutting tool in the end. And the camera's a lot better. It's an artificial insect eye, so it's ultra-wide-angle. It can see almost everything around it."

Andrew coughed slightly. "Maybe instead of Eye Spy,

you should have called it"—and he paused for effect—"*the Eye of the STORM.*"

Gaia groaned. Will suppressed a grin.

Andrew pretended to be hurt, but he was smiling. "I thought that was a good one."

Shaking his head, Will slipped the box back into his pack. He turned to Gaia. He was curious about something. "And maybe now Gaia will show us what's in *her* bag."

She blushed. "Clothes."

"I mean that one." Will pointed to the black bag resting on her hip. It was oblong, and semi-rigid. Like a camera bag.

"Gaia?" Andrew said with curiosity.

She was silent for a moment. "Actually, I have been working on something. Not like your devices," she said to Will.

"What something?" he asked.

She unzipped the bag, and from the padded interior produced an old-fashioned fountain pen. Very carefully, she unscrewed it. She pinched the gold nib between her fingers and slowly lifted it away from the casing. Attached to the nib, Will and Andrew saw a standard rubber reservoir, which looked full of black liquid.

"So now I'm *dyeing* to know what that liquid actually is," Andrew said as he sat down beside her.

"Ink," Gaia said, ignoring Andrew's bad pun. He looked disappointed. "Obviously it isn't ordinary ink! But I can't show you on the plane."

"Why not?" Will asked.

"Why do you think?" Gaia said. "What do I know about? Knowing me, what could be special about this ink?"

Will could make a pretty good guess. "It's *explosive.*"

She smiled.

"How explosive?" Andrew asked, eyes shining.

"Explosive enough for me not to want to expose it to the air right now."

"But what's in the ink?" Will asked.

"Tiny particles of aluminum and copper oxide. Epoxy varnish. Alcohol. And a sodium-based trigger. Once the ink dries out—which takes about five minutes—it explodes."

"That's brilliant," Andrew said softly.

Gaia smiled. She put the two halves of the pen back together and slipped it back inside its protective padding. She looked at Will. "You still haven't shown us what you used to listen in on that meeting. Unless the Eye of the STORM has a bug in it?"

Will shook his head. "But I really don't think you'll to want to see."

Gaia narrowed her eyes at him. *"Show us."*

Will held up his hands defensively. "All right." He found the cigar box. Brought it back to the table. Slipped it across to Gaia.

She picked it up and read the side panel, which was written in Spanish. "Vegas Robaina Don Alejandro cigars . . . Can I open it?"

"If you're sure you want to," Will said.

Three seconds later, he regretted his decision.

Gaia lifted the lid. For a moment, she was transfixed. Then revulsion rippled through her body. She dropped the box, shaking loose the plastic seals.

Eleven roaches scattered, fast as shrapnel—under the seats, into the food cabinet, even into the cockpit.

After fifteen minutes with the pheromone stick, Will managed to collect all the roaches.

Gaia looked at him, embarrassed. "Sorry," she said.

"I did warn you."

"Why did Vanya use *cockroaches*?" she asked.

"They hide. They like darkness."

"No wonder, when they look like *that*."

Will smiled and crossed to the window.

They were coming in to land. The narrow valleys and snow-topped cliff faces of the Alps looked spectacular.

Interlaken airport was tiny. Most people bound for the town flew into the main airport at Zurich and took a land transfer. But then, most people didn't arrive in a private plane.

Gaia followed Will as he headed for the exit. She could hear Andrew behind her, talking to Abigail, letting her know they'd arrived.

"Gaia! Will!"

Andrew lowered his phone. "Abigail's asking if we want a car."

Will thought for a moment. It could certainly make life easier. But then Gaia voiced the concern at the back of his mind.

"If she gets us a car, she could make the driver tell her exactly where we are and what we're doing. I don't want her coming out here and getting in the way. Or some driver asking questions."

Will nodded. But Andrew hesitated. He didn't like telling nice people things they didn't want to hear. Not that he wouldn't, he just didn't like it. "Ah, thank you, Abigail, that's a very kind offer. But I think we'll make our own arrangements. I'm sure it'll be easier . . ."

Will kept walking, and blinked as the glass doors slid open, letting them out into the sunshine. He took a deep breath— and gasped. The fresh air seemed to slash his lungs. After the pollution of London, it was almost painful. He looked up. The sky was powder blue, jagged through with sharp mountains.

A single taxi was waiting. Andrew jogged over to it. He put his suitcase down. "I'll just find the address. Hold on." He started to hit keys on his smart phone, looking for the stolen e-mail with Wickett's last-known address.

But Gaia strode past him. "You've forgotten something," she called to Andrew as she opened the passenger door.

He looked thrown.

"My photographic memory." She smiled and turned to the smartly dressed driver. "Blaustrasse 14, Kleinkirchen."

Crags jutted. The Jungfrau massif soared, gray and white against the luminous sky. Will stared out of the cab window. He'd never seen anything like it. But running against that brilliant backdrop were other, darker thoughts.

Project FIREball—what was it? And how was InVesta involved?

Fir-covered mountainsides swept past. Will caught glimpses of a lake, clear and blue as the sky. He saw white wooden houses with neat red roofs. Gray churches, their steeples needle-sharp. And he thought about David Wickett.

He was out there, somewhere. If he hadn't already been captured. Or hadn't fled the country, taking his extraordinary knowledge with him.

After the roaches had been safely secured back in their box, Will had scoured the Internet for more information about those six scientists.

At first, they seemed to have little in common, except that they were all physicists. But it turned out that each had been thrown out of at least one top-level lab. Two had been physically attacked at conferences. Edmund Pope had been expelled from the Academy of Sciences—though the reasons were murky. David Wickett had been publicly booed at an international symposium. Strange, Will thought.

There was another similarity: All were acknowledged by their peers as brilliant. To their supporters, they were mavericks; to their enemies, geniuses who unfortunately had gone off the rails.

Before he left England for Switzerland eight months ago, Wickett had been employed as a lecturer by King's College, London. His old staff web page had been cached by Google. At the bottom was a dry list of his research interests. But no mention of a Project FIREball, of course.

Another hour on the Internet had produced nothing. Type "FIREball" into Google and you got information on racing boats, an album by a band called Deep Purple, and pages and pages on meteors.

They still had no idea what the project was all about. But perhaps now they'd find out.

For the past ten minutes, the taxi had been weaving down the side of the mountain. Suddenly it swerved to a halt.

"There," the driver said, in English. He was pointing up a steep track.

The scene looked frozen. To their left was a mound of brown earth and a pile of logs. Two yellow Bobcats were motionless in the cool sunshine. A building site. Below, another road ran dementedly down to a still, sapphire lake, semicircled with fir trees.

Will followed the driver's finger. At the top of the track, he could just make out a red roof and the tops of two white-painted windows. Beside the house, a silver stream poured out of a ragged gray cliff face, the heart of the mountain erupting and vanishing into a drain that had to run under the road. A faint breeze blew. In the distance, Will could hear cowbells.

At Will's request, the driver had stopped about three hundred yards from Wickett's house. "You want go up now?" the man asked.

"No," Will said. "We want to walk."

"Walk?"

"We live in London. We like this fresh air," Andrew said.

"I wait?"

"*Nein*," Gaia said as she got out. She didn't know as much of German as she did of some other languages, but a photographic memory was invaluable for internalizing a phrasebook. She knew just about enough to get by. "*Danke. Mein Freund hat die Geld.*" She pointed at Andrew.

Andrew paid the fare, and the cab pulled away.

They turned to peer in the direction of Wickett's house.

"We do know there's no chance Wickett will be there," Andrew said. "Not when five of his colleagues have just been killed."

"Yeah," Will said. "But this address is the only place we have to start. Maybe we'll still find something useful."

"Like a notebook describing the details of Project FIREball?" Andrew asked, with just the faintest trace of sarcasm.

Will looked at him, surprised, and Andrew regretted his tone. Sarcasm wasn't really his style. "I mean—yes, okay, you're right—this is the only place we have to start . . . So what's the plan?"

Will thought for a moment. "*If* InVesta is after Wickett, they'll have already checked the house. They could still have people there now. It would be safer if just one of us went." Will focused on Andrew, who looked blank. Will continued to regard him silently. Andrew's blue eyes suddenly blinked.

"Me?"

Will smiled. "Relax. I was just getting you back. I'll go. You both stay here."

"I could go," Gaia said.

Will patted his backpack. "I have Eye Spy."

"I could always take it." But she could anticipate Will's response. It was an unwritten rule that, unless he gave permission, no one should touch Will's inventions, except him.

"*Maybe,*" Will said, as though the idea was just about conceivable. "But the only audio gear I have on me has legs and antennae."

Gaia grimaced. "I'll wait here."

Andrew smiled at her. He sat down on the scrubby grass and stretched out, tilting his face to the sun. "There are worse places to wait," he said. "Take your time, Will. Make sure you give it a thorough examination. Don't miss a thing." He breathed deeply.

"Yeah, yeah," Will said as he slung his backpack over his shoulder. "Just don't get too comfortable. If I find bad guys up there, you might have to be ready to run."

The ground was uneven. Rocks. Tufts of spiky grass. Will's breathing quickened as he climbed. When he got within clear sight of the house, he crouched and watched. He could see nothing moving. Hear nothing, except a gentle swish of the breeze in the grass, and the cowbells in the distance.

The house looked well-kept. Window boxes at each of the four front windows were bursting with pink and orange flowers. Poking out from behind the back wall was a woodpile, the logs neatly stacked. But from here, Will could see little else. Net curtains screened his view of the interior. He'd have to get closer.

Will dashed across the open ground, heading straight for the back of the house. He skirted the woodpile, edged around a bicycle, and then another bike—or rather, a hybrid between a bike and a scooter. Will knew what it was, though he'd only seen them on TV before. It had cross-country wheels, but in place of pedals and a seat, there was a low platform to stand on. A Trottibike—popular in the Alps for racing down mountainsides. This particular bike was also fitted with a small motor to drive the wheels. Was it David Wickett's? Then Will froze.

He'd heard a sound. It had come from inside.

Will crouched low. He inched forward. If he tried to look in through a window, there was a chance he'd be spotted by whoever was inside. What was Eye Spy for, if not covert visual surveillance?

Will pulled the device from his pocket. He used the control pad to extend the tendril and watched it unfurl, like the tentacle of an octopus. The titanium joints gleamed. A red switch on the base of the device activated the cutting tool, with its diamond tip, five hundred microns thick. This was old-school technology, but STASIS had the equipment needed to grow the diamond sheets—and solid diamond was still supremely hard. Will flipped the switch. At once, the cutting blade vibrated. He aimed the gadget right at the wall, between two planks of knotted wood.

The blade caught at once. It made only the slightest noise as it burrowed into the wood. A small cloud of brown dust formed in the air. Then Will felt the resistance against the tip ease. Eye Spy was in. He pulled his smart phone from his pocket and watched the video feed.

Eye Spy's lens was based on a dragonfly's. It was a molded plastic dome, one-tenth of an inch across. In the surface of the dome were thousands of miniature micro-lenses. Incoming light passed through each of these micro-lenses, and on to the center of the eye via tiny channels.

The vast number of minute lenses provided an incredibly wide field of vision. In practice, this meant that Will could push the lens just inside the room—and he'd be able to see everything from the wall on the left-hand side of Eye Spy's tip, all the way around the room to the wall on the right.

On the screen now, Will saw a fridge. A wooden cupboard. It was open. A dark shadow. The shadow moved. Will used the remote to reduce the magnification. He saw a blue skirt. A white belt. A blouse. A girl.

Holding his breath now, Will adjusted the angle of the bug-eye camera until he found her face. He saw short dark hair. Pink cheeks. She was sixteen or seventeen years old. And she had something in her hand. With just a fraction of a movement, Will shifted the lens. Could it really be . . . surely not . . . a *duster*?

Will breathed again. This girl looked like a housekeeper, and if InVesta henchmen were close at hand, she'd hardly be dusting. The only noise so far had come from the kitchen. He had to assume she was alone.

When Eye Spy was safely back in his pocket, Will retraced his steps. He peered around the side of the house and caught a flash of light from the direction of the road. The sun reflecting off Andrew's glasses, Will realized.

He *could* call them up. But perhaps it would be better if he handled this alone.

13

Greta Studer made a final swipe of the window ledge, carefully folded her duster and put it back with the other cleaning tools, under the sink.

She cast her eyes around the spotless room. Every Monday and Tuesday for the past eight months, she had come to clean and prepare food for the British scientist. That morning, she had been peeling potatoes, when her mobile phone had rung.

Herr Wickett's voice had sounded strange: "Greta! Thank God!"

Then he'd asked her if there had been any visitors, and he'd told her he was in trouble.

Herr Wickett *was* an eccentric. This was not the first time he had failed to come home at night. But why had he talked about the *police*?

Greta had kept her phone in the pocket of her apron, to be sure she wouldn't miss another call. She had cooked two casseroles, split them into portions, and put them in the freezer. Then she had dusted the living room. This was her second time around the kitchen. In five minutes, she would go home to her mother.

And then there was a knock.

Greta took a deep breath. Wiping her hands on her skirt, she peered through the spyhole.

She opened the door two inches. "Yes?"

"I'm looking for David Wickett."

The girl looked afraid, Will thought. She squinted her black eyes.

"He isn't here. Who are you?"

"Can I come in?"

"I am busy. What do you want?"

Will hesitated. There were various ways he could go about this. But the best approach was probably honesty.

"My name is Will Knight. I'm here because the niece of someone David Wickett was working with asked me to come. Yesterday, her uncle was killed in an explosion at a farmhouse not far from here, with four others. I think David Wickett should have been there too. Somehow he managed to escape."

Greta couldn't conceal her surprise. Of course, she had heard about the explosion. An accident. Or at least, that's what everyone said. The names of the dead had not been revealed. But what did this English *boy* know about it all? Why should David Wickett have been there?

"I want to find him, to see if we can help," Will said. "My friend is worried. She doesn't know what her uncle was involved with."

Whoever this boy was, he seemed to know a great deal, Greta thought—if what he was saying was the truth. But Herr Wickett had made her promise to tell no one anything. To carry on as normal.

"He comes and goes as he pleases," she said tersely. "I clean. That is all. I don't know where he is." She slammed the door shut.

Inside the hallway, Greta's thoughts raced. The explosion . . . And David Wickett *should have been there*? What if? She couldn't help it. The thought stuck in her mind.

What if he was involved? What if he had killed those others and he was on the run? But then why tell her to call the police if she didn't hear from him? Unless he feared vengeance from someone else?

Ludicrous! Or was it? Her stomach knotted.

But she deserved answers. If she was aiding a criminal, she had to know.

She was only his employee, only his housekeeper. And he was asking too much.

For a few moments, Will waited outside the slammed door.

He could try knocking again. But the girl was taking him seriously. Perhaps it would be best to retreat, and watch.

Quickly, he retraced his steps down the mountain to where Andrew and Gaia were waiting. He told them about his conversation with the housekeeper.

"If she doesn't know where Wickett is, she knows something," Will said. "I think we should wait here and see what she does." Then he turned, raising himself so he could just see the front of the house. He stiffened.

The girl was coming out. She vanished around the back. A moment later, she reappeared, pushing the strange bike. Andrew and Gaia crept closer for a better look.

"What *is* that?" Andrew said.

"It's called a Trottibike," Will said. "And this one's *motorized*. We have to follow her."

They should have held on to their taxi, Andrew thought. "We don't have a car! What are we supposed to do?"

The girl was pushing the bike across the track that led from the front of the house to the main road.

Will half stood. He scoured the landscape. His eyes rested on something.

Gaia followed his gaze. "*Will—*"

Andrew only nodded. "We have few options, Gaia. There's an old saying: needs must."

She shook her head. "Then you *must* be insane."

14

"Can you even drive it?"

Gaia was running behind Andrew and Will.

"I've done it before," Will shot back. Which was true. Once. Two years ago, on the farm next to his old home in Dorset.

He was heading straight for the building site, his backpack bouncing on his shoulder. The Bobcat was parked up by a pile of logs, close to the road.

"She *will* see us!" Gaia said. "You don't think she'll notice a bulldozer following her?"

"The bike doesn't have any mirrors," Will replied.

"Then she'll hear us! And even if the keys are in there, there's no way we're all going to fit!"

If the girl did hear the Bobcat, would it really matter? Will thought. She wouldn't suspect the machine was actually following her.

But Gaia was right when she said they wouldn't all fit inside. The cabin could take only one person. But there was a rail on the back, above the engine cover. Someone could hold on to that.

"You'll have to get on the back," Will said to her. "Andrew, you'll have to ride in the tray."

Andrew's eyes opened wide.

"There's no time to discuss this! If we don't do it, we'll lose her." Will craned his neck. Down the hill, he could see the girl on the bike, still on the grass, about to hit the main road. Half bike, half scooter, designed for whizzing down slopes. They had to *hurry*.

Will jumped into the tray and stepped up, through a door in the front of the cabin, to the driver's seat. He pulled down a black restraint bar, of the sort used in roller coasters. His eyes shot to the ignition. The key was in it.

Gaia was groaning, but she climbed onto the back of the Bobcat. She slipped underneath the boom rail and twisted, so she was sitting facing backward, holding tight to the rail. Gingerly, Andrew began to climb into the tray. It was four and a half feet wide, easily big enough for him to fit inside. As he sat down, he noticed a hazard sticker. It read: *Danger. Avoid Death. Never Use Loader as a Man Lift. Never Carry Riders.*

Andrew shook his head. He looked up uncertainly at Will, who had just turned the key. At once, the engine rumbled and an orange light on the roof of the cabin started flashing.

There were two steering levers, like giant gearshifts, one on each side of Will's seat. The left-hand lever controlled the two left-side wheels, while the other did the same for the right.

To move forward, Will remembered, you pushed the levers dead ahead. To make a left turn, you had to push the right-hand lever forward a little, while pulling back on the left. If you pushed both levers hard in opposite directions, a Bobcat could spin on the spot.

But first Will had to lift the tray off the ground. He pushed his heel down on the left-hand pedal.

Nothing happened.

He heard a thump on the roof of the cabin.

"What are you waiting for?" Gaia yelled.

What was wrong? Why wasn't it working?

Will nudged the two steering levers forward. *No response.*

He wiped his hands on his jeans. The engine was running, so why wasn't the machine responding? Then he remembered. His eyes scanned the touch pad next to the front window. There was the green Press to Operate button. Will hit it. Again, he pushed his heel down on the left-hand pedal—and the tray jerked upward.

Andrew's white face popped out of the top.

"Get down!" Will shouted. "Hold on tight!"

He pushed the steering levers forward and the Bobcat responded at once. The sixteen-inch wheels, with their heavy-tread tires, started to roll down the grass. A moment later, the bulldozer hit the road with a bang.

Will heard a yelp. Gaia. He glanced back. She was still hanging on.

Now that they were on asphalt, Will pushed an orange handle at the side of his seat, from a symbol of a tortoise to a rabbit, for maximum speed. He shoved the levers full ahead and squinted. The Trottibike was a good quarter mile ahead. The girl's skirt ballooned in the wind, a big blue ball.

The Bobcat gained pace, but it wasn't exactly fast. There was no speedometer, but they couldn't be going more than eight miles an hour. Even though the girl was only on a scooter-bike, at this rate it would still be hard to catch her.

The asphalt hugged the mountainside. Will glanced

down the slope. He could see that the main road ran in one long hairpin bend, down toward the lake. But there were at least three turnoffs. There was no predicting where the girl would end up.

All he could do was focus on the Trottibike and urge the Bobcat on.

Or was it?

Could he take a chance?

He had to.

"Hold on!" he yelled, hoping Gaia and Andrew could hear him.

Will pulled back on the right-hand lever and pushed the left forward. At once, he heard a bang on the roof. Gaia's fist. *"Will!"*

"It's all right!" he shouted back. "I know what I'm doing!"

As the Bobcat left the road and hit the grassy slope, Andrew's head jerked up from the tray. He could see Will's face, set, and focused dead ahead. They were angling down fast, at thirty degrees now, at least. As the terrain suddenly got rougher, Andrew started to bounce. The tray was vibrating. His teeth clattered. He peered cautiously past the metal spikes. He was barely two feet off the ground. His fingers gripped tighter to the edges of the tray. Suddenly the Bobcat hit a mound, and Andrew felt himself almost flung out of the tray. *"Will!"*

Will looked down. He was on a spring-suspension seat, which absorbed the rocks and the ruts. But he'd seen Andrew's legs fly up—and now Andrew's terrified face, his glasses askew.

"Go back to the road!" Andrew yelled.

"Just hold on!" Will shouted.

With this maneuver, they would cut across the hairpin. If the girl didn't turn off, *if* she was still on the main road, he would slash the distance between them. It was a calculated risk. He glanced back. Gaia's hair was flying. Her head suddenly knocked against the rear window. He heard her curse. But they were nearly there. They were nearly back at the road. Just another thirty feet.

Suddenly, the slope steepened. They had to be at forty degrees, Will thought. Then forty-five. How far could he push it? The Bobcat seemed to lurch forward. Will felt a sudden rush of nausea. *If it went over—*

He stopped the thought.

Almost there, he told himself. Almost there.

And the front wheels finally hit tarmac. A soft bang—at least, for Will—and the rear end was on the road. And there, barely three hundred feet in front of them, was the Trottibike.

Will exhaled hard. The gamble had paid off.

He twisted in his seat. "Are you all right?" he shouted to Gaia.

"Just look at the road!" she yelled back, her eyes blazing. "Which, by the way, you're meant to stay on!"

Will smiled and turned. Very slowly now, Andrew's head rose from the gray tray. With a trembling hand, he adjusted his glasses.

"All right?" Will shouted.

For a moment, Andrew didn't respond. Every limb was battered, he felt as though someone had kicked him in the neck, and as they'd hit the road, his funny bone had smashed into metal. His elbow was still screaming. So the answer was no. But Will didn't need to know all that. Andrew gave him the thumbs-up.

Will grinned and waved Andrew down, concentrating on the road.

They had closed the gap on the Trottibike, so Will eased up on the steering levers. If the girl looked back, he didn't want her to see his face.

But she wasn't looking back. Ahead now, she was taking a hard left onto a narrow track. Will followed its route. It led south, to the lake. To a falling-down hut.

Dead ahead, beside the main road, was a dense patch of firs. As soon as they hit the trees, Will let go of the levers. The Bobcat ground to a halt. He turned off the engine.

Sudden silence made Will's ears ring. But he breathed easily. They were hidden. Under cover. For a few seconds, he just sat there. His body was tingling, rushed through with adrenaline

Gaia jumped down. She rested both hands on her knees, breathing hard.

From the tray, there came a shaken voice: "Remind me never to drive with you again. Ever." Awkwardly, Andrew clambered out. Dirt and grit clung to his clothes. He wiped damp sand from his cheek.

Will slung his backpack over his shoulder and jumped down from the cabin. "What did you want me to do? Lose her?"

Andrew rubbed his elbow and swallowed hard. "After all that, we'd better not. So what are we waiting for?"

Will smiled. "Gaia?"

She nodded. But she wasn't smiling.

Will walked quickly back along the road, to the very edge of the woods. From here, he had a clear view down to the lake. He could see the Trottibike, lying on its side on the grass beside the hut. Andrew and Gaia closed in behind him.

"She's in there," Will said. "Come on."

Between the trees and the hut there was nothing to use as cover. As he ran, Will kept his eyes open. He could see no one. A sports car sped past on the road behind, engine roaring, and it went on, growling into the distance.

Will passed the Trottibike. He was running so fast, he almost collided with the wall of the hut. Andrew and Gaia caught up. Will listened. He could hear nothing, except their breathing. See nothing—just the faint ripple of the breeze on the turquoise water of the lake. Everything seemed peaceful.

Cautiously, Will edged around to the front of the hut. A wooden door with rotting holes in the planks hung almost off its hinges.

Will touched it. It responded at once. As it swung back, he saw streaks of light through darkness. Then, as his eyes adjusted, he saw her—the girl—kneeling on a tarpaulin beside an open trapdoor.

Greta's head shot up. Her mouth dropped open. Her gaze skittered across Gaia and then Andrew.

Andrew took a step forward. "My name is Andrew. This is Gaia. You already met Will. We only want to help."

"Did you expect to find Wickett here?" Will asked. "We know he's in trouble. We know his life's in danger. You have to trust us. Do you know where he is now?"

Greta stared, her brain reeling. It wasn't only the appearance of these three kids that had thrown her, but a note. A note that Wickett had left under the tarpaulin—and which she had read quickly and pushed into her pocket moments before the door had swung open. Why had he left a note? Why hadn't he called her? And what did these words mean!

"He was here this morning," she said. "He called me—he told me he was in trouble—and now he has gone." She turned and scowled at them. "Why are you here? What do you want?"

"We want you to tell us everything you know!" Gaia said impatiently.

Greta pressed her hands to her eyes. She didn't know what to think.

David Wickett couldn't have killed those people. And now, he had left this note. It made no sense!

She *had* to talk to someone. "How do I know you are not enemies of David Wickett?"

Will considered using the asthma inhaler to soften her up. But the cartridge contained only two doses, and he'd already used one getting into the conference. "Do we look like enemies of anyone?" he asked. "We want to help Wickett. We want to find out what happened at that farmhouse—why those scientists were killed."

"We want to find Wickett and make sure that he's safe," Andrew added. "We think he's in danger. We're not out to hurt him. You have to help us."

Greta took a deep breath. Made a decision. "All right . . . But you tell me everything about you. Who you are. How exactly you know all these things!"

"Fine," Will said. "But not here. Come with us."

Will led the way.

They covered the ground quickly, heading toward the shelter of the dense patch of fir trees beside the main road. The girl had come here looking for Wickett, so perhaps other people would too. Perhaps someone was watching them right now . . .

Will's eyes scanned the horizontal plan, darting across to the lake, back to the hut, ahead, to the main road, and to the trees.

He didn't look up.

If he had, he'd have seen an eagle. Circling.

Three hundred feet up, the Eagle's head swiveled. The left iris dilated.

On the banks of the River Tweed, Shute Barrington squinted at the images from the high-res camera. They were streaming back to his monitor. He'd just received an instruction to alter the Eagle's surveillance sweep, and she was flying at high altitude over the lake. But what were those figures doing? They were *running*.

Barrington increased the magnification of the camera's lens. And his eyes opened wide.

"Will! Andrew! Gaia! What the hell are you doing there?"

Ten seconds later, Will's phone rang. They had just made it around the edge of the woods. The Bobcat was in sight.

He stopped. Checked the name on the screen. Answered the call: *"Barrington?"*

Andrew, Gaia, and the girl were close behind. *"Shute?"* Andrew whispered.

Will nodded. He hit the loudspeaker button, so they could all hear.

Barrington's voice boomed: *"Will, what exactly are you doing?"*

"Shute. Where are you?"

"It doesn't matter where *I* am. I know where *you* are. 46.5 degrees north, 7.89 degrees east. Sound about right?"

Will's brain raced. How could Barrington possibly know their location? Unless he'd somehow discovered that they'd headed to Switzerland, and the longitude and latitude were a guess—

Will stopped himself. Barrington didn't make guesses. "But how—"

"Look up, Will. Recognize anything?"

The yellow sun stunned Will's eyes. He blinked. Then he saw a shadow. A raptor, circling high above. And he remembered the Eagle! Barrington had been talking about the project the last time he was at Sutton Hall. But he hadn't realized the Eagle was operational—and why would Barrington be following him? Why had he phoned only now? The questions stuck in Will's throat.

"I'm listening," Barrington said.

Will wasn't sure what to say.

Andrew had followed Will's gaze. But he hadn't understood Will's shock. "It's just a bird," he whispered.

Will covered the mouthpiece of his phone with his hand. "A robotic bird with cameras for eyes! It's the *Eagle*—I told you about it. Barrington can see us!"

"I can also hear you," came the powerful voice. "And you haven't answered my question."

Will hesitated. Yes, they had told Abigail they wouldn't go to MI6. But Barrington knew they were in Switzerland. And Will had to act according to his own conscience, not anyone's instructions. He trusted Barrington. Now that the man had made contact, he couldn't lie.

Gaia nodded, as though she had read his mind. "Tell him," she whispered.

"I'm not sure where to start," Will said.

"Oh, you'll work it out," Barrington replied.

And so Will told him—about the meeting with Abigail Pope, though he didn't name her, about their visit to InVesta's London HQ, about Andrew's printer hacking, the list of dead men, even Greta and the hut.

Will spoke rapidly, but Greta kept up. By the end, she was openmouthed.

"So you can see why we're trying to find David Wickett," Will said at last.

"You and about a dozen of our field officers, six Swiss agents, three CIA men, four EU representatives, and I dread to think who else." Barrington's voice was heavy as lead. "This is bloody serious, Will. You don't work for me, but I'm giving you an order: Leave Wickett. Let us find him."

"Why?" Will said quickly. "What's he working on? What's Project FIREball?"

Silence. Then Barrington said: "I can't tell you. And if you want to know the truth: *I* don't even know what FIREball is. It's got an Alpha classification. Which means that only the Prime Minister, C, as the chief of MI6, and the defense minister would have access to the full dossier."

"*You've* got the Eagle out here."

"Under orders! I'm the *tech support*, Will. The bloody geek! I'm feeding images straight back to MI6 Operations Control to help them search for Wickett and coordinate the field team." Barrington took a deep breath. "I've got a pretty good understanding of the way you think, Will, so I'm going to make this plain: Leave Wickett. If you don't, consider whatever relationship there is between STORM and STASIS over."

Will froze. That last sentence hung in the air. Barrington was serious. And you couldn't argue with him. Will knew that. But Barrington was asking an awful lot.

Will looked at Andrew.

Very slowly, Andrew nodded. If Barrington was ordering them to leave Wickett, on the pain of ending their relationship, they had to do it.

Will's eyes shot to Gaia.

She looked at him. At last, she shook her head. "He said it: We don't work for him," she whispered. She liked Barrington, and she respected him. But they were free agents.

Will squeezed his eyes shut. He didn't like being told what to do any more than Gaia did. But he had a decision to make. Right now. "All right," he said.

Gaia's gaze hardened. Will avoided it.

"That's the right choice, Will." Barrington was clearly relieved. "Now take Andrew and Gaia and go eat some fondue. Check out the sights. The mountains are quite something."

"*Yeah*," Will said. And he cut the connection. He could stomach agreeing to obey Barrington, but not his condescension. Not even as a joke.

As Will slipped the phone back into his pocket, his face flashed his irritation—not with Barrington's line about the fondue, but with the decision he'd been forced to make.

"Don't even think about it," Andrew said at once. "We've agreed now. It's unfortunate, I know. But we have no choice. We have to leave Wickett."

Greta looked confused. "What is happening?" she asked. "Who were you talking to? Who are you?"

Will ignored her.

"Will?" Gaia said. She could see what he was thinking. He was still weighing it up.

"Will, it isn't worth it," Andrew said quickly. "You trust Barrington, don't you? We have to let it go. If he's sure it's for the best—"

"Best for him," Gaia said.

Andrew stiffened. "Gaia, don't you think Barrington would do what he thought was best for Britain?"

"You have a lot of faith in him," she said flatly.

"Yes, I do! And what reason has he given you to doubt him?"

Gaia thought about it. None, in fact. Except that he was warning them off a scientist missing from a top secret project. Could there be reasons other than the fact MI6 was already chasing him?

Will took a deep breath. "We'll leave Wickett," he said. Then he added: "But that doesn't mean this is over." He'd been thinking. The e-mail that Andrew had intercepted in London had been sent from something called the Black Sphere. And someone in that meeting with Evelyn Hughes had mentioned a Sphere. Whatever this was, it had to be linked to Project FIREball. "We can still find out about the Sphere," he said.

Except he had no idea what it was.

And now they couldn't ask Barrington.

Will turned to Greta, who was watching them silently. "Do you know what Wickett was working on?"

She shook her head. "Why would he tell me? All I know is that yesterday morning he was very happy. He said he'd done it. I don't know what! Then at half past twelve, he went out."

"Have you heard of something called the Sphere? Or the Black Sphere?" Will asked.

Greta looked blank. Shook her head.

Another long shot, he realized. And without Barrington's help, they were alone. It had made sense to turn down Abigail's offer of a car, but some local knowledge might be useful.

Who could they go to? Not the police. Not a journalist. They might have their ear to the ground, but they'd ask too many questions. Suddenly Will remembered Vanya's letter—and his association of retired spies.

"When Vanya sent me the roaches, he sent a letter. He said, if you need help anywhere, I know people—call me. Last month, he told me about an association of retired spies. He's the chairman. He has contacts all over the world."

"*What?*" Gaia said. "Retired spies have an *association?*"

"Yes."

"But who's in it?" Andrew asked, eyes wide. "What do they do?"

"They meet up. They swap stories. You can ask Vanya all about it at the wedding!" Will was impatient. He understood why they were interested. And he'd spent one long night asking Vanya all about it. But now wasn't the time to elaborate. "Look, if Barrington won't help, perhaps Vanya can."

Greta had been concentrating hard. She'd understood most of what they'd said—at least she'd understood the actual words. But now they were no longer talking about Wickett, and after what he'd written in the note, she was afraid for him, and for her own safety. She took the note from her pocket and held it out to Will. "He left this at the hut."

Will frowned at her. "*David Wickett* left this? Why didn't you tell us before?"

"I haven't had a chance!"

Andrew hurried over to Will to take a look. Gaia leaned around his other shoulder.

Kleinkirchen at risk. Evacuate. Get EVERYBODY OUT. Tell—

What was Wickett talking about? And why had he stopped in mid-sentence, Will wondered. Had he been interrupted?

"Why evacuate Kleinkirchen?" Gaia asked. Wickett was in danger. But why should the village be too?

Greta hesitated. There was something else she hadn't told them. Perhaps she should go the police, or to the university. But perhaps David Wickett was a murderer. Or he was mad. These kids knew more than she did. If she told them, then it would be in their hands, and she could go home. She could talk to her mother, and tell her about the note. "I know where his notebook is," she said at last.

Will stared at her. Two stunning pieces of information in as many minutes.

"I clean for him!" Greta went on. "I know where he keeps it. The pest control people who came—they did not find it. I looked at it once. But it does not seem to be in English. There are lots of numbers. As though it is in code."

Andrew's eyes shone. "Equations?" he asked. "Does it look like physics?"

Greta shook her head. "I don't know."

"But you can get it for us?" he asked.

" . . . Yes. He keeps it behind the woodpile. I found it two months ago when I was leaving traps for rats. I knocked the logs. Some of them fell—and I saw it."

Will remembered Andrew's attempt at sarcasm when they were wondering what they might get out of a visit to Wickett's house. "A notebook describing the detail of Project FIREball," he said to Andrew with a raised eyebrow. "Exactly what we'd hoped to find."

On a black desk in a dark room, a telephone was ringing.

Gustav Pritt ran to answer it. He was a tall, long-limbed man with a large paunch. His black trousers were too short for him. They showed an inch of white socks. Pritt pulled his pipe from his mouth. *"Ja?"*

The voice was cold. "Wickett is no longer answering his phone. You were supposed to call me when he made contact with you to reconfirm."

Pritt knew what his boss wanted to hear. But it wouldn't be the truth. Pritt searched his English vocabulary. Nervously, he rubbed his gray mustache. "Unfortunately, sir, that eventuality is yet to occur. But of course—"

"Silence!"

It was agonizing. At least for Pritt.

"But he is still alive? Don't tell me that you've messed up again! If Wickett is dead—if anything has happened to those plans—"

"Sir, I can assure you . . ." Pritt's voice trailed off. In fact, he wasn't in a position to assure his boss of anything.

Another agonizing silence.

At last, his boss said: *"Hudson's report?"*

Here was good news! "Yes, sir. I have just e-mailed you a copy, as requested."

"And Hudson?"

"He is in the building. He will be dealt with."

"Make sure of it, Pritt. Or I've a mind to lock you in a room somewhere in Kleinkirchen!"

Pritt shuddered. "Wickett will do as he has been instructed, sir. He understands what will happen if he fails to produce the documents. He will be in contact if—"

"It's not really an issue of *if,* is it Pritt?" the voice said. "For your sake, let's say it's *when* . . . I'm in the air. I'll be there in an hour. *Meet me with good news.*"

16

Greta ran back to the hut to get her Trottibike. From the woods, Will and Andrew watched her, while Gaia called a cab to take them back to Interlaken.

Will knew that, for a while at least, Shute Barrington would probably keep an eye on them with the Eagle. The robot could track moving figures from an altitude high enough to be practically invisible to someone below, so they wouldn't even know it was there.

But Barrington was carrying out official business. If the Eagle wasn't following a route proscribed by Operations Control, they'd want to know why. Barrington would have to get back to work soon enough.

The plan was for Greta to go back to the house to get the notebook. Meanwhile, they would head into town and find somewhere apparently innocent to wait. Barrington would think they'd done as he'd asked and—hopefully—stop watching them. Then they'd call Greta with the location, and she'd bring the notebook to them.

Will felt impatient for answers. Barrington's call had only increased his desire to find out exactly what was going on.

Thor, one of the STASIS techies, had told Will about the report classification system one evening at Sutton Hall. As head of MI6's science and technology unit, Shute Barrington had clearance for the vast majority of the intelligence passing the desk of C, the MI6 chief. An Alpha classification meant Project FIREball had to be one of the hottest projects going. What could be so important? And why would it interest InVesta?

And why was Wickett so scared—not just for himself, but for Kleinkirchen too?

Their best bet for at least some answers was the notebook. But if it didn't reveal *everything*, if Vanya could come up with someone who could provide some local assistance, it would still be worth meeting them. Maybe this person would have information that Barrington could not—or would not—share. *Maybe* they'd be able to throw some light on the bizarre note.

But how could he ask Vanya for help without giving the game away?

"The cab will be here in fifteen minutes," Gaia said as she joined Will and Andrew. "Have you called Vanya?"

"Not yet," Will said.

"What are you waiting for?"

"If he wanted to, Barrington could listen in on all my calls."

"ECHELON?" Andrew asked.

Will nodded. ECHELON was a secretive surveillance network led by the U.S. and the U.K. intelligence agencies. When Will had once asked about it, Barrington had been cagey on the detail, but in theory ECHELON could be used to intercept telephone calls, e-mails, faxes, and radio and satellite communications practically anywhere across the globe.

"So if you ask Vanya for help, Barrington will know," Gaia said.

Will nodded. "If he's listening. And given the conversation we just had, he probably is."

"So what do we do?"

Will thought for a moment. He held down number nine on his keypad. It would connect him straight to Vanya's cell. "Vanya used to be a spy," he said. "Hopefully if I sound strange he'll catch on—"

"*Slooshayoo.*"

"Vanya!"

"Will! What a surprise! You are calling no doubt to thank me for the gift. Or perhaps to discuss the color of your page boy suit? Or the grandson speech you will make at the wedding?"

His *grandson speech*? But perhaps he could use this. "Yeah, thanks for the present—and I did want to ask you about the speech. I'm on holiday with Andrew and Gaia, in Switzerland. It looks like I've got some time on my hands, so I can work on it. And you said if I needed help with it anytime I could call you? *Anytime, anywhere?*"

There was a pause. Then, "That's right. Yes, of course." Vanya still sounded jovial. But the slight change in his tone told Will he understood something was up—and he was playing along. "So, you are in Switzerland?" Vanya said. "You are enjoying the views?"

"Yeah, we were thinking of going to have a closer look at the Jungfrau this afternoon."

"So you are in . . . Interlaken?"

"That's right," Will said. "So you can *help me* with the speech?"

"You *really* need help with it?"

"Yeah. If that's possible."

There was a slight pause. "Of course, yes. Then let me think about it, and I will get back to you. And you know, I spent three weeks in Interlaken last summer. I went to many delightful restaurants. If my favorite spot is open for lunch, you must go there. It'll be worth it. I will text you to let you know."

"Thank you, Vanya." Will hoped all his gratitude made it through in those three words.

"Take care of yourself, grandson. I will be in touch."

Will flipped his phone shut, relieved. But only someone who knew Vanya would realize his tone and his sentences had been off . . . *I went to many delightful restaurants.* The normal Vanya would never say anything like that. And Barrington had met Vanya. Perhaps he even knew about the retired spies' association, Will thought. Barrington was far from stupid. There was a chance he would translate the conversation. Will hoped not.

Andrew and Gaia were looking doubtful.

"Vanya *understood* all that nonsense?" Andrew asked. "What did he say?"

"He knows we're in Interlaken. He knows we want help. If one of his contacts is available, he's going to text us a place to meet."

Andrew smiled. "Good old Vanya."

Will grinned. "Never let him hear you say that."

STASIS Headquarters, Sutton Hall, Oxfordshire

Charlie Spicer pulled out his earphones, unsure what to do. Six minutes ago, he'd gotten an urgent call from Shute

Barrington telling him STORM were in Switzerland and that he'd warned them off Wickett. Then Barrington had asked Spicer to monitor Will's, Andrew's, and Gaia's mobile phone conversations. Barrington had access to the main STASIS network from Scotland—but not to ECHELON.

Spicer had immediately logged in. Now he'd just heard Will talk to a man called Vanya (location, the computer said: St. Petersburg), about restaurants.

Whatever was going on, they weren't talking about Wickett or FIREball. So there wasn't exactly anything Spicer could pass on. Maybe Will had listened to Barrington, and was obeying? Stranger things had happened.

So why did he feel so uneasy?

Maly Prospect, St. Petersburg

In the parlor of Will's grandmother's apartment, Vanya Safronov rubbed a hand through his white hair. That had been a most unusual conversation.

"Vanya?" Elena was coming in with two cups of coffee. She took them to the table. "That was Will? What did he want? Didn't he want to talk to me?"

"Yes, that was Will," Vanya said. "And what he wanted was help."

"What sort of help? Vanya? What is it? Should I call Anna?"

"Leave his mother out of it," Vanya said. "The boy can look after himself"—he plucked a coded address book from the desk—"with just a little assistance from me."

5:11 P.M. Will, Gaia, and Andrew were in a cab, passing

through a valley flooded with golden light. Will didn't notice. He couldn't stop thinking. And it was getting him nowhere. The questions were starting to rub at his brain.

His phone vibrated. Will pulled it from his pocket. The text message said:

Grand Restaurant Schuh, Hohweg 56, 6 pm.

Vanya had come through. At least, they had a location and a time.

Beside him, Gaia asked, "Vanya?"

"Yeah."

Quickly, Will keyed in the number that Greta had given them. Her phone rang once, twice—

"Greta? We're heading into town now. Do you want to meet us?"

"Yes. Yes, of course."

"Great. I'll text you the address. Get there as soon as you can."

Will flipped his phone shut. Anticipation rushed through his veins. David Wickett's notebook! They'd unpick the equations. They'd find out about FIREball. Within the hour, surely, they'd be able to tell Abigail Pope what her uncle had been working on—and why he had died.

17

Grand Restaurant Schuh. 5:30 P.M.

Pink carpet. Matching tablecloths. Crystal chandeliers in a 1960s style. Old men with long hair, dressed in ties and blazers, were tucking into gateaux. A table of stout ladies wearing broad-heeled shoes and heavy eye makeup sipped coffee and nibbled at marzipan tarts.

In an annex to the dining room was a chocolateria, the shelves piled high with chocolate blocks, their wrappers showing old-fashioned trains steaming through the Alps. Beside them nestled a pile of chocolate logs tied up with orange ribbon. "You sit down," Andrew said as he headed toward the counter. "I'll join you in a minute."

Will took a table by the window. A group of laughing hikers strode past outside. As Gaia sat down, he glanced at his watch. "Half an hour till Vanya's contact's due."

"What do you think he'll be like?" she asked. "What should we tell him?"

"It depends if Greta gets here first with the notebook. And what the notebook says. We might not even need him."

"I'm thinking white hair, six feet tall, big Adam's apple, lumberjack shirt."

He smiled. She'd just described Vanya. "I'm guessing not all retired spies look like Vanya."

"Or act like him, I hope."

Will frowned. Yes, Vanya could be overbearing and rude, but he was also loyal, smart, and brave. "He came through for us in St. Petersburg. Maybe he will here too," Will said quietly.

Gaia's cheeks flushed red. "Will, I didn't mean—"

"Chocolate logs!" Andrew announced. He dropped the package on the table and pulled out a chair. "I couldn't resist."

As Andrew sat down, movement by the door caught their attention. It had swung open, and now Greta dashed in. She looked around wildly, saw them, and hurried over. She was clutching a paper bag.

The elderly woman at the table next to them stopped with a forkful of cake halfway to her mouth. Greta was oblivious.

"I cannot delay," she said. "My mother is expecting me. We are going to stay with my aunt in Bern. Just in case. Here is the notebook. You will let me know what you find out? And if you find the village really is in danger?" She fixed her black eyes on Andrew.

"Of course," he said. "We'll phone you. And if David Wickett gets in touch?"

"Yes," she said, "I will let you know."

She turned to go.

"Thank you," Andrew called after her.

Greta glanced back. Nodded. And was gone.

"Short but sweet," Will said as he picked up the paper bag.

"What—Greta?" Gaia asked him, still smarting after their exchange about Vanya.

Will only smiled. Then he lowered his gaze to David Wickett's notebook. His heart pounded. At last, they were getting somewhere.

Andrew looked impatient. "Go on, Will, open it."

Will was about to do exactly that. Then he held it out. "You're better at math than me. You take the first look."

The surprise was clear in Andrew's blue eyes. But he wasn't about to argue. He grabbed the book and flicked it open.

"Well?" Gaia asked.

For two whole minutes, Andrew had been silent. He'd been leafing through the pages, a frown knotting his forehead. Will was leaning over his shoulder, giving about as much away.

"*What does it say?*" she demanded. A waitress bringing coffee stopped in her tracks and frowned at them.

Andrew looked up at Gaia. "I have absolutely no idea."

"Will?" she asked.

Three cups were deposited on the table. None of them noticed.

Will shook his head.

"It seems Greta was right," Andrew said wearily. "It is *actually* in code."

He dropped the book on the table and turned it so Gaia could see. "Look—these numbers mean nothing. Even the equations aren't right. Somehow, he's encrypted his workings."

"But you can break it, right?" Gaia asked quickly.

"Maybe. In a few days, or a few weeks, or a few *years*. It

totally depends what sort of encryption he's used, and since he's no slouch in the intellectual department, I'm guessing we're in trouble."

"So—no," she said.

"If you want the short answer." Andrew turned the book back around and stared at the pages till the tiny red letters and numbers seemed to merge. A sudden ringing made him jump.

Gaia checked her phone and looked annoyed. "It's Dad," she said. Without another word, she got up from the table and headed outside.

Andrew was still poring over the encrypted notes. "I just don't know," he said, half to himself. "I can't make anything of it. The equation here looks like it should make sense, but then . . ." He turned the page and shook his head.

Will reached out. Gently he pulled the notebook away. "Give yourself a break," he said. He slid the menu over. "We should eat. And I mean something more substantial than chocolate logs. Then we'll have another look."

Sighing, Andrew nodded. He opened the menu and cast an eye over the offerings. Beetroot-turnip-cabbage carpaccio. Smoked wild boar ham with green apple salad. Game pâté with pistachios. Suddenly he didn't feel hungry. Outside the window, he noticed, Gaia was pacing. Tourists were colliding with her, apologizing and waiting for her to reciprocate. It didn't happen. Gaia's expression was black.

Andrew closed the menu. He looked thoughtful. "Has she told you about her dad?"

Will wondered what Andrew meant, exactly. The last he'd heard, her dad had been doing a bit better. "What about him?"

"He went back into the hospital last week."

". . . Right." The news left Will with a mix of feelings. He knew that no matter how badly she and her dad got along, he was still her dad. She still cared about him. But why had she told Andrew about the hospital and not him? Will clenched his fists under the table. He wished she'd confided in him. She should have wanted to confide in him.

Andrew pushed his glasses back up along his nose. A familiar anxious gesture. "There was something I wanted to run past you." He paused. "I was thinking that if anything did happen to her father, I could ask Gaia if she wanted to live with me. Perhaps my father could become her guardian. If she wanted. She could be my sister." Pale blue eyes regarded Will uncertainly. "What do you think?"

For a few moments, Will said nothing. Andrew had surprised him. Gaia could be his *sister*? Will wasn't sure how to respond. So he bought some time. "Have you talked to your parents?"

Andrew shook his head. "But they're home now. For a few weeks, anyway. I was planning to. I mean, before we came here."

"Your parents aren't home much."

Andrew looked slightly taken aback. "No . . . but that's all right." His fingers played with the edge of the menu. "I don't have any issues about it. I don't have any *neuroses*. Maybe if I did, Dad would be more interested—"Andrew blushed. "He would be interested in Gaia, that's for sure." And he smiled quickly, trying to cover his embarrassment.

The atmosphere felt suddenly thick. Will wasn't sure what to say.

"I meant to ask," Andrew said, eyes on the table. "I mean, you don't have to tell me. But I've noticed. You—you . . . and Gaia," he said at last. He raised his eyes. Fixed them on Will.

Will could only look back. *Him and Gaia*. Now it was his turn to blush. Then the door swung inward. Gaia was striding toward them, plunging her phone into her pocket.

Will picked up the menu quickly.

Gaia scraped back her chair and sat down heavily. She noticed their strained expressions. "What's wrong?" Her gaze shot to the notebook. "Have you found something?"

"Ah," Andrew said. "No. Unfortunately. No. We were just thinking we should eat. I think I'm going to order the turnip carpaccio."

Gaia raised an eyebrow.

Will still had the menu. And Andrew, who didn't want to look at Gaia, grabbed the notebook again. He opened it at random. Sighed. Flicked over the page . . .

Frowned.

Stared.

Thought: *Hold on a second . . .*

"Although . . ." Andrew said.

There had been an edge to his voice. Will had heard it before. He dropped the menu.

Andrew was peering hard at the book. "Hold on—I recognize that—"

"*What?*" Will asked.

Andrew looked up at him, his face rigid. Then words started tumbling out: "I read a feature in a magazine. It wasn't a journal. I mean it wasn't peer-reviewed. It was an idea—

and I checked it out, and I saw that diagram. Something a bit like it, anyway, I'm sure."

"*What feature?*" Gaia asked.

"It was theoretical, but—it would explain a lot. It could explain Project FIREball . . . If that's what they were up to. It could explain why InVesta are seriously interested . . . Why they'd want to get their hands on the research!" Absorbed in his thoughts, Andrew had raised his voice. Diners at the surrounding tables had stopped eating.

Gaia was very fond of Andrew. But this was exasperating. "Andrew, tell us—"

"*Greetings!*"

Three pairs of eyes shot up.

A woman had appeared by their table. A woman like none of them had ever seen before.

"I think that you are expecting me. My name is Elke."

The tattoo. That was the first thing Will noticed. Then the long black ponytail, streaked with gray. Elke's eyes were the color of emeralds. They burned from her taut, pale face. It looked expressionless, stretched over strong features.

It was obvious that the woman cared about her body. Biceps bulged beneath the turned-up sleeves of her red T-shirt. Her thigh muscles strained against black denim. Will noticed red toenails poking out of black flip-flops. He was staring, he knew, but he couldn't help it.

As Elke pulled out a chair to sit down, Will got a better look at the tattoo. It covered her forearm. A snake. Scaled, fork-tongued, in striking black and red. Will was so surprised by Elke's appearance that for a moment, he even forgot Andrew's excitement about the notebook.

"My middle name is Adelinda," Elke said, her eyes flicking to her tattoo. "It means *noble serpent*. In training, they thought it suited me." She paused. "They called me The Snake."

The dramatic introduction left its impression clearly on Andrew's face. He looked stunned. "They call me, er, Andrew," he said awkwardly. "This is Gaia, and this is Will." He put Wickett's notebook on his knee.

Elke nodded. It was a violent gesture, like a horse irritated with a bit. She folded her hefty arms in front of her. Her hands were huge, Andrew noticed.

Andrew was desperate to tell Will and Gaia what he had found. But it would have to wait. It would hardly do to blurt it all out in front of Vanya's strange-looking contact. And there were no guarantees he was right. Maybe he was seeing things. Belatedly, something occurred to him. "When you say *they* called you The Snake, who do you mean?"

Elke laughed—a short, brittle sound. She didn't answer him. "You," she said to Will. "You do not look much like Vanya."

"He's not a blood relation. He's marrying my grandmother. How did you know who we were?"

"Pale, brown-haired boy, with the Russian cheekbones. Boy with glasses. Half-Italian girl with curly hair. Did Vanya get it wrong? Or is there another such trio lurking here?" Elke made a show of pretending to scan the restaurant.

Will nodded. She was right: It had been a stupid question. But he still felt thrown. In fact, like Gaia, he *had* been expecting someone a bit like Vanya. It wasn't as though he'd encountered many retired spies. "How long have you known Vanya?" he asked. "How did you meet him?"

Her eyes sparkled. "I was twenty-three years old, and I was in Cairo, in the old market. I was chasing a target, a woman I had been after for a week. We were racing down a street. It was hot with the fires of blacksmiths. I was close. She was slowing, tired. She turned down an alley, but I knew a shortcut." Elke clapped her hands. "I had her. Then slam! Someone was in front of me! I ran right into him. I didn't see his face. The next thing I knew, he had slipped behind me. He grabbed my right arm and pushed it up behind my back. My shoulder was about to dislocate." She grimaced in remembered agony. "He had me pinned tight. Then I heard his voice in my ear, his cheek rough with bristles: *Let me introduce myself, Elke Hahn. My name is Vanya. I work for Russia. And your target is mine.*"

Elke stopped, breathing hard.

Will, Andrew, and Gaia had been watching her intently. Now that she'd finished, no one spoke. Elke laughed.

"Come," she said. "Our chitchat is over. You need to tell me why I am here. Let's walk—and let's talk."

The Grand Restaurant Schuh opened onto the high street. Ahead, on the other side of the road, Andrew saw the aptly-named Grand Hotel, with its ironwork balconies and mushroom-colored awnings. Above its fluttering green flag, jutting mountains soared into a clear blue sky.

Elke strode on with Will, and Andrew took the opportunity to hang back. The notebook was safely in his satchel. Now there was something he *had* to check. He brought out his smart phone and connected to the Internet.

"What's going on?" Gaia whispered.

Andrew frowned at Elke's back. "It looks as though they're talking."

"I mean, with the notebook! What's FIREball? Do you really know what it is?"

He didn't look up at her. "I have an idea. But I need to check something. And I can hardly tell you now, when"—he lowered his voice—"The *Snake* could hear."

Ahead, Will was concentrating hard on Elke's face. He'd just told her most of what they knew—leaving out the notebook and his contact with Barrington, and, so far, the Sphere. When he'd mentioned Project FIREball, he'd seen a flash of what looked like recognition on her face.

"You know about FIREball?" he asked.

Elke paused. "No . . . I have heard the name. And I knew there were scientists here working on something—something big—but that's all."

"No rumors about what they were working on?" Will asked.

"Lots of rumors," Elke said. "None worth the breath to repeat them—"

"But—"

"*Idle rumors.* If any of my contacts really knew about the project, I would too. You can count on that."

Will hesitated. He wanted to push her, but she didn't seem the sort of woman to be pushed. "So," he said, "Abigail Pope wants us to find out what happened to her uncle—what he was working on, why he was killed, and who did it. We think David Wickett is still out there somewhere—but we don't know where."

"Ah!"

Will glanced back.

"Ah," Andrew said again, this time more quietly, his blue eyes blinking fast. "Sorry—it's nothing. Carry on!"

Will and Elke reached the Grand Hotel. Now he asked: "Have you ever heard of something called the Sphere? Or the Black Sphere?"

"*The Black Sphere!*" Elke stopped short. The intensity of her voice got everyone's attention. "I have not heard it called that in years. At least, not by most people around here. Not since the black sphere itself was torn down. It was a military listening post. Like a giant golf ball, later painted black. The sphere was demolished in 1994 and the site was sold."

"So what is the Sphere now?" Will asked. "The e-mail that we found in London came from it."

"It is no secret," Elke said. "And, given what you have told me, I think you are going to be very interested."

The woman was worse than Andrew, Gaia thought.

In a low whisper, Elke said, "It is eight miles from here. Built high into the mountainside, as impenetrable as any fortress. The European research and development institute of InVesta Corporation."

Will's brain raced. In many ways, this made sense.

A research and development center employed scientists. At the Sphere, the researchers would presumably be working on new types of weapons, or improved methods for extracting natural gas—anything relevant to the multinational's interests. But they might also have met the six physicists attached to Project FIREball.

Scientists liked to discuss their work, as Will knew from his own experience with his mother and her friends. What if InVesta had found out about FIREball, and didn't like it? Or if the FIREball scientists had discovered a commercial secret that the InVesta bosses wanted kept? Both could be reasons to kill.

Will was more desperate than ever to question Andrew. He almost asked him outright what he thought he'd seen in Wickett's notebook. But they had only just met Elke. Will wanted to keep control over the flow of information.

Andrew and Gaia were looking at him, he realized. Waiting for him to respond to Elke's revelation about the identity of the Black Sphere.

"It makes sense," he said at last.

"So you suspect that InVesta really is after David Wickett?" Elke asked. "That *they* want to silence him, like the others, for whatever he has learned?"

"Or invented," Andrew put in.

Will glared at him.

Elke cracked her oversized knuckles. "Look," she said. "In my circle, rumors have been spreading for weeks. Let's say I am interested too in finding out about FIREball and why the scientists were killed. Let's say we can work together. Vanya has told me all about STORM. Twice, when we were in competition, Vanya saved my life. I owe him. I will help you. So now you have this information. Now you know about the Black Sphere. The question is: What do you want to do about it?"

Will glanced at Gaia. Then at Andrew, who had shoved his phone back into his pocket and was shaking his head, still half in his own world.

Will thought for a moment. No matter what information the notebook contained about Project FIREball, they would have to look for proof that InVesta had killed Edmund Pope and the others. The e-mail was not enough. They needed hard information either to go back to Barrington, or at least to take to Abigail. "What we want," Will said, "is to get into the Sphere."

To his annoyance, Elke laughed. The noise was like a machine gun going off. "Once," she said, "I got as far as the security office. As a *guest*. There are fingerprint checks, iris scans, the latest technology!"

Andrew was about to correct her, but he held his tongue. Now wasn't the time to discuss developments in biometric security.

"So you're saying it's impossible?" Gaia asked. This was a challenge to Elke—and both Elke and Gaia knew it.

Elke's smile vanished. She looked at Gaia. "Perhaps. Perhaps there is a way. But you would be crazy."

"What way?" Will asked quickly.

Elke seemed to gather her thoughts. "A man I know—or, rather, I knew—he talked about a route in once. He said he'd bought it from an old woman whose father had mapped it when she was young. Before the Black Sphere was even built. This man—my acquaintance—he said one day he would try it. I don't know if he ever did. He was crazy, but he did not have a death wish."

Anticipation made Will's heart pound. *What route?*

Emerald eyes bored into his. "I don't know. Not exactly. But this man—*if* I can still find him, *if* he isn't vanished or in jail, and *if* he will speak to me—I think he does."

Shute Barrington gazed hard at the lake. His brain was so feverish, he was almost surprised not to see the water start to bubble and boil.

At first Barrington had acted as Will had expected. Using the Eagle, he had tracked Will, Gaia, and Andrew into a taxi and on to the road to Interlaken. In fact, Barrington had had every intention of continuing to follow them. For two reasons: A) he doubted Will would actually listen to him, and B) there was a chance STORM just might find something useful. It had happened before. He could always tell Operations Control the Eagle was acting up.

But then his cell phone had gone off.

It was Charlie Spicer. An MI6 field officer had just called in a possible location for David Wickett near Grindelwald, high up in the mountains. The Eagle was needed.

Barrington didn't disguise his irritation. But there was something he wanted to ask. Somehow, this situation—Project FIREball, the missing scientist, the huge field search, the top-security classification—it all felt slightly *odd*. This was a gut instinct. Which he'd learned to trust. "Charlie—" A pause.

In theory, Barrington could speak freely. His phone wasn't bugged, he was 100 percent sure of that. After all, he was the guy who came up with the bugs—*and* the bug-screening devices. And this particular handset was supposedly ECHELON-proof. *But . . .* But he was in Scotland, dammit, without access to the full STASIS systems, and Spicer was a big boy. If he didn't want to help, he only had to say so.

". . . Sir?"

Barrington swallowed. "Charlie, what do you know about a Project FIREball?"

"Those six scientists were working on it, and Wickett's the only one still alive. That's all I know."

"Charlie, what could you *find out* about a Project FIREball? Given that our guys designed the MI6 computer network, but that it's got an Alpha security classification, and that if anyone found out you were sticking your clever nose where you shouldn't, you'd be kicked out of STASIS and probably right into prison."

A pause. "I could do a little careful digging."

Good. Barrington had expected Spicer to rise to the challenge—even this one. "And could you check which field officer was handling David Wickett?"

"Yes. Sir—"

"No questions, Spicer," Barrington said. "Sorry. Not yet."

Then Barrington threw down his phone and snatched up the Eagle controls.

Whichever MI6 field officer in Switzerland did have responsibility for maintaining a link with Wickett, he or she deserved to be a STASIS Advanced Weapons test subject. First, they'd let the scientist almost walk into a deadly explosion. Then they'd lost him, requiring a full-scale search, which Wickett had so far evaded. A very poor performance for an officer with Britain's "intelligence" service.

A *surprisingly* poor performance, in fact.

20

Will watched Elke stride off across the street, her ponytail swinging. She'd parked her car a couple of blocks away, she'd said. She'd collect it, then she'd take them to the man who might know how to get into the Black Sphere. Will waited until he was sure Elke was out of earshot. "Right, Andrew, spit it out."

This time, Andrew didn't delay: *"Cold fusion,"* he said.

Will's first reaction was disbelief. Then disappointment. Either Andrew was totally wrong or those scientists were wasting their time.

Will knew all about the theory: that colliding and fusing the nuclei—the hearts—of atoms at room temperature could generate cheap and clean energy. The world would no longer have to rely on fossil fuels. Dirty power stations—and their impact on global warming—would vanish. A home could create its own energy, and heat itself.

Cold fusion was a scientific Holy Grail. And every researcher that had gone in search of it had been torn apart by fellow academics. In some scientists' eyes, those who peddled the idea were in the same bag as the ancient alchemists who had believed base metals could be turned into gold.

"Andrew, it's crank science!" Gaia exclaimed.

"Every single respectable scientist in the world thinks it's impossible," Will said.

"Not quite," Andrew said patiently. He waited until a couple of hotel guests had passed. "It's just that the work has gone underground. Labs around the world still spend millions of dollars on cold fusion research every year. Respectable scientists have published really promising results—just not usually in the really respectable journals, because they refuse outright to touch anything to do with cold fusion."

Andrew paused, looking from Will to Gaia. They just stared at him. He went on.

"In 2006, Brian Josephson—he was a Nobel Prize winner at Cambridge University—he did an interview with *New Scientist* magazine. He said"—Andrew pulled out his smart phone and scrolled to the right paragraph—"and I quote, 'I reckon that cold fusion will be accepted in the next year or so.' What if they've actually done it?" Andrew's face was shining now. "Cold fusion. Clean, abundant energy. An invention like this—it would put InVesta out of business. If even just the news of the invention came out, their stock market value would crash overnight!"

Will glanced at Gaia. She didn't look convinced. But Andrew was very rarely wrong. If he believed cold fusion was possible, Will thought, perhaps it was. "This notebook explains how to do it?" he asked.

"Well, I don't think it actually describes a technique," Andrew conceded. "It looks more like background. Wickett's drawn a diagram of the model from a 1989 cold fusion experiment involving deuterium. It's been messed around a bit, but it's not easy to encode a diagram. Then a bit later, there are three big red stars, and an exclamation mark, as though he's made some kind of breakthrough."

"But there's no proof that they've actually invented a method that really works," Gaia said.

"There's no *proof*," Andrew said. "But remember what Greta said? Yesterday David Wickett was happy. He'd said he'd done it. What if that *it* is cold fusion? Even if those scientists were just *working* on cold fusion, if they were getting close, InVesta would have good reason to want to get rid of them."

"Maybe," Will said. But he was thinking. InVesta *could* kill the scientists, but would that really put an end to FIREball? Wouldn't replacement scientists be recruited? And if other labs really were spending millions on cold fusion research, what if one of those teams succeeded?

Will turned to Andrew. "What if InVesta was waiting until FIREball did it?" he asked. "What if they wanted Wickett alive—at least until he'd explained how his technique worked? What if they never *wanted* to kill Wickett? If InVesta could get their hands on a technique for cold fusion, they could patent it. They could *own* it. That would be better than trying to prevent it."

Now he remembered the Wikipedia entry he'd found on the way over to Switzerland. "InVesta gets eighty-three percent of its income from fossil fuels," Will said. "Those fuels aren't going to last, so that income isn't going to last. In that welcome video they were talking about renewable energies being the future. What if they really meant it?"

"If they thought *cold fusion* could replace their coal and gas?" Gaia asked.

Will nodded.

"It's possible," Andrew said.

"So is this what we're going with?" Gaia asked, still half disbelieving. "That FIREball was set up to develop cold fusion? And they've actually done it? And David Wickett might have the plans?"

Andrew took a deep breath. "Look, we already know that FIREball is something very special. Otherwise Barrington would know about it—he'd probably be *involved* in it. So it would have to be something *like* cold fusion for it to be classified at an Alpha level, surely? Edmund Pope was a specialist on electrochemistry, and that's crucial to all this. At least, it was crucial to that 1989 experiment. That must have been why they wanted him on board. I can have another look through all the papers published by those scientists, but I bet I'll find that somehow there are links if you're looking for cold fusion."

"You didn't spot that earlier, when you *were* actually looking for a link," Gaia said.

"I'd never have considered cold fusion! Who would? But if they *have* done it—it would change everything. The environmental implications alone could be huge."

Andrew was right, Will thought. But exactly how the world would change would depend on who was in control of the technology—whether it was owned by a private company, like InVesta, or made freely available.

If it was owned by InVesta, Saxon Webb, who was already very influential, would become one of the most powerful men in the world. He wouldn't even need to build cold fusion plants—

The full impact of it suddenly hit Will like a punch in the chest. Saxon Webb could lock the plans away in a safe and extort billions from other energy companies and oil-rich nations in return for a promise to keep them there. Or he could license the technology, so that it would actually be used, and he would become rich beyond even his wildest dreams.

Suddenly Will recalled the note that David Wickett had left in the hut. Who was it for? And why had he written that Kleinkirchen should be evacuated? What did that have to do with cold fusion—or InVesta?

Perhaps those answers could be found in the Sphere.

A deep mechanical growl suddenly grabbed his attention. A car rocketed past the Schuh restaurant. It was a Maserati. A Quattroporte. Literally a "four-door" sports model, and dark purple, sparkling like an amethyst. A split second later, the Maserati stopped abruptly outside the Grand Hotel. The driver's window wound down and a dark head popped out. "Your chauffeur is here," Elke said with a smile that didn't reach her eyes. "Get in."

"Four-hundred-brake horsepower," Elke said proudly. "Six-speed sequential semi-automatic gearbox. Top speed of a hundred seventy miles per hour. Zero to sixty in five point two seconds."

Andrew was in the front seat. As they shot out of town, his eyes ran greedily over the luxurious interior. "This is the Sport GT," he said. "The engine computer was reprogrammed—I read about it. It delivers faster gear shifts."

Elke raised a black eyebrow. "Thirty-five percent faster."

Andrew's eyes shot to the steering wheel. "That's carbon fiber?"

"Yes. Along with the emergency brake cover. The pedals are aluminum. My retirement present to myself. But you wait until I show you what's in the trunk."

"What?" Andrew asked eagerly.

"I said, you *wait* until I show you," Elke said, but she was grinning. "Now, if you want to adjust your heat, your ventilation, even your massage—see there?—each seat is individually controlled."

Will found his controls. First the private jet. Now the Maserati. STORM was traveling in style—well, if you didn't count the Bobcat. He hit the massage function.

"Well?" Elke said. "What do you think?"

"It's impressive," Will said.

"You want impressive"—Elke put her foot down, making the car roar—"how about that!"

The scenery raced past.

Will saw wooden farm sheds with sloping roofs. A neat guesthouse with a yellow awning. Painted signs for companies advertising hiking tours, spas, even extreme sports. In the distance, tiny roads glittered like streams. Real streams shot like lightning forks down the mountainside. On either side of the road, fir trees grew thickly.

Elke was talking to Andrew about cars, but Will was absorbed in FIREball. If Andrew was right, *if* Wickett did have the key to cold fusion, no wonder Barrington had been edgy. *If* he actually knew what FIREball was all about. And Will had to suspect that he did. Yes, it was Alpha classified. But Barrington was head of MI6's science and technology division. If Barrington was determined to, surely he'd be able to access even the most sensitive information. Right?

Beside Will, Gaia was silent. She was thinking too, about cold fusion and InVesta. And trying not to listen to Elke, who was telling a story about a car chase across Puerto Rico, when she'd totaled a Porsche 911 and ended up diving into a phosphorescent lake.

The Maserati slowed. Elke made a ninety-degree turn up a narrow side road lined with rocks. This road had only one destination.

They were closing in on a single-story whitewashed building with brown shutters. In front, there was an expanse of dull gravel with half a dozen battered red plastic tables and chairs. They were unoccupied. In fact, the place looked abandoned, Will thought.

Elke pulled onto the gravel and cut the engine. Outside, nothing moved. The silence echoed in Will's ears. "Where are we?" he asked.

A pause. Then, in a low voice, Elke rasped, "The Black Sphere is built right into the mountainside, as I told you. But there are people who know these peaks inside out, and their fathers and grandfathers before them. They know every stream. Every cavern. They have secret routes even through the bellies of the mountains, which they would die to protect—or charge a king's ransom to share."

"Shepherds?" Gaia asked.

Elke laughed. "No, you fool! Not shepherds. Smugglers."

"Smugglers?"

"That's what I said! Inside, over there. This is an old-time bar."

"And the man you talked about with the map—he's in there?" Will asked.

"While I went to collect the car, I put in a few calls," Elke said. "Yes, he should be in there." She rested her huge hands on the steering wheel. "But if you want his knowledge, you will have to pay—and still there are no guarantees. I know this man. If he doesn't feel like helping you, he will not, no matter what you offer him. I advise you to give me the money and let me do the deal. I will go and find him. If he agrees, I will bring you instructions. Perhaps, if you are very lucky, even a map."

Elke was looking at Andrew while she talked. Vanya must have told her about his money, Will realized.

Andrew was thinking. Yes, they *could* give her money. But just because she was Vanya's friend didn't mean he completely trusted her. "No," he said, pleasantly but firmly. "If *we* have to pay him, *we* want to meet him."

Elke's eyes narrowed. She read Andrew's determination. "Very well. But I warn you. These are hard men. And this bar—it is not the Grand Restaurant Schuh. You will not find old ladies sipping tea. Understand?"

Saxon Webb stepped out of his stretch limousine and onto a neatly paved path.

As he strode along it, his eyes clocked the chrome sign staked into the ground:

INVESTA CORPORATION
EUROPEAN RESEARCH AND DEVELOPMENT
INSTITUTE

Known to its employees as the Black Sphere.

Webb took the black marble steps at a jog. Glass doors slid open silently, admitting him into a vast foyer. The only sound was a trickling from the ornamental Zen water garden. A woman behind the reception desk looked up.

"Good day, sir."

Webb nodded. He headed straight for the corridor that led into the body of the building. Anyone trying to enter without permission would be stopped here by an automatic barricade. Steel doors would slam shut, sealing off the corridor. Alarms would go off, triggering an instant armed response.

Webb himself had signed off on the security system. He knew how it worked. The instant he'd stepped into the foyer, an array of twelve miniature cameras had locked on his face. They'd scanned the unique patterns in his irises—the freckles, pits, furrows, and stripes across the colored part of his eyes. By the time Webb reached the corridor, a hidden computer had confirmed his identity and cleared him for access to all areas.

Webb stomped on, heading for the office of Gustav Pritt, the director of the Sphere. Pritt had called moments before Webb had arrived. Urgent inspections of the experimental drill sites were required. Pritt would be back in his office as soon as possible.

Webb doubted that any such inspections were required. Pritt had made the whole thing up, Webb guessed, in the hope that he would escape the first wave of his boss's fury.

Webb found the door marked *Direktor: Herr Gustav Pritt*. Inside, the office was small. Webb saw a black desk with a laptop and a phone and an executive swivel chair. Beside the desk was a glass-fronted bookcase stuffed full of textbooks and journals.

Webb sat down. He slammed his briefcase on the desk and withdrew two files, both of which he'd printed to reread on the flight to Switzerland.

The first was on Wickett.

Webb shook his head. Of all the six scientists working on FIREball, Webb had thought Wickett the least likely to crack cold fusion. Webb himself had chosen to put Bailey on the payroll. In the event that he—or any of the other team members—succeeded, Bailey would receive fifteen million dollars, so long as he gave InVesta the tip-off before the European Union bosses were informed.

Gustav Pritt had been put in charge of managing Bailey, and monitoring FIREball's progress. And then Bailey had called with the news that Wickett had done it—Wickett had called in the instruction to meet at Assembly Point Zebra!

Webb had ordered Pritt to send men to the farmhouse to kidnap Wickett. In case the other scientists were close to their own methods for cold fusion, he had ordered them to be exterminated. Then, once Webb was satisfied that he understood the technique, Wickett would be disposed of too. And Webb would have his hands on an invention that would make him incalculably powerful and wealthy.

But the goons that Pritt had hired to do the job had fouled it up. The explosive had gone off far too early, killing not only four of the scientists, but also the idiots themselves, who had been hiding in the kitchen. Bailey had tried to escape—and Pritt had used a Frisbee to kill him.

Wickett *had* escaped.

It was a miracle no one had noticed the Frisbee, Webb thought. Pritt was fond of the new robot—and Pritt was a fool! But Pritt was also loyal, and he was trustworthy. Webb would wait to get rid of him until this business with Wickett was over.

His eyes flicked back to the file.

DAVID AUGUSTUS WICKETT

Age: 37

Nationality: British

Family: none

Friends: none identified

No one to kidnap and hold for ransom in return for the plans for cold fusion, in other words.

Which was why Webb had been forced to turn to this, the second report.

It had been prepared three months ago, duly noted, acted upon, and filed. Only, in the present circumstances, the contents were much more riveting . . .

Webb read the cover page.

CONFIDENTIAL
UNAUTHORIZED POSSESSION IS A CRIME
A. HUDSON, CHIEF ENGINEER

Webb had met Hudson once or twice. He remembered steel-framed glasses. A dark suit. Someone trustworthy, dependable, and honest. Perhaps too honest. Hudson had insisted on presenting this report to Webb in person. Webb could still hear the engineer's earnest voice: *"You must act at once, Mr. Webb. It must be stopped."*

And now Webb intended to do just the opposite.

As he swiveled in the chair, he caught a glimpse of himself in the glass of the bookcase. He saw a successful man. What did other people see?

A pug face. An expensive suit. A St. Tropez tan and dazzling white teeth.

A murderer?

Webb smiled at his reflection.

It grimaced back.

Gaia translated the small wooden sign nailed above the door:

The Smuggler's Rest

Smuggling must have been a lucrative business, she thought. During the Second World War, perhaps, when Switzerland had been a neutral country. Perhaps smugglers were like the South China Sea pirates she had seen on TV recently. Perhaps they were making a comeback. If they were, it didn't seem to be very successful.

Gaia was right behind Will, who was following Elke. As they headed in, Gaia made out varnished pine tables and yellow, smoke-stained walls. A loud voice was ranting in German. It took her a moment to realize it was coming from an old TV, which sat on the bar itself, toward the back of the room.

The only voices came from that TV set. If the customers had been talking, they stopped when Elke, Will, and Gaia entered. Fourteen pairs of hostile eyes were fixed on the intruders. A middle-aged man with spiky brown hair glared at them over his mug of beer. A sidelong glance told Gaia he had a gold hoop earring and sideburns. Two tattooed birds were fading on his forearm. Beside him sat an older man in a stained red polo shirt. Gaia caught the glint of metal studs in the man's leather belt. His hair was long at the back, cut in a mullet. Gaia jumped. Andrew had just grabbed her arm. He clutched his vibrating phone in his hand.

"It's Abigail," he whispered.

"Call her back later!" Gaia hissed, annoyed. Partly because Andrew had startled her. Partly because a call from Abigail was the last thing they needed right now.

Andrew nodded. "All right—*Gaia!*"

She followed his gaze. A man was striding toward Elke and Will. He had stringy white hair. His mouth was wide and downturned, like the mouth of a fish. Suspenders held his gray trousers up over his swollen stomach. But his chest was broad and his arms were thick as tree trunks.

"Elke Hahn!" he yelled, then continued aggressively in a language Gaia didn't understand. The local dialect, she thought. The man suddenly raised a fist. He pulled it back. He was going to punch—

But Elke, who looked irritated rather than afraid, simply reached out and closed her fist over his. Gaia saw the surprise on the old man's face as Elke swung, taking the force of the punch, then raised a knee and jabbed it hard in his groin. She twisted his thick arm hard behind his back, kicked his legs out from under him, and scowled as he fell, facedown, onto the dirty linoleum floor. Before he could get up, she stamped her foot between his shoulder blades. Red nail polish glinted in the dim light.

"I come here if I want, and I bring who I want," she said in high German—which Gaia could understand. "Anyone else want to take issue?" Elke's eyes flashed as she glared around the room.

No one spoke. The man in the red polo shirt looked down at his beer.

Slowly now, Elke removed her foot from the man's back. "Try anything else," she said calmly, "and it will be much worse for you next time. And look—so embarrassing—these children are watching!"

Will glanced back at Gaia. She raised an eyebrow. Smiled slightly.

The man staggered up, his stomach wobbling. He shot Elke a black look. But if he was thinking about having another go, he thought better of it. Swearing under his breath, he stomped out of the bar.

"Ha!"

It had been a female laugh. Now Gaia noticed a pinch-faced woman behind the bar. She was about Elke's age, and she was resting pointy elbows on the beer-stained pine.

"Elke Hahn," she breathed. "It has been some time since we have witnessed your particular brand of entertainment. Come, before I lose all my customers, tell me why, after all these years, you are back?"

Elke went over to the bar and leaned over it. Then she began to talk in a low voice.

Will, Andrew, and Gaia watched, somewhat stunned. Andrew's eyes were shining. "It looks as though she has some history with this place," he whispered, obviously impressed. "Perhaps she betrayed a smuggler for the good of Switzerland—but the others in this bar wouldn't forgive her, so she couldn't come back."

"Perhaps she just punched too many people," Will said,

then took a step forward. Elke was beckoning them over.

"He is in the back room," she called. "Follow me."

The door had been concealed by the bar. Now, as they followed Elke, Will saw a low-ceilinged, rectangular room with four pine tables. A man sat alone. The bulb of a mock-Victorian iron lamp, riveted to the wall, showed a hefty pair of forearms and huge hands, holding up a newspaper.

Elke coughed. The newspaper dropped three inches to reveal a man in his forties with short, vivid black hair. Dyed. He had a broad face with a thick black mustache. Cold, black eyes glared out from under hooded lids. He said nothing.

"It has been a long time," Elke said at last. "I wasn't sure I would still find you here."

The man's eyes grazed Will, then Andrew, then Gaia. He turned back to Elke. "Elke Hahn. If only I could say you haven't changed. But you look old. What do you want?"

If Elke took offense, she hid it. Hands on her hips, she said, in English: "Only the map you said once you would not dare to use. The way into the Black Sphere."

There was an icy silence. The man folded his newspaper. He took his time, smoothing out the creases, making Elke wait. Now his upper body was in full view. He was in good shape. His black T-shirt stretched tightly across his pectoral muscles.

"Why do you want it?" he asked. "Why do you bring children? Why does The Snake want the map?"

"What does it matter, Dirk? Just tell me your price."

"Why? For old times' sake?"

"Old times are gone," Elke said. "And I, for one, am glad. Now, tell me your price."

Dirk's black eyes narrowed. "Tell me why you want it, or it is not for sale."

Will glanced at Elke. The conversation didn't seem to be going well. And this was their business, after all. "*We* want it," he said.

Elke flashed him an angry glance.

The man's black eyes shifted to Will. "Then I ask you the same question: *Why?*"

"We can't tell you why," Will said. "But we have money. We can pay."

Dirk said only, "*No.*"

"We have money," Will said, more firmly. "We could pay you well—" He felt someone tugging at his backpack. Gaia had edged behind him. She was unzipping the side pocket. *What was she doing?*

The smuggler had noticed too. He was watching her closely. Good, Gaia thought. She coughed theatrically. "It's the smoke in the bar," she said. She sidestepped Andrew to stand right in front of Dirk, and added, "I have asthma."

"Gaia, no!" At the exact moment that Gaia lifted the inhaler to her mouth, Andrew grabbed her arm. But Gaia had already pressed the button. An invisible chemical cloud was spreading fast. It caught Andrew before enveloping Dirk's face.

Gaia scowled hard at Andrew. "What did you do that for!"

Andrew blinked. He coughed a little. Whispered,

"There's only one dose left . . . And this is dangerous. I was trying to keep you out of trouble." He took a deep breath. Gaia watched him closely.

"What is going on?" Dirk shouted. He thudded a fist on the table. "Elke Hahn, what is going on?"

Andrew had gone pale. He took a deep breath and turned to Will. "Will, I feel strange."

It doesn't work that fast, Will thought.

And yet the formula was experimental—and Andrew was a lot smaller than the CIA officer at Bushell House. Without doubt, the anxiety was fading from Andrew's face.

Will frowned. Gaia had used their last dose of the formula without asking him. But perhaps she'd been right. They needed this route in, and Dirk hadn't exactly been falling over himself to help them.

"You know, money really isn't a problem," Andrew said to Dirk. "We do have plenty." He dragged a heavy chair over from the next table and sat down opposite the smuggler. "Look, let's just talk. You can trust us. We can work it all out."

Andrew was *smiling.*

Will glared at Gaia.

"He got in the way!" she whispered.

Elke hissed, "What is going on? What have you done?"

Will didn't answer. He couldn't leave Andrew to try to handle the situation alone. He dragged over another chair. Determined to sound calm, he said to Dirk: "It's true. We can pay for the map. *If* you have it."

Dirk blinked. He looked up at Elke. "Of course I have it."

He rubbed his forehead. Again he looked at Elke. The hostility had vanished. "The map for the Black Sphere, you say."

"Yes," Will said steadily. He felt his pulse start to speed. "The way into the Black Sphere."

"The route through the caverns?"

"*Yes*," Elke said. "The route through the caverns." She looked again at Gaia, a suspicious expression on her face.

"Well, I *do* have it." The smuggler was nodding at Will. He rubbed his thick mustache thoughtfully. He was starting to look almost genial.

"That's . . . great," Will said. Now he had to push. But *gently.* "You know, it's fine to give it to us. We can pay you well. It's the right thing to do."

Dirk shrugged his bulky shoulders. "I don't know."

"No, really," Andrew said. "We're all friends here. All good people."

Gaia tensed. Andrew was laying it on a bit thick. Suddenly, she jumped. Again Dirk had thumped a fist on the table. "All right. If you like. But not for old times' sake," he said, wagging a finger at Elke.

"Well, that is wonderful news!" Andrew exclaimed. He was smiling inanely. Gaia clamped a restraining hand on his shoulder.

"You know, we would quite like it now," Andrew managed to get out, despite Gaia's tightening grip. "Ow!" he said loudly. "Gaia, please, don't." But he was still smiling. He turned back to Dirk. "Is the map close by? We could go and get it."

"No need. I have it here." Dirk tapped his forehead and

swept his newspaper onto the floor. "Bring me paper. I will sketch it out."

Shaking her head in disbelief, Elke said, "I'll get some. No one go anywhere." She turned to go to the bar, then hesitated. Whatever Gaia had just done, it had made Dirk astonishingly compliant. If she didn't try to take advantage of that, she'd be a fool. "By the way," she said casually, "last year, I heard it was you who got hold of those black market Chinese microprocessors. Who sold them to you?"

"Microprocessors?" Andrew said loudly. "Who cares about those? It's the map we're after!"

Elke shot him a fierce glare. At the time, the microprocessors had caused a stir. Millions of Swiss francs were reported to have changed hands.

"Yes," Dirk was saying, waving a hand dismissively. "Never mind the processors. We are concerned with the map!"

"But—" Elke started.

"*I'll* get the paper," Will said. he got up and edged past Elke.

"But—" Elke said again.

Dirk had refocused his gaze on Andrew. "So, you know *my* name now. You are?"

Andrew beamed. "I am Andrew! And this is—"

"Jessica!" Gaia said, clamping her hand again on Andrew's shoulder. She glanced around at Will, who was returning with a paper napkin and a pen. "And this is *Steven*."

Andrew looked up at her, surprised. Gaia glared back at him.

Dirk seemed oblivious. "I am pleased to meet you. Ah, Steven. The paper. Thank you. Where shall I begin? The hidden entrance? Is that the best spot?" Evidently these were rhetorical questions, because he continued: "There is an underground water system, with an entrance *here*."

Dirk scribbled down the latitude and longitude. "The water flows right through the mountain. If you follow my map, you will take the branch that empties out into a waterfall that drops into a dam in a courtyard at the back of the institute—behind the spot where the old black sphere used to sit."

Dirk was sketching quickly. Now he jabbed at the paper.

"You will need floats to get through the caverns. The journey becomes violent. Here, the channel splits, and the current could smash you to the roof. Here is a jutting rock. It could slice a head in two. A boulder blocks the way here." He jabbed with his pen. "But there should be room—just—for you to slip through. Soon you find yourself in a large cavern. Make sure you follow this route *exactly*. There can be no drifting. At two points, here and here, where the tunnel splits, you must go to the right." Dirk fixed his black eyes on Will. "Go the wrong way and you could get sucked into the mountain, into whirlpools, into oblivion.

"But if you follow this faithfully," Dirk continued, "you will come out in a waterfall that plunges down to InVesta's dam. It is thirty feet, perhaps. It will make you fearful, but it is nothing to the waterfall that flows on beyond the sluice gates at the far side of the dam, down into the reservoir of

Kleinkirchen. A one-hundred-eighty-foot drop. At least. The water thunders, the air is thick with spray. You could be drowned, or *crushed*."

Will saw Andrew's mouth fall open. But he had to concentrate on the practicalities. They'd follow the map. They'd get out at the dam. They didn't need to worry about the one-hundred-eighty-foot drop.

They should be able to get hold of tires easily enough, Will thought. They could use those as floats. Then he remembered one of the signs he'd noticed on the journey to the bar, for a company called Alpine Adventures. Will didn't have Gaia's photographic memory, but he remembered some of the extreme sports on offer: Paragliding, Zorbing, dry slope skiing, Trottibiking, hydrospeeding . . .

Hydrospeeding.

Dirk considered his map. He nodded. "That is it. Yes. That is all."

"Thank you," Gaia said. She reached out for the napkin. Dirk let her take it.

"You've been most helpful," Andrew said. "How much do we owe you?"

"How much do you have?" Dirk asked.

Andrew felt for his wallet. He pulled out a wad of notes. He didn't even check them. "Is this enough?"

Dirk only beamed. "Now you will need good luck," he said. "The journey—it is dangerous. The rocks—they are sharp."

"The microprocessors—" Elke said again. She couldn't help herself.

"Microprocessors?" Dirk said. "What microprocessors? You have some to sell?"

Elke forced a clenched smile. She had to try her best to be patient. "No, last year, the Chinese microprocessors—"

"Never mind that. You want to join me for a beer? I would do that for old times. The drinking we did, Elke, you remember? Me and Elke Hahn! The Snake! The prettiest mercenary this side of the Alps! You remember our song—it was your favorite, when you were younger, before you got all these big muscles, before you got wrinkled . . ."

Dirk launched into what Will presumed was their old drinking song, and Elke exhaled hard. "Some other time," she growled.

23

Alpine Adventures, 6:30 P.M.

The kiosk was in the middle of a field, backed by raw crags with snow on the peaks.

Will gave a teenaged salesclerk two hundred Swiss francs. In return, they got a six-hour hire of three hydrospeed floats plus extra-thick wet suits, flippers, and crash helmets fitted with flashlights. When the clerk had finished piling up their equipment, he dug a brochure out of a drawer and gave it to Will and Gaia. "This guide you have hired, he is very experienced? He is licensed?"

"Yeah," Will said. He grabbed his bright red float and glanced back toward the parking lot, where Elke was waiting.

"Now," the teenager said, "remember: Read the brochure thoroughly. Your guide will explain everything, but you can read this on the way. Hydrospeeding is the most exciting thing you can do. Like white-water rafting. But you're on your own and you're right down there, on the water. Exhilaration like you would not believe. Have fun—and stay safe."

"Thanks," Will said.

The boy nodded and turned to a pair of customers who were approaching the kiosk.

Gaia picked up her float. It was about three feet long and

a foot and a half wide, made from polyethylene, and filled with polyurethane for extra buoyancy. There were hollows for your elbows, and two handles to hold on to at the front. The idea was to go down white water headfirst, with your chest resting on the board. "Have you ever done anything like this before?" she asked.

Will shook his head. Gaia glanced at Andrew, who was scanning the list of sports on the blackboard outside the kiosk, hands on his hips. He looked awed. Clearly the inhaler drugs hadn't worn off yet.

"He's a good swimmer," Will said. "Are you?"

"Good enough. I *hope*." She smiled cautiously. This was going to be fun, but dangerous.

"Hey." Andrew waved to them. "Zorbing! I'd like to try it. Imagine: rolling across the land. It'd be like flying, but . . . on land." He grinned. In other circumstances, it might have been amusing, Will thought. But not now. Well, maybe only slightly.

"Next time," Will said. "Right now we have to do something that's like flying but . . . through water."

Andrew's grin broadened. "Even better!"

"How long does this stuff last?" Gaia asked Will.

Good question, he thought. "In theory, about fifteen minutes. But I don't know if the formula was actually finished. I got it from the development lab. And they were perfecting it for a man weighing two hundred twenty pounds."

"What's that? Like twice Andrew's weight?" Shaking her head, she called out to Andrew: "Come and get your stuff. And try to look normal. *Please*."

The hydrospeed floats sat piled on the front seat of Elke's Maserati.

In the back, Andrew, Will, and Gaia were squashed together. Andrew looked almost smothered by the flabby neoprene wet suits and the other gear, but he didn't seem to mind. He hummed along to the radio, which was blaring a German pop song.

Will's brain tuned out. He was thinking about their plan. If they did get caught at the Sphere, they could always play the kid card. Suspicious security officers would usually try to grab kids, not shoot them. At least, that's what Will had told Elke. And if they *did* get into serious trouble, Barrington would help them. Will was sure of it. MI6 would somehow get them back to Britain.

Barrington might refuse ever to deal with STORM again, but at least they'd be alive. And at least they'd have tried to find out exactly what was going on. If InVesta wanted to get its hands on cold fusion, STORM had to stop them. No single company could be allowed to own a technology that in theory could be used to hold nations to ransom.

But there was no denying it: The journey to the Sphere would be extraordinarily dangerous.

Dirk's map was clear enough. Almost the entire route would be white water. They'd have to negotiate some nasty bends. A few of the drops were near-vertical. If they strayed from the route into other channels, they could easily get lost. Deep underground.

Then, if they actually made it out of the mountain, they'd have to tumble down the waterfall into InVesta's dam both intact and unnoticed. Apprehension made Will's pulse race.

But the self-hardening body armor would come in very useful, he thought. The roaches should, if well wrapped, survive the journey. He couldn't risk Eye Spy, though. They'd also have to communicate with Elke somehow, but how could they protect their phones?

"It's so beautiful," Andrew murmured next to him. He was pointing across the valley below. Pale grass was sprinkled with candy-colored wildflowers. Picture-book houses nestled against the slopes.

In some ways, Will thought, STORM could be about to embark on their toughest challenge yet. He needed Andrew's full mental concentration. Which he did not have.

"Yeah," Will said. "Isn't it, *Gaia*?"

"It wasn't my fault!"

"And you still haven't told me," Elke said as she swerved the Maserati around yet another steep bend. "What exactly was in that inhaler?"

"A secret formula," Gaia said.

"I see. A secret formula. *Alles klaar*! You know, I do have some *items* of my own. You spill your little beans, maybe I will spill some of my own."

"What items?" Will asked.

"Now you are interested! Give and take—that is the rule of any relationship, remember. Although, it is true, I prefer to take than give." She chuckled dryly. "In my experience, it is safer."

"In your experience as a mercenary?" Will asked, remembering what Dirk had said back at the bar.

Elke scowled. "The man is full of nonsense. You cannot believe a word he says."

"So he could have made up the map?" Will said.

"Not that! No, believe me, not that. Dirk is many things, but when it comes to business, he plays fair. So, the formula?"

"I honestly don't know," Will said. "But it makes people trusting. At least, that's what it was designed for."

"It wasn't designed by you?"

"No," Will said. "A . . . friend gave it to me."

"You have useful friends," Elke observed.

"So do you." Will glanced out the window. They were climbing fast on a road cut into gray rock. He could hear rivers, but he couldn't see them. They passed through a series of tunnels. When they came out, Will saw streams rushing, and a waterfall cascading behind a small shop.

They seemed to be above the tree line now. The only green was from shrubs and grass and pale lichen spreading over bare rock. Will saw an altitude marker: 5,700 feet. He blinked at the sunlight reflecting off the runnels of ice above them. The stripes looked like rays. They were blinding white.

Elke rolled the steering wheel to the right and pushed a black flip-flop on the brake. She cut the engine. The silence was sudden. Andrew's eyes were closed now, Will noticed. He might actually be asleep.

"We're here?" Will asked.

Elke nodded. She pointed up the mountainside. "The entrance is somewhere over there."

Will got out of the car. At this altitude, it was cold. He shivered. For a few moments, he surveyed their surroundings. They were high, and the view was impressive. Will could see right down a long valley to the lake at the bottom. Something seemed to be rolling across the water. A Zorb ball, he guessed. From here, there was no sign of any buildings.

Elke and Gaia stood close by. Andrew had gotten out. He was crouching, shielding his eyes against the sun, gazing at the lake.

"So where's the Black Sphere?" Will asked Elke.

Elke peered across the valley, squinting. "You can't see it from here. It's down, round that slope—over there. It's built on a ledge. An aerie."

An aerie. *An eagle's nest.* Will glanced up. He couldn't help hoping that perhaps Barrington's robot *was* up there somewhere, keeping an eye on them.

Elke cracked her knuckles loudly. "So, you are sure you want to do this?" she said to Will.

"Yeah." He glanced at Gaia, who nodded. And a thought that had struck him after Venice resurfaced. In St. Petersburg, they had risked their lives. They'd felt they had no choice. And it hadn't been easy. Every single second of their fear had cut right to the bone. Then in Venice, situations that should have made him afraid, if not terrified, had barely registered. They'd gotten away with so much. They'd taken risks, and those risks had paid off. Every time.

What if they were getting overconfident? What if they'd had a run of good luck? Play dangerous odds, and in the end they catch up with you. His father had known that.

But they were here. In Switzerland. They'd come so far already. And Will knew why they were about to try to break into the Sphere. It wasn't for the thrill. Or, it wasn't *only* for the thrill. "I need to take another look at the map," he said.

"I could lead the way," Gaia said. "My memory is better than yours, for something like this. I could easily memorize the map."

Will hesitated. But she was right. "I'll get it." He turned back to the car and was struck again by the problem of how they'd take their phones down with them. "Do you have anything hard and watertight?" he asked Elke. "We have to take a phone with us."

"I have some boxes," Elke said. "They are plastic, with loops. Perhaps you can attach them to belts? But they are not watertight. You will be underwater sometimes, you know. The journey will not be smooth. I don't think a phone will make it."

"But we need to stay in contact with you," Will said. "If there are problems, we'll need to ask you for help."

"What about the bugs?" Gaia asked. "If the roaches get a bit wet, they'll be all right, won't they?"

"Roaches?" Elke said. *"Cockroaches?"*

Will wasn't listening. He'd just followed Gaia's thought process. Leave Elke with the earphone, and talk to her via the mike in a roach. It was a good idea—except for one thing. "I'll need the earphone in there," he said to Gaia. "I'll be using the roaches for audio."

Gaia glanced back at the Maserati. "Elke, you said you had kit. Do you have a laptop in that trunk?"

"I have a fully functioning mobile surveillance unit in that trunk." Elke clamped her hands onto her hips. "At our annual meeting last year, Vanya mentioned a project he wanted to pursue—implants in the exoskeletons of cockroaches. I thought he was drunk."

"He might have been," Will said. "But he did build them."

Gaia wanted to ask about the annual meeting. *Later,* she told herself. "So, Elke, you have Internet access?"

"Yes."

"So we need to divert a signal from one of those roaches to a website, or somehow directly to Elke's laptop," Gaia said. She looked down at Andrew. His eyes were closed, his face tilted to the sun. Gaia sighed and crouched beside him. "Andrew, there's something I need to ask you. Can you concentrate—"

"Can I reroute a signal from one of the insects?" he asked, almost absentmindedly.

"You *were* listening! Could you?"

There was a pause. Then his blue eyes opened and he beamed. "I can try."

Hotel Lindrick, River Tweed

Shute Barrington was walking fast. His rod was over his shoulder. The river was rapidly receding.

He had to get back to his room. Get to his computer. Log into the STASIS network. See what he could find out. Charlie Spicer had been too long—

He stopped and reached for his phone, which was finally ringing.

"Spicer—"

"Sir, sorry to disturb you. I know you're on holiday. I hope the fishing's going well?"

An insult rose in Barrington's throat, but he swallowed it. Spicer wasn't stupid. If he was talking in this way, obviously he suspected someone else could be listening. *Who?* Barrington thought. His phone was secure—wasn't it? Who on earth could interfere with STASIS communications?

"Oh, fabulously," Barrington replied, not missing a beat.

"That's great, sir. I'm only calling because something's arrived by courier, addressed to you and marked urgent. I thought you might want me to open it at once."

Barrington understood. "Ah . . . No, no, Spicer, don't worry. I'll take care of it when I get back."

"All right, sir. By the way—that transmitter I gave you. You said you'd taken it with you, didn't you?"

Spicer knew full well he had. It was still in the pocket of his leather jacket, which was back at the guesthouse.

"Yes, Spicer. Apologies."

"No, that's fine, sir. I just wanted to double-check. I won't keep you from the fish."

The line went dead.

It had been a curious conversation. As he strode across the grass, Barrington picked it apart.

Spicer had something to tell him, and for some reason he was afraid to discuss it over the phone. So Spicer had dispatched a message by courier. Risky? Yes. More dangerous than a phone call? Certainly not. At least, not if Spicer was sending it on one of his modified laptops.

The computer would appear to be normal. But part of the hard drive could be activated only by an encrypted radio-frequency code transmitted by the owner. Spicer had modified two laptops already. They were back in the lab. One, Barrington suspected, was on its way up to Scotland.

Barrington broke into a jog. That morning, it had taken him an hour and a half to walk to the river. If he ran, perhaps he could do it in thirty minutes. Spicer would have used an urgent air transfer, he thought. By the time he got back to the hotel, it could be there.

But would the prototype transmitter actually work?

And, most importantly, what did Spicer have to say?

25

Gaia gripped her board tight against her chest. There in front of them was the river. The water frothed as it thundered past, then vanished into a jagged black hole in the side of the mountain.

"You ready?"

Dirk's warnings echoed in her mind. She wasn't sure now if it was better or worse to know what lay ahead. But they had no choice. She nodded.

"We'll be right behind you," Will said.

Gaia looked past him at Andrew, who was holding his board and blinking up at the sun.

"Right behind you," Will repeated. "I promise."

She took a deep breath. There was no point delaying the inevitable.

"See you at the Black Sphere," she whispered. Her legs trembling, she jumped.

Cold. The air rushed, pummeling Gaia's face. Spray blasted into her eyes. Icy water flooded her wet suit. She hurtled into blackness, fear ripping through her. She could hear her own breathing, her pulse in her ears. The flashlight in her helmet shone brightly, but she was moving so fast she couldn't get a fix on anything. She glanced up. Registered a slimy arc of black roof—and then, ahead, a boulder, half blocking the channel. The boulder! Dirk had marked it!

A third of a mile in, before the first right-hand fork and before the cavern. There was just enough room for a person to slip past. As she hurtled forward, Gaia suddenly leaned hard to the right, re-angling the nose of her board. She kicked. Her foot caught the wall. Her ankle scraped rock. But she was at the boulder. And she was through!

The current blasted her forward. Gaia angled down, the water rushing into her face. She blinked hard and glanced back quickly. She saw a yellow light flash on the roof. Then another. Will and Andrew. They were still with her.

Any second now, she should see the first fork in the tunnel. She gripped tight to the handles and kept her body weight just to the right-hand side of the board. Not so far that she'd unbalance herself—just enough to keep her on course.

The tunnel was wider here, nine feet across. Gaia's eyes strained. The air seemed stale. She coughed. And there it was—her one-watt flashlight showed the river splitting into two. The water crashed repeatedly up against the junction of the two channels. Above the din, she heard a cry.

"Yeah!"

Andrew was *whooping*? Gaia wanted to yell at him to focus, but there was no time. She bounced violently over the water. It was so icy, she could hardly feel her fingers anymore. She swiveled her body, and her board rocked dangerously. *Hold on*, she told herself. *Hold on*. And there was the split. She leaned hard—and raced, skidding over the water, on track!

No time for relief. Gaia's blood pounded in waves.

Concentrate, she told herself. *Picture that map.* In five seconds, they'd take a second right-hand fork and enter a high cavern. Then the roof would close in as the river raged on.

Will's board bounced relentlessly. It jarred his skull, making his vision blurry. But he had to keep his eyes on Gaia. Three seconds ago, they'd shot along the second right-hand fork. Will had seen the light of her flashlight flicker and disappear, then reappear as he sped on after it. Now from behind him, Will could hear Andrew, still shouting with excitement.

"Andrew!" Will yelled. *"Shut up!"* Andrew probably couldn't hear. But it made Will feel better. Then suddenly he gasped. Ice water had breached his float and washed over his face. He spluttered and blinked hard. When his vision cleared, he saw the roof was dipping. He was about to collide with the wall! Will flinched. His knee hit rock. He prepared himself for pain. But the liquid between those seven layers of Kevlar in his armor had reacted at once, forming a solid barrier. He'd whacked his kneecap, but it was only stunned, not gashed. In the darkness, Will smiled. It worked. His device worked!

"Ow!" Andrew's voice.

Only this time he'd sounded different.

"Ow! *Will!*"

That had been a *yelp*.

Will glanced back. His flashlight picked out a deathly white face.

"I can't see!"

Will heard a gurgling sound as Andrew swallowed water.

"I've got your glasses!" Will yelled back. They were in one of Elke's plastic boxes, hanging with the roaches from his belt. The drugs must be wearing off. "Hold on, Andrew. *It's all right!*"

He looked ahead and saw Gaia's light jerk. Any second now, the tunnel should open up. "You're all right, Andrew." Will shouted over the roar, *"Hold on!"*

The channel began to widen. The current slowed. The water no longer rushed so wildly over his board. They had to be entering the cavern.

Gradually, the roof started to rise. Will jerked his flashlight, trying to build up a picture of his surroundings. The beam caught a flash of something pale. Will tried to keep it steady. He stared. It was a stalactite! And another. They were bristling. *Hundreds* of them, glimmering in the flicker of his flashlight.

Will's breathing came fast—from excitement now, not fear. They could be the first people to see this in decades! His eyes ran over the walls. Moisture glistened.

Ahead, Will could just make out the yellow of Gaia's flippers. "It's beautiful!" he called.

Her light shot around. "Yeah!"

They were moving slowly now. The current swept him gently forward. It was almost like being on a fairground ride. Except that these sights were real—like the danger.

Will peered ahead. According to Dirk's map, the cavern was about 150 feet long. They had to be close to the other end. Will glanced back. "Andrew, are you okay?"

Silence. Then a cough. "Are you hoping I'll say yes?"

"But look at this place!"

"It's a bit difficult, Will, when I don't have my glasses, *and* it's pitch-black!"

Will smiled. He gazed up, kicking to help propel himself along. Then Gaia screamed, and Will froze.

He peered ahead. Her flippers had vanished. Her beam had gone. "Gaia!"

No response.

"Gaia!"

The current nudged the edge of his board. The river was beginning to pick up speed again. Will heard a rushing noise. Getting louder. White water. *Raging.* Will's heart raced. He called back: "Andrew, hold tight—" Suddenly, Will's board dipped and he bounced up. His head hit rock. There was a crunching sound. His flashlight.

Will plunged into darkness. The walls closed in. A jag of rock caught his board. It spun him hard. The force tore his right hand away from the handle. His arm flailed in the blackness. He started to roll. He was on his side. Water rushed over his face. He gasped. Panic started to pulse through his veins. He *had* to find that handle. He had to pull himself back—

Again, the board ricocheted off rock. Above the rush of the water, Will could hear Andrew yelling. He made out a jerking glimmer ahead. Gaia's flashlight. Will was back on his side. He was about to go under. *Reach,* he told himself. *Reach.*

He clenched his fists and threw himself forward, stretching for the handle. He touched plastic. Fumbled. Coughed as river water sloshed into his lungs. He reached again. He felt the rope. But just as his fingers gripped the handle, the channel dropped, and Will with it.

26

Gravity made Will's stomach lurch. Again his hand was thrown free from the raft. It smashed into rock. He felt his knuckles tear. His hand was on fire. Nausea rose. He was going to be sick. Then he screwed up his eyes. Ahead, the beam of Gaia's flashlight exploded into a ball of white light.

Suddenly, the water fell away.

That light was the sky.

They were *out*.

But all Will saw was white. He was spiraling down. He felt his heart thud.

Then nothing. The world was silent.

He was underwater, plunging down into darkness. Desperately, his eyes sought light. Found a speck. Will reached for it. A second later, his injured hand broke the surface. He blinked. Coughed hard. And then he saw Gaia, already at the concrete shore.

Will tried to make sense of their surroundings. They were definitely in the dam. At the far side, he could see the top of a sluice gate. Above him was the hole in the mountain, which they'd just burst through, down a thirty-foot drop. At eye level, across a stretch of flagstoned yard, was a low building constructed from brick and chrome.

The Sphere.

Andrew had reached Gaia by now. She helped him out and waved at Will. "Hurry up!" she called.

Will kicked hard. Gaia grabbed his hand, and he clambered onto land. Andrew was already running toward a small brick hut halfway between the dam and the institute. Will and Gaia raced after him, into what seemed to be the pumping station for the dam. One small window was cut at head height. It was dark inside the hut, and damp. But they were hidden.

They dropped their floats. Will was shivering. The gash in his hand looked bad. But right now there was nothing he could do about it. Andrew sat down, breathing hard. Gaia pushed her tangled hair away from her face. Then she noticed the blood. "What happened?"

"I hit my hand on a rock," Will said. "It's okay. Are you all right?"

She nodded quickly.

"Andrew?"

Andrew only blinked. He was still breathing hard.

"We have to make sure no one saw us." Will peered out the window. He couldn't see anyone. And if someone had noticed them, surely they'd know about it by now.

The Sphere's security was focused on the main entrance, Elke had said. Around the edge of the yard, Will could see fifteen-foot-high wire fences. Bright yellow signs with black lightning forks indicated that they were electrified. Security probably didn't even know it was possible to get in through the river. Will couldn't help but smile.

With every second that passed, he felt safer. But Andrew was pressing his dripping hands to his face. The armor and the wet suit made him look unusually bulky. He was shivering.

"Andrew," Will whispered. "Are you okay?"

For a moment, Andrew didn't react. Then he dropped his hands. "What did we just do? What were you thinking? Are you *mad*?"

Will glanced at Gaia. "We had to get into the Black Sphere—remember? This was the only way in."

"I don't remember actually agreeing to water torture!"

"Well, you did," Gaia whispered. "Welcome back, by the way."

Andrew looked confused. For a moment, Will was afraid the spray had messed with his memory. Then Andrew peered hard at him. "What exactly is in that inhaler?" He looked at Gaia. "*What did you do to me?*"

"It was an accident," she whispered. *Well, actually it was your fault,* she thought. But there was no point getting into it now.

"You're all right," Will said. He undid his belt and started to slide off the boxes.

"You call this *all right?*" Andrew said. But then he sighed. "I'm sorry. It's just—I haven't ever felt like that before. I felt *blurry*. I can hardly even remember. I—"

"It's all right," Gaia said. "You're all right." She touched his shoulder. "The spray worked, Andrew. We got the map. We're here."

Will handed Andrew his glasses. The cigar box was damp, but the roaches were scuttling around happily. "We'll have to hide the wet suits in here," Will said. "But keep the armor on. We'll put our wet clothes back on top."

When they had changed, Will nudged open the door to

the pumping hut. He could see a single door into the Sphere. They'd have to hope it wasn't locked, but there was little reason to lock a door in what was meant to be an impenetrable yard.

Beside him, Gaia fidgeted. This waiting around was making her more nervous. "Are we going now?"

"Are you in a hurry?" Will said.

She looked at him. "To find proof that InVesta killed those scientists, and to stop them getting their hands on the plans for cold fusion? I don't know, should I be?"

"But what if someone actually does see us?" Andrew whispered.

"Improvise," Will said. "You're the nephew of one of the scientists. You came in with him, and you got lost. No one would believe a fourteen-year-old kid could actually break in. Remember what Elke said: The security here is meant to be the best."

"Though luckily for us it isn't *watertight*," Andrew said with a wan smile. "All right, apart from being wet, cold, and still fuzzy in the head, I'm ready. What are we waiting for?"

Will smiled. "Nothing," he said.

27

The door opened easily. On the other side, a corridor gleamed. Will saw eight white doors. At the far end was another one of solid, mesh-toughened glass.

The plaques beside the doors reminded Will of Sutton Hall. He read:

HYDRO 2A
DRILL-RIG BETA: COMMS
AUTOMATION

Laboratories, Will thought. "Let's split up," he said. "You two check out these labs. I'm going to see what's through the door at the end. Meet me back here in thirty minutes."

Andrew looked at his own watch. "We should synchronize."

Gaia and Will exchanged glances. Clearly Andrew's brain still wasn't working properly. Thirty minutes was thirty minutes whatever time their watches showed.

"Not necessary," Gaia whispered, and took his arm. "Come on."

Will headed off, moving cautiously.

Through the glass door he found himself in another

corridor. Sunlight flooded in through porthole windows along both walls.

On the left, Will saw yet another door, painted white, and then a series of framed photographs. They were similar to those in the London offices. Bone-white blades of a modern wind mill looked stark against a bright green field. Two Indian toddlers smiled up at a telephone kiosk. Sonar panels on the roof were stamped with the logo of InVesta.

Will shook his head. These photographs gave the impression that InVesta cared about people, and about the environment. They didn't show the less pleasant side of a multinational corporation. The sell-outs. The secret deals. The murder . . . ?

Edmund Pope's mortuary picture flashed through Will's mind. Then he thought about David Wickett. Where was he, right at that moment? Perhaps Barrington had already found him. Of course, Will hoped so. If InVesta got its hands on cold fusion, once they understood exactly how it worked, Wickett would no longer be needed. He'd be as good as dead. Five of the brightest minds of Wickett's generation were already gone.

Will reached the end of the corridor—and stopped. Through the meshed glass, he'd seen movement.

He quickly backed against the wall. Just in time. The door swung open, and a stocky, bald man with a tanned neck strode through. *Saxon Webb*. Will recognized him from the welcome video. Hard on his heels was an overweight man wearing too-short trousers and white socks. Neither one of them saw Will.

So Webb's here! Will thought. His heart thudded.

But where was he going?

A moment later, Will had his answer.

Webb pushed open the white door and headed into unknown territory.

Will waited twenty seconds. Took a deep breath. Then he followed.

Andrew peered at the machine. He didn't recognize it exactly. But from the instructions on a label on the side, he could make a fair stab at its function. "Well, this seems to be an energy lab," he said quietly. "But I don't think we're talking energy for power . . . Gaia?"

She was at the far end of the untidy Automation laboratory. Between them, three stainless steel workbenches overflowed with gear, including two laptops, both of which were switched off. This suggested, Andrew hoped, that whoever had been working in the lab had left for the day. Boxes and cables were strewn across the floor. Beside a large cardboard box, Gaia had found a lumpy pile covered by an old sheet.

"Gaia," Andrew whispered again. "Did you hear me?"

Gaia nodded. Then she grabbed a corner of the sheet and pulled it off. She gasped.

"What?" One of the benches was in the way. Andrew couldn't see. He hurried over, almost tripping on a coil of electrical cable. Then he stared.

Three pairs of eye cavities stared back.

The faces were made of silicone. They were attached to silicone torsos. Androids. Instead of arms, they had what looked like nozzles.

"What are they?" Gaia whispered.

"I'm guessing you're looking for an answer other than 'robots,' in which case I don't know."

Gingerly, he touched the face of one of the androids. Then the jet nozzle. He grabbed it, gently pulling the torso forward so he could see the back. "There's space here for something to slot in. A canister maybe. It could fire its contents through the nozzles."

Andrew thought for a moment. "You remember what we read about InVesta? One branch deals in energy for power, the other in arms? What if this is actually an arms lab? Look over here."

Andrew let the robot fall back against the wall, and he dodged the high-tech obstacle course back to his machine. Gaia followed.

"This machine generates laser beams. And look over there." On the opposite wall was a copper sheet with a solid metal pad behind it. The copper was pierced with smooth holes.

"This isn't a *laser* weapon?" Gaia said.

"Well, that's what it looks like. At least, this kit could be used for research into laser weapons."

Something struck her. "Remember Wickett's note? Do you think it could have something to do with all this? What if InVesta is blackmailing Wickett—unless he hands over the plans, they'll attack Kleinkirchen with laser weapons?"

Andrew thought for a moment. "Blackmail sounds possible. But why threaten Kleinkirchen? Why not kidnap his family?"

"What if he doesn't have any family? And they'd be

talking about an *entire village*. Wickett would *have* to do what they wanted."

Andrew nodded slowly. "All right—but I don't see how they could use something like laser weapons on a village and hope to get away with it. I can believe they could blow up a farmhouse and either dupe the police or even pay them off. But taking out an entire village . . . ? If they really are blackmailing Wickett with a threat to Kleinkirchen, the weapon would have to be a lot more subtle."

"Like what?"

Andrew shook his head. "I have no idea." He looked at his watch. "Fifteen minutes until we're supposed to meet Will. Maybe we should finish checking this lab and head to the next one."

Gaia nodded. Where *was* Will? she wondered. In St. Petersburg and Venice, they had used the tooth phones to stay in touch. It felt strange, not knowing if Will was all right. "Do you think he's okay?" she asked. "I wish we had the tooth phones."

Andrew smiled gently at her concern. Of course he shared it. But was hers just the concern of a friend? Now wasn't the time to consider such things. He decided to disguise his smile. "Mental note," he said. "Next time we go on a last-minute international mission, we *must* be better prepared."

Bugging InVesta was becoming a habit.

Will had followed Webb and his companion down yet another silent corridor. Then he'd watched as they'd entered a room marked *Direktor: Herr Gustav Pritt* and slammed the door shut.

Now, very slowly, Will reached for Vanya's cigar box. Holding his breath, he peeled back one corner of the seal, reached in, and grabbed a wing case.

Quickly, Will checked the number on the belly and he released the insect at the base of the door. It scuttled in at once.

Will pulled out the earphone, then ducked past the director's office, looking for somewhere to hide. It didn't take long, and the coincidence almost made him smile. Another InVesta office—and another fire door. Only this was the ground floor, so it had to lead directly outside.

Will pushed through it, into sunlight. He was at the side of the building, he realized, on a path bounded by electrified razor wire. Will listened hard, in case the door was linked to an automatic alarm. He didn't hear any alarm. What he heard was this:

"Half past nine, as we said. I will be in position. If Wickett does not come . . ."

". . . problem, sir. Unfortunately, there has been no recent contact. He could have been seized already. Or killed."

"Well, if he has, what use are you to me? I can get rid of you, like the others! You want the same fate as Bailey? I can arrange it!"

Will listened hard, one hand pressed to his temple. *I can get rid of you, like the others.* Webb *had* to mean that he'd ordered the murder of the FIREball scientists. And it wasn't hard to guess what he was talking about now. A meeting with Wickett, scheduled for—Will checked his watch—ninety minutes' time. And if Wickett didn't show? Then what, exactly? What was the threat to Kleinkirchen? Was Webb planning something if Wickett failed to turn up?

". . . pumps activated. I want the drill rig ready to go at my command. Now get Hudson out!"

Will frowned. The drill rig? This partial conversation was triggering more and more questions, and painfully few answers. He'd have to speak to Vanya about improving the audio.

Then came a shout of disgust: *"Ugh!"*

A second later, the audio cut out. Will could guess what had happened.

Cockroach number eight had just died on active duty.

28

Barbour jackets lined the porch. Shute Barrington threw his rod against them as he raced in. He heard it clatter to the floor but he didn't go back. He was already halfway across the grand entrance hall, mounted with stag heads, and he strode on, to the oak reception desk.

A blond woman in a tweed suit was on the telephone. She smiled pleasantly and raised a hand, indicating that he should wait.

"Has a package arrived for me?" Barrington demanded.

The woman's forehead creased. "Yes, madam, we do have a room—"

"A package," Barrington interrupted. "For Shute Barrington. It's urgent."

The receptionist placed her hand across the mouthpiece. "Sir, I'll just be a moment—"

"No, you won't," Barrington said. "I don't mean to be rude, but when I say urgent, I actually mean it."

Barrington's bluntness finally got through to her. That and the way he swerved around the edge of her desk and through a door bearing the words *Staff Only.*

"Madam, I'm sorry, I'll have to put you on hold." She pressed a button and hurried after Barrington into the delivery room. "Sir, you really aren't supposed to come in here!"

Barrington didn't answer. He was making his way past a cart piled high with boxes of apples and two hams to an old wooden school desk. On top were newspapers, letters—and two packages.

The first was addressed in spidery writing to a Colonel somebody. The second had been delivered by courier. Barrington recognized Spicer's neat capitals at once. He snatched it up.

"Sir, *please*—if you could—"

"Leave?" Barrington said. "Of course. This *is* addressed to me, by the way." Clasping the parcel to his chest, he swept past her. "You've been most helpful." He made a dash for the stairs, taking two in each leap.

As soon as he was inside his room, he ripped the wrapping open. When the paper, cardboard, and polystyrene fell away, he found a mound of bubble wrap. Inside was a computer the size of a paperback book.

Barrington put the computer on his bedside table and switched it on. While it booted up, he found his leather jacket and the transmitter. Then he sat down on the edge of the four-poster bed, his palms damp. "What have you got for me, Spicer?" he murmured to himself. *"What have you got for me?"*

At last, the desktop settled. Barrington held the transmitter tight in his palm. He pulled off the cap and pressed a black button. At once, the screen flickered.

Barrington moved the cursor to My Computer. Selected the secret G drive. Double-clicked.

Two seconds later, he was in.

There were four files. The first was a Word document, titled *Read Me*. Barrington clicked on it.

Check out the file called <u>Project</u>, Spicer had written. *It explains what those scientists were up to. Then look at Rendezvous. It contains details of Wickett's MI6 handler—and his latest contacts. If I need to get more information to you, I'll send it by e-mail, using the encryption key in the document called Key.*

I just generated the key. I haven't logged it on the STASIS system. No one knows it but you and me. If I'm right about why I'm not telling you all this over the phone, I'll e-mail you. I need to check something first.

Despite the run across the fields and the race upstairs, Barrington's blood felt cold. Sweat froze on his forehead.

He had worked for STASIS for sixteen years.

This was totally unprecedented.

Whatever Spicer had discovered had to be desperately serious.

One step at a time, Barrington told himself. And the next step was *Project*.

The file seemed to take an interminable time to load. When Barrington saw the first three lines, his brain raced away on unfamiliar tracks.

Classification: Alpha

Project: FIREball

Objective: Fusion in a room-temperature environment

Cold fusion.

How hadn't he known about this?

Had the scientists actually *done* it?

And, almost more incredibly, why hadn't C, his boss, consulted him?

He was director of STASIS. Head of science and technology at MI6. And yet apparently this project was too secret even for him? What was C thinking? Why hadn't he consulted him? *What the hell was going on?*

Three minutes after cockroach number eight was crushed, Gaia and Andrew finished their search of the Automation lab. Apart from the unfinished robots and the laser machine, they'd found little else of interest.

Andrew was about to open the door, when he froze. They'd both heard the shout. Then someone stomped along the corridor, in the direction of the other labs. He opened the door a crack. Just in time to see a fat man in black trousers disappear into Drill Rig Beta: Comms.

"What's going on?" Gaia whispered.

"Hold on," Andrew whispered back. "I just saw someone." He put his ear to the space between the door and the jamb. He could hear a voice. And then another gruff shout, in German.

"Nein, Hudson. Jezt, komm mit!"

Two pairs of feet stomped along the floor right toward them. Andrew pushed the door shut. He and Gaia waited, holding their breath.

"Wo ist Herr Webb?" This was a new voice. It had to be Hudson's. *"Wo ist Herr Webb?"*

"Where is Mr. Webb?" Andrew mouthed questioningly.

Gaia nodded. She listened hard as Hudson rattled off a series of rapid-fire questions. "It sounds like they're taking him away," she whispered.

The footsteps got quieter. When he couldn't hear them anymore, Andrew peered out into the corridor. He saw no one. But the door to Drill Rig Beta: Comms was standing open.

"They've gone," he whispered. "Come on."

Andrew inched his way along the wall to the lab. He peered in. Saw no one. The lab was smaller than Automation. And much tidier. Four modern wooden desks were kitted out with desktop computers, fans, and jars for pens. Toward the back of the room was a large whiteboard.

The computer on the nearest desk was switched on, Andrew noticed. He pointed to it. "I'd like to take a look. Could you keep watch?"

Gaia hesitated. She wanted to investigate too. But she nodded.

Andrew dashed to the computer.

He moved the mouse, and the InVesta screen saver vanished, revealing a Word document. This document was written not in German, but English.

It seemed to be a list of concerns, ordered in bullet points.

Junior Engineer Schwarz has reported your order to raise tapped water flow by 150 percent. I understand this has been carried out for the past 24 hours, and was to be kept from me. Please could you explain this?

Engineer Schwarz also reports your order to recommence drill rig preparation. Again, could you explain this? Reference report of April 22nd (attached).

What was this? Andrew wondered. A draft of an e-mail to someone? To Webb? What did increased water tapping mean?

Perhaps nothing.

But perhaps he should find that report from April 22.

Quickly, Andrew opened up My Documents. He scrolled through the dates of the files until he came to April 22.

Underneath Summer rosters, he found: *URGENT! Severe risks*.

Andrew double-clicked on it. The egg-timer icon appeared.

Come on, he urged the computer.

"Andrew!" Gaia's voice had been low. She was backing away from the door, jabbing a finger toward it. Her meaning was clear, but the report! Andrew's pulse throbbed. At last, the file opened. He saw the front page.

URGENT: Severe risks associated with drill-point experimentation in quadrant B5.

Confidential. Unauthorized possession is a crime.

A. Hudson, Chief Engineer.

"Andrew!"

Gaia was making for the whiteboard at the rear of the lab. With a trembling finger, Andrew closed the document and he double-clicked on the Outlook icon.

Out of the corner of his eye, he could see Gaia waving frantically from behind the whiteboard. He could hear two voices getting louder—getting closer. But he had to have this report. Somehow, he *had* to.

At last, the e-mail software loaded. Andrew instantly created a new e-mail, hit INSERT, then FILE—and he heard the door handle judder as someone grabbed it from the other side. *One more second*, he thought. *Just one more second*.

He attached the report, typed in his own e-mail address, and hit SEND.

As the door opened, Andrew shut down Outlook and flung himself to the floor. His breathing was coming fast. He tried to slow it. Almost coughed. Gaia wasn't far away. But he didn't dare try to join her. He was paralyzed by the two voices. One was a curious mix of English and American. Saxon Webb.

"I thought you told Schwarz to meet me here!" Webb barked.

"Yes, sir, I did." Heavily accented German. The man in the black trousers they'd heard a few minutes ago?

"So how can I trust that Hudson has been dealt with?"

There was a pause. "I swear my life on it, Herr Webb."

Hudson! The engineer, and the author of the mysterious report. The man who had just been "escorted" out of his lab. And Schwarz . . . the draft e-mail had mentioned a Junior Engineer Schwarz.

Andrew heard a grunt.

"The rig must be prepared for action, Pritt. I am not in the habit of making empty threats!"

"It will be done, sir. I will see to it personally."

"Ensure you do. And be ready to leave for the Nest in one hour. If Schwarz does not have everything ready—"

"He will. I will stake my life on it, Herr Webb."

"You are very ready to stake your life, Pritt. And I will hold you to it."

Andrew watched one pair of legs pivot. Then they stomped out of the room, followed by Pritt, who was shouting, presumably into a radio: *"Wo ist Schwarz? Nein! Ich bin . . ."* Pritt's voice faded as he raced back along the corridor.

Andrew finally let himself breathe. Oxygen rushed to

his brain. He pushed himself up and saw Gaia emerge from behind the whiteboard. She pointed toward the door, eyes wide.

Andrew nodded.

She could have meant either:

They've gone.

Or:

We need to get out of here.

Andrew was in agreement with both.

They had what they needed. At least, he had to hope they did. As soon as they were somewhere safer, he could read through that report. Hopefully he'd be able to work out what Webb was threatening Wickett with, how the drill rig fitted in, and what Hudson was so concerned about. But what was "the Nest"? Where was Webb going?

One step at a time.

Step one: Find Will.

Step two: Get out of the Black Sphere.

Will's watch showed there were six minutes left until he was due to meet Gaia and Andrew. Perhaps he should try to check out the route they'd need to follow to the foyer—and the way out.

The security measures were there to stop people from getting in, not leaving. They'd be spotted, of course, but they wouldn't hang around, and Elke had promised to be close by in the Maserati. They'd stride out together, and into the car . . .

If he could imagine it happening, perhaps it really would work.

At least the trip, and the risks, had been worthwhile, Will thought. Now he was as sure as he could be that Saxon Webb was behind the deaths of those FIREball scientists. And he knew that Webb was planning to meet Wickett. If Andrew and Gaia had managed to learn anything else, it would be a bonus.

Will looked through the razor wire to the mountainside beyond. He shivered. It was bare up here. The evening sky was clear.

But what was that . . . ?

What was *that?*

It was black and circular. And it was spinning right at him.

"Herr Pritt? *Herr Pritt?*"

At his desk in the closet-sized surveillance suite in the bowels of the Black Sphere, the security officer peered harder at the screen. He grabbed his walkie-talkie. "Sir, Unit 1 on routine patrol has detected motion at perimeter in zone C9. Repeat—"

"I heard you!" Pritt roared, furious. He was striding away from the staff common room with Junior Engineer Shwarz. "What do the cameras show?"

"Thermal imaging shows human form . . ." The officer's eyes narrowed. "Video imaging shows . . . a boy? Wait." The officer switched the controls from auto to remote. He'd seen something else. Unit 1 hovered for a moment, then shifted. The officer's eyes widened. The boy was closing in on two more humans in the region of the dam. "Correction: Two boys. Repeat: Two boys. One girl."

"*Children*? Who are they? How did they get in here?" Pritt's angry questions tripped over each other. "How long will it take you—"

"I am on to it."

"Hold them. *Do you understand?*" Pritt's voice was raw. If Webb heard about this . . . "*Contain them.*"

Back in the surveillance suite, the officer nodded. He understood. Contain them. At all costs.

Beside the option *Weaponry* was a button marked *Active*. It was gray. De-selected. The officer double-clicked.

The button flashed red.

"What *is* that?" Andrew was staring.

He and Gaia had just emerged into the yard, looking for Will—and they saw him, racing toward them. Then Will stopped dead in his tracks. Nine feet above his head a black disc was . . . *spinning*. What was it? A reconnaissance drone? It had to be. They'd been spotted!

Will jabbed a finger at the pump hut. "In there!"

Gaia and Andrew right behind him, he raced to the hut. In the second before they threw themselves inside, Andrew noticed a red flash on the rim of the disc. Was it infrared? Suddenly, a bloodred beam shot to the ground, inches from the door. The flagstone cracked. Dust billowed. That wasn't infrared!

"A laser!" Andrew cried, pulling the door shut.

Will's back was to the wall. "We need to get out of here!"

"But what *is* that thing?" Andrew said. "It just shot you with a *laser*!" He rushed to the window. The armed disc—it looked like some kind of robotic Frisbee—was still there, fifteen feet away. It was motionless now. Hovering. "I've never seen anything like it!"

Gaia joined him. "What's it doing? Why is it just hanging there?"

"Maybe it's waiting for us to make another move," Will said. "Or it's waiting for backup." He ran through their options. They could try to make it to the foyer, but it was too late now to try to slip out unnoticed, and the Frisbee was *armed*. Surrendering was a possibility. No—it was a last resort.

Will reached for the cigar box. "I'm going to contact Elke. She can call the police, or she can come herself and create a diversion." His fingers fumbled. At the exact moment he found the roach, the Frisbee suddenly slid toward the window. It was right outside. Something bad was about to happen. Will could feel it.

Suddenly, four lights flashed around the rim. Whoever was controlling that thing was preparing to shoot!

"We have to get out of here!" Andrew cried. "We have to run for it!"

"*Where?*" Gaia asked. "*Run where?*"

But Will knew the answer. They had only one choice. "The waterfall. We'll jump down it, into the reservoir."

Andrew stared. "It's a one-hundred-eighty-foot drop! That's crazy!"

Will shook his head. "It's our only chance."

"The fall will kill us!" Andrew cried.

The Frisbee started to spin again. Gaia hissed, "And this thing won't? Will's right!"

"We've got the armor," Will said. "It'll help protect us. *We have no choice.*"

Gaia took Andrew's arm. "Andrew, we're going now. Okay? Together. *Now.*"

Will kicked the door open. Instantly, a beam flashed. It hit the space Will's right foot had just occupied, tunneling a hole in the concrete. If Will had doubted whether InVesta would actually shoot at them, he didn't anymore. "Come on!" he yelled. He veered through the door. Gaia was right beside him, still holding on to Andrew.

Will fixed his eyes on the narrow path that led around the edge of the dam. They'd have to race along it to the sluice gate—

He ducked. Two beams burst over his head. He could smell burning. Had they caught his hair?

The black disc spun sideways. Will glanced back to track it and caught the edge of a flagstone. He stumbled. He saw another red flash. Before he could throw himself out of the way, a beam pierced a path through the air—*right to him.* It caught him in the chest, throwing him backward, into Gaia. They fell together. He coughed. His ribs felt as though they were on fire. He looked down.

A black line was burning through his T-shirt.

"Will!" Gaia scrambled out from under him. With Andrew's help, she dragged him up. When she looked back, the Frisbee was zooming toward the institute. What was it doing? "Will? Will, are you all right?"

"I'm okay," he said. He coughed again. It hurt like crazy. But the armor had taken the impact. He couldn't see any blood.

Andrew stood staring behind them. The Frisbee was spiraling back, coming right at them. And it was being followed! A man had just dashed out of the institute. He was running in their direction. Black trousers, white socks, a gray mustache. And a revolver. He was carrying a *revolver*.

"*Halt! Jezt!*"

Pritt.

Will saw him. Pritt was aiming his gun. Will heard a bang and ducked.

They *had* to get out of there. "Come on!" Will yelled again.

He ran, and realized that somehow he was still holding the cockroach. He hissed into it: "We're coming out down the waterfall, Elke! Meet us at the reservoir! We're being chased by a—a flying disc. It's armed!"

He suddenly ducked right as a red beam hit the fence. Sparks flew from the electrified wires. Andrew and Gaia were ahead of him now. Will ran to catch up.

At last, they were at the sluice gate. Will grabbed Andrew's shoulder and peered over it. From here, he could see right over the crashing edge of the waterfall. Brown water rushed. It disappeared down in the distance into a violent cloud of spray. The drop was sheer. That cloud could conceal rock ledges jutting from the cliff. It seemed impossible to believe, but their exit from the Sphere was going to be even more dangerous than the way in.

Pritt was yelling again. The Frisbee whizzed toward them. Will glimpsed a flash of red and reached for Gaia. "One." He grabbed Andrew with his injured hand, taking the pain. "Two. *Three!*"

● ● ●

Will saw gray. White. Cliff face. Thin air. Then spray smothered his face. The world seemed to move in fractions. It was as though he'd been broken into pieces. He tried to shout out, but his lungs wouldn't work.

Andrew. *Gaia.* They'd been wrenched away from his grip the instant they'd jumped.

Will felt a sudden *thwack.* The air was thumped from his body. He felt himself plunging, water parting around him. He struggled through a glassy darkness. For a moment, time stood still.

Finally, Will exhaled. A stream of bubbles pummeled his cheeks. He blinked. *He could see.*

He twisted his neck and made out a frothy glare of white. That had to be up. Will reached. Kicked. Reached again. Finally breached the surface.

Air rushed into his lungs. Will spluttered. Coughed. Inhaled water. Coughed again. He was kicking hard, away from the raging behind him. When at last he stopped, he saw the reservoir, bright with evening sunlight. It was stretching right in front of him. It looked luminous and vast.

Will heard a shout. *Gaia.* He squinted. She was already at the bank. Andrew was pulling toward her. They'd made it. *They were all right.*

Will took a deep breath—and saw something else. Near the top of the road that zigzagged up behind the reservoir, someone was standing by a car, clutching what looked like a shotgun. *Elke?* What was she doing?

Will's heart thudded. He saw a flash of black. The Frisbee. It was zinging down the mountain, spinning away from the waterfall. Elke darted. A red beam scorched the asphalt. She crouched. Took aim.

Will kicked for the shore. He felt Andrew's hand grip his. He looked back. For a moment the Frisbee hovered motionless, a deadly black sun. Then it started to spin again. It suddenly cut through the air, racing back toward Elke.

Something happened then. The Frisbee trembled. Then it dropped. Will saw it hit a rock and smash into fragments. Elke must have fired, but Will hadn't heard a shot. He scrambled out of the reservoir.

And he heard Elke's voice, ringing through the air. *"Gotcha!"*

Will's eyes were closed. He knew he was moving. And he knew he was in a car. He could hear the hum of the engine, and he could feel the warmth of Gaia, squeezed up beside him. And he could feel the throb in his hand and the ache in his chest. He wasn't asleep, but he was barely awake. It was the daze of aftershock.

Will wasn't sure how long it lasted. After climbing out of the Kleinkirchen reservoir, the next thing he was properly aware of was Elke, cutting the car engine.

Then he was outside, in cool air. Dark firs draped the mountainside. Gaia was beside him. Elke was hurrying them toward a wooden house with maroon shutters. She had their bags. She turned a key in a lock. "Easy, now. You will all be safe in here."

Will stepped inside. At last, his mind settled, returning more to normal. The dark hallway was cluttered with skis and skates, even an old Trottibike. Elke directed them into a living room with thick lace curtains, a gray sofa, and a threadbare rug. One of the walls was a stiff concertina, Will noticed, dividing a larger space into two.

They stood there, soaking wet, shivering. Unsure what to do.

"Don't worry about the furniture," Elke said. "This is my

brother's place and it is old. Sit down. I will fetch towels."

Andrew looked uncomfortable. He blinked at her. His glasses were long gone, smashed to bits in the fall. But his spare pair should be safe in his satchel. He reached for the bag. "We've already drenched your car," he said.

"If it makes you feel better," Elke said, "I will charge you for expenses. Now sit down. The sofa is ugly. If you ruin it, my brother will have to buy a new one, and I will thank you."

Andrew slipped on his glasses and sat down, but on the floor, with his back to the sofa. Gaia half collapsed on the rug. His chest aching, Will sat down beside her.

Elke hesitated at the door. *Laser-firing robots.* InVesta had shot at children, in clear view of the village. "You would like something to drink?" she asked. "Water? Tea?"

Andrew looked at her wearily. "I don't care if I never taste water again."

Elke smiled. "Tea, then. And I will try to find a first aid kit. And those towels."

"One question," Will said. "That gun you used. I didn't hear a sound. What was it?"

"If you did not recognize it, I do not blame you," Elke said. "I had it custom made by a friend who is a researcher at the university. It shoots microwaves. They can burn skin. They can also wipe out electronics, like the chip inside that disc."

Andrew had been rooting around in his satchel. Now he stopped and stared at her. "*Microwaves?* I thought a hand-held microwave weapon was still on the drawing board."

"Well, now you know otherwise." Elke slipped out of the room.

Andrew noticed that Gaia was shaking. Her neck was covered in goose bumps. Will still looked dazed.

It was interesting that they had all taken up positions on the floor, he thought. Psychologically speaking, it made a lot of sense. There was safety in solid ground. But were they *really* safe? Pritt had seen them. He'd tried to *kill* them.

Andrew rubbed his head. It ached.

"Are you okay?" Gaia said.

He nodded. "You're shaking," he told her.

"It's just the cold. When I'm dry, I'll be fine." She looked at Will. The laser had burned his T-shirt. "You were hit."

"It's all right," he said. It had to be. "We did it," he said. "We got out in one piece."

"Just," Gaia said softly.

"So," Will said, "did you find anything useful?"

Andrew nodded. "A report. I e-mailed it to myself. It was from an engineer named Hudson—it seemed to be about a risky drilling project."

"I heard Webb talk about Hudson, and a drill rig," Will said. "He wanted it activated. And he definitely ordered the killing of those scientists. *And* he has plans to meet Wickett at a place called the Nest." Will looked at his watch. "Pritt's leaving in an hour. I guess Webb will be with him."

Andrew gripped his smart phone. "Then I'd better check out this report. I'm hoping it might tell us what Webb will do if Wickett doesn't actually turn up. Or at least what's he's threatening to do."

"You think Webb's threatening to attack Kleinkirchen if Wickett doesn't turn up?" Will asked.

"It must be something like that," Andrew said, glancing

at Gaia. "We were thinking perhaps Wickett doesn't have any family to threaten, so Webb thinks Wickett would have to respond to a threat against an entire village. Though I don't know what Webb could actually do against a whole village."

Will looked up. Elke was coming back into the room, towels slung over her right shoulder. She was carrying a plastic carrier bag and a tray with three mugs. "Tea," she said. "And in this bag, there is a first aid kit. If you need anything else, you tell me." She put the tray on the floor and threw the towels on the sofa.

Gaia grabbed one. "Thanks," she said. She picked up her backpack and disappeared around the concertina door to change.

"Yeah, thank you," Will said. "For everything, I mean."

Elke stood with her hands on her hips. "You were lucky to get out of there alive. So, was it worth it? Did you find anything useful?"

Andrew looked up from his phone. "We're not sure yet," he said. "I'm just checking something I e-mailed to myself."

But Elke deserved more than that, Will thought. She had risked her own life to help them. She'd destroyed the Frisbee.

Gaia pushed back the concertina door, in dry jeans and a long-sleeved black top. She sat down on the sofa as Will began telling Elke about Wickett's note. And about how they thought InVesta was blackmailing Wickett. He explained about the meeting scheduled for half past nine.

Elke's emerald eyes burned. "*Cold fusion,*" she breathed. "And they've done it? Wickett knows how to do it?"

"It looks like it," Will said. "I'm sorry. We should have told you more before."

"Maybe you should have. Maybe you were right not to trust me. It is my personal rule never to trust anyone."

"To take and then give," Will said.

"The world is not a nice place," Elke said, shrugging. "I play by its rules. So—where is Webb hoping to meet Wickett?"

"A place called the Nest," Will said. "Do you know what that is?"

"No . . . but it should not be too difficult to find out. I must call my brother to let him know we are here. Then I will try a few contacts. See if they have heard of it. Then we work out what to do. Yes?"

"Yes," Will said.

Elke slipped back out of the living room, and Will started to get up. He winced. Gaia noticed the flash of pain across his face.

"Did the laser cut through?" she asked.

Will looked down. He pulled open the hole in his T-shirt and touched the scorch mark in the self-hardening fabric. "I don't think so." Slowly, Will pulled off the T-shirt, then he eased off the top.

Gaia almost flinched. A bright purple bruise was spreading just below the apex of his ribs. There were two more bruises on his right bicep. A red welt jagged down across the center line of his chest.

In the background, Gaia could hear Andrew talking to himself, oblivious, his eyes glued to his phone. "Come on," he murmured.

Will touched his chest gingerly. Again he winced.

"Do you need a bandage?" Gaia said softly.

"Not for this. Maybe for my hand." He inspected the long red gash. The flesh between his second and third knuckles had been torn by the underground rock.

Gaia went to the bag and dug into the first aid kit. She found a tube of antiseptic ointment and a bandage. She held them out to him.

He took the antiseptic first. "Thanks."

She crouched beside him. "You should probably get stitches."

"It'll be all right," Will said. He took the bandage roll from her.

"Do you want help?" She waited until he looked up. Met her eyes. Nodded.

After Will had smeared the white cream across the cut, Gaia unrolled the bandage and began wrapping it around his hand. She weaved it between his fingers, then across the palm. "Hold it there," she said, and she grabbed the scissors and a safety pin from the first aid kit. Then she cut the bandage. Secured it in place. Inspected her handiwork. It wasn't exactly neat, but it would keep the cut clean.

"Thanks," Will said. And despite all the other thoughts racing through his mind, he couldn't help remembering what Andrew had said in the Grand Restaurant Schuh.

It was true: No other girl came close to Gaia. She was loyal and smart and he trusted her with his life. She was also beautiful, in a fierce kind of way. The impulse to tell her rose in his throat. She was looking at him. He met her gaze. Her dark eyes were giving something away, but he wasn't quite sure what.

"Ah!"

Andrew's voice. His eyes were still glued to his phone. He was absorbed in his task. But the interruption sent Will's thoughts into hiding. There was no time to think about those things now. Webb was leaving to meet Wickett *in an hour*.

"*Ah!*" Andrew said again, louder this time. His head shot up. "I think," he said, "that you'd better look at this."

URGENT: Severe risks associated with drill-point experimentation in quadrant Beta.

Confidential. Unauthorized possession is a crime.

A. Hudson, Chief Engineer.

Andrew scrolled down to an introduction. "Blah blah," he said. "This is all background. I've just been wading through it. It's about some new drill heads they've been testing at the Sphere. But hold on. Yes, look at this bit."

Will and Gaia sat down on either side of Andrew. Over his shoulders, they read:

If drill head testing continues in this quadrant, the risk of seismic activity will be increased. I estimate the risk of Richter 5 at 89 percent.

A Richter 5 event would have devastating consequences. A landslide of approximately ten billion cubic feet of earth and rock would plunge into the reservoir above the village of Kleinkirchen. This would displace an estimated two billion cubic feet of water. The resulting flooding would destroy the village. See diagram 1B.

Will stopped reading. "Webb cannot be threatening to create an *earthquake?*"

"That's what it looks like," Andrew said.

"Can you really do that?" Gaia asked.

Andrew nodded. "I wasn't sure, so I just searched a few news sites. And there are precedents. In America, research in Utah recently concluded that underground coal mining could induce earthquakes. In Taiwan, there's a skyscraper called Taipei 101, which some geologists think has reopened an ancient earthquake fault line and triggered two quakes. In Indonesia right now there's a mud volcano erupting, and scientists think it was triggered by drilling for gas." Andrew remembered one of the bullet points he'd read in the lab in the Sphere. "This engineer, Hudson, was preparing a memo or an e-mail to Webb just before he was seized. He was asking why more water was being diverted from the inflow for storage in InVesta's dam."

"And?" Gaia said.

Andrew blinked. "Push water into an injection hole and you increase the risk of a rupture."

"An earthquake, you mean."

"Yes."

Will shook his head. "This is what they're blackmailing Wickett with—an earthquake that would wipe out the village?"

Andrew scrolled down to the diagram. It showed the likely epicenter of the rupture. Hudson had marked the current level of the Kleinkirchen reservoir. An arrow showed ten billion cubic feet of earth sliding into the reservoir at a speed of approximately seventy miles per hour. The result would be an eight-hundred-foot-high wave. Kleinkirchen would be obliterated.

"But they wouldn't do that!" Gaia said. "They'd kill thousands of people!"

"Two thousand forty-three," Andrew said. His face was white. He minimized the report, revealing the home page of the Kleinkirchen tourist information office. It showed a pretty square with a gray church and a fountain. Two small blond girls with bikes were smiling outside a baker's shop. In English, at the top of the page, were the words: *Welcome to the Friendliest Village in the Alps!*

"So if Wickett doesn't make that meeting—" Will stopped. Two thousand forty-three people would die. They had to do something, fast. "But I can't believe MI6 hasn't found him yet."

"We should double-check they haven't," Andrew said. "Barrington might tell us. If Wickett's in custody now, obviously he won't make that meeting. And if that's the case, someone has to let Webb know, or he'll unleash the quake. We have to tell Barrington everything." His head shot around. The door had opened.

Elke strode back into the living room. She took in the three pale faces. "I thought the English only needed tea to feel better."

"Did you find out about the Nest?" Will demanded.

Elke crossed her arms. The snake flexed. "As a matter of fact, yes."

Shute Barrington whistled. He'd read the file titled *Project* twice.

It listed the academic backgrounds of each of the six scientists, their addresses in Switzerland, and, for the two British physicists, Edmund Pope and David Wickett, the name of their MI6 contact.

Project FIREball was an international effort. Run, at least officially, from the European Union headquarters in Brussels. The funding also came from the EU. And the results of the research—*if* there were any—were to belong, at least notionally, to the same body.

The primary aim of the project was to free Europe from financial and political obligations to oil companies and oil-rich nations, Barrington read. To create a cheap, plentiful, *locally available* source of power. Once the technology had been perfected, the EU would release it to anyone who wanted it, for a nominal license fee.

Barrington had snorted. He could guess how "nominal" that might be.

Such was the sensitivity of the project that it had been classified Alpha, which meant the detail was known in the UK only to three people: the prime minister, the minister of defense, and the chief of MI6, C.

Pope and Wickett had been told not to reveal anything about FIREball to their MI6 contact—who, in theory, had no knowledge of the actual aim of the project. But this officer, code-named Thatcher, was to be alerted if they had any concerns about their own safety, or if they feared the project had been compromised in any way.

Impatiently, Barrington clicked on the second document, which obviously had been put together by Spicer, whose technological dexterity in even obtaining the information on FIREball deserved a bloody medal, Barrington thought.

It seemed to be a brief biography of Thatcher. And it included dates and times of contact with Pope and Wickett.

Codename: Thatcher

Name: Ian Birch

Date of birth: 19 February, 1971

Strengths: Fluent French, German and Mandarin. Firearms, Level 10. Kung fu: Jinlong (Golden Dragon—highest level). Proficient in Korean swordsmanship.

So far, so run-of-the-mill, Barrington thought.

He flicked through the notes, until he got to the contacts record, which was asterisked and marked by Spicer: *Alpha-classified*.

Even the *contact record* was Alpha-classified? Barrington could hardly believe it.

Pope's name appeared seven times. He'd had one meeting with Thatcher in April, then five toward the end of June. Neither the reasons for these meetings nor the outcomes were recorded.

Wickett's name didn't feature at all. Perhaps he'd never even met Thatcher.

But just as Barrington was about to close the document, he saw that he hadn't come quite to the end. Frowning, he brushed his cursor down over the scroll bar. A single line on the final page appeared.

Wickett. July 16. 09:25

July 16. That was *today*.

Wickett had met Thatcher today?

That had to be a mistake, Barrington thought at once.

Because if Wickett had met Thatcher, surely Thatcher would have taken the scientist straight to a safe house. So why were MI6 field officers still scouring the countryside looking for him? And why was Barrington operating the damned temperamental Eagle?

He had to call Spicer at once. An envelope icon suddenly appeared at the bottom of his computer screen. He had mail. And if he had mail on *this* computer, it had to have come from Spicer.

At once, Barrington brought up the e-mail software. He found a single item, titled *STASIS Training Results*.

Barrington's heart started to race.

He read three lines of apparently meaningless type.

Encoded.

Quickly Barrington found Spicer's decryption key. Applied it.

The lines immediately resolved into something meaningful. In fact, the meaning was so astonishingly stupendous that at first Barrington's brain did not take it in. It was so unlikely. It was *impossible*.

"No!" Barrington exclaimed. "Spicer, you need your damn head examined!"

If this was true, it would mean—

He ran a hand through his hair. Wished he bit his nails.

Spicer had to be wrong. He absolutely had to be. In his technological meanderings, he'd messed up. Got the decryption key wrong. Anything. *Anything* but *this*.

Blood rushed in Barrington's ears. He dialed Spicer's number and did his best to muster a relaxed, vacation tone. He failed miserably.

"Spicer, just had a thought. That, er, budget you sent me. Are you absolutely sure that's the bottom line?"

There was a slight pause. "Yes, sir." Spicer's voice was grim. "I'm afraid so."

"But the implications—"

"I understand, sir. But I'm afraid we have to face the fact."

"There's no possibility of error in your calculations."

"None, sir."

"I see. Well, thank you, Spicer. I should get back to the fish. Just couldn't get that budget out of my head."

"No problem, sir. I hope they're biting well."

Barrington stood up and began to stride around the bare floorboards of his room. He couldn't think in here.

But he damn well had to.

His eyes flicked back to the mobile phone, which he'd tossed onto the bed.

Now, apart from Spicer, there was only one other person Barrington could ask for help. But his phone wasn't safe. Barrington rifled through the pockets of his jacket and found two pound coins. He grabbed his door key, then ran along the hallway and down the stairs. There was a public pay phone in the corridor between the restaurant and the restrooms. He'd use that. He'd just have to hope the mobile phone he wanted to call wasn't being monitored by someone using ECHELON.

Too risky, he thought, halfway down the stairs.

Barrington dashed back up to his room. He ran to the computer and typed an e-mail: *I need you to get ECHELON deaf to Knight's mobile. If you can't do it within two minutes, call me.*

Knight's was a civilian phone. Spicer was a technological whiz, and an MI6 employee. He should be able to do it.

Barrington encrypted the e-mail, using Spicer's key. Then entered Spicer's e-mail address and hit SEND.

Something else occurred to him.

Barrington made a decision. It wouldn't immediately solve anything, but it might help later. In an ideal world, he'd leave for Switzerland, but Spicer was a good deal closer. Plus, there were two aircraft stationed in the STASIS hangar.

He wrote another e-mail:

Go directly to Interlaken. Take all necessary computer equipment. If anyone asks, say you're needed to fix problems with the Eagle. Call as soon as you arrive. Leave everything else to me. I have a plan.

Barrington sighed hard. A "plan" implied a carefully considered procedure for achieving a goal. Did he have that? No. But these were desperate times—and his desperate, lunatic idea would have to do.

"The Nest does fondue," Elke said, in the doorway. "Three types. And excellent steak."

"The Nest is a *restaurant*?" Will said.

"An exclusive one, and very remote—or so I hear. It is up in the mountains, at least half an hour's drive from the nearest village. Apparently it is popular with businessmen treating their mistresses. For those with large expense accounts, there is a private dining room in a glass dome on top of a tower, which they call the Bubble. It has views all over the valleys."

Making it an ideal place for Webb to lie in wait for Wickett, Will thought.

If Wickett was still out there, they had to stop him from meeting Webb—but then they'd also have to stop the quake. They needed Elke. He should tell her the rest.

So he explained about Hudson's report.

Elke paled. "Creating an earthquake? That is really possible?"

"I think so," Andrew said quietly. He pushed his smart phone back into his satchel. They really should have told Barrington before Elke, he thought.

"And you are sure that David Wickett is still free?" Elke asked.

"No," Will said. He watched her closely. "You haven't heard anything? You must still have contacts in the Swiss secret service."

Elke cracked her knuckles. "Two or three, even now. But I left the service many years ago. For most of my career, I worked freelance. So to speak."

"So you *were* a mercenary!" Andrew exclaimed.

"Oh, so pompous! What are you—*MI6*? I don't think so!"

Andrew flushed. "We don't work for the highest bidder."

"Then you are exceptionally stupid or exceptionally lucky," she said. "Most people are obliged to!"

"And you?" Andrew said, his voice tight. "Right now— are you working for money? Is Vanya paying you? Did he promise that we'd pay you?"

"I am *re*paying Vanya," Elke said angrily. "This is the abolition of a debt."

"Look," Gaia interrupted, "we need to get back to Wickett."

"*Yes*," Will said. "We need to talk to Barrington. We have to ask him what he knows."

"Though he probably won't tell us," Gaia said. "Not after that last conversation."

"Who is Barrington?" Elke asked.

"Someone who *does* work for MI6," Will said.

He should have contacted Barrington right away, he thought—as soon as they'd gotten to this house. Or earlier, when Andrew had figured out that Project FIREball was about cold fusion. But Barrington *had* to know that. He had told them he didn't know the details of the project because they were secret, not because he didn't *actually* know them. Surely.

Will got up, his ribs aching. He dug into his backpack for his phone.

But just as he picked it up, it started ringing.

The southern corridor of the Hotel Lindrick was lined with heavy oil paintings of strong men in tartan kilts. Shute Barrington's eyes flicked back to his watch. He was sitting on a leather chair next to the public pay phone. In his right hand, he gripped the Bakelite receiver and watched the seconds tick down.

Thirty.

Twenty.

Five.

Zero.

Two minutes had passed with nothing from Spicer. Barrington had to assume Spicer had done the business with ECHELON, and whatever he told Will Knight would be private.

Hurriedly, Barrington keyed in Will's number. He heard a shuffling from behind. An elderly gentleman in an Arran sweater and moleskin trousers nodded.

Barrington cupped the receiver. "This is a private call."

"This is a public telephone," the man pointed out in a Scottish brogue. "And I am only waiting my turn."

Barrington reached into his pocket. Threw his mobile phone at the astonished man, who caught it. "Go elsewhere and use that. It's on me."

He turned his attention back to the digital rings.

"Shute?"

"Will. Good."

"I was just about to call you," Will said.

"Why?"

Will told him everything: the notebook, their visit to the Black Sphere, the engineer's report, the threat to the village of Kleinkirchen, the Nest.

Barrington listened hard. STORM had been busy. He cursed his own ignorance. But what mattered now was what he did with this information. And what Will did next.

"So—is Wickett still on the run?" Will asked.

A pause. "No."

"You've got him?"

"Not exactly. But I know where he is."

"Where?"

Another pause. Barrington's thoughts rushed through his brain. All he had in Switzerland were STORM and his Eagle. He didn't want to ask Will, but this was *cold fusion*. It was vital that the technology didn't fall into the wrong hands. An invention like this threatened global stability. Countries would go to war over it.

"Will, I need to ask you something. If I tell you where Wickett is, and if I tell you I could provide you with backup, would you . . ." Barrington hesitated. "Would you go there? Would you see if it's safe? If you could get him out? Then escort him to a secure location and make him wait for more instructions from me."

"Shute, what's—"

"Don't ask me now what's going on. I will explain everything later. I promise. I wouldn't ask you if I didn't think it was the only option. No offense. And if you agree, you must keep this *secret*. Apart from Andrew and Gaia, if necessary, no one else must know."

If necessary. Of course it would it be necessary to tell Andrew and Gaia, Will thought. He was glad he hadn't pressed speakerphone. Somehow, he would have to keep this from Elke. Will saw that Andrew and Gaia were watching him impatiently. "All right," he said.

Barrington's sigh of relief was clearly audible. "Good. But *only* go to Wickett if it's safe. If I'm right, there's only one man guarding him. And I have the Eagle. You'll need to get close, and then when I've incapacitated that guard, I'll alert you. Then go in and make Wickett believe in you. Do whatever you have to do. Get him out of there. As soon as I can identify a safe house, I'll let you know. Make sure Wickett gets there. Whatever you do, don't let him go."

"What about the meeting? The earthquake?"

"I'll handle it. Send me the engineer's report. I'll get people to the Sphere and the Nest. Webb will be arrested."

"Okay," Will said cautiously. But he trusted Barrington. If he said he would do something, he'd do it.

Spicer's e-mail had contained a map reference for Wickett's location. Pressing his mouth close to the receiver, Barrington said: "Now, I'm going to text you Wickett's coordinates. Then I'm going to send in the Eagle. When I get a visual ID, I'll be in touch again. *Do not* go in until I give the all clear. Understand?"

"I understand," Will said.

33

David Wickett groaned. The concrete floor was cold, and his arms were numb. His wrists were pinned behind his back with plastic handcuffs. Whenever he tried to move them, the cuffs tightened, digging into his flesh.

This was torture. But whom could he complain to? Certainly not the red-haired man sitting on an upturned bucket, smoking a cigarette.

A low-watt lamp and the glow of that smoldering cigarette cast the only light. But it was enough for Wickett to realize he was in an old milking shed. He could just make out the outline of a rusting milk cooler and discarded buckets. Near the door, there was a pail of water, which his guard drank from. Other than that, the building was empty.

He'd had plenty of time to build up a picture of his surroundings. Three hours, in fact.

Four hours before that, while he was still back at the hut, he'd made up his mind to get in touch with his MI6 contact. First, he'd called Greta. Then he'd taken the call summoning him to a meeting at the Nest—or else two thousand people would die.

The line had gone dead. Wickett had started to shake. But he'd already decided to call MI6. He had to trust his task officer. Everything would be all right.

Wickett had been looking in his address book for the number when a noise had made him freeze. The door to the hut. It had opened. Wickett had heard feet on the wooden floor. There were gaps in the boards. If he had tried to make a call, the person up there would have heard! What could he do?

Wickett's notebook had been on his lap still. Quickly, he'd started to scribble. If he was abducted or killed, he wouldn't be able to call Greta later. She would call the police, and they would come. They would find his note.

Kleinkirchen at risk. Evacuate. Get EVERYBODY OUT. Tell—

Then the trapdoor had been yanked open. A man with a black handgun had jumped down. He'd hit Wickett hard in the spine, making him crumple.

The man had pulled the memory stick from around Wickett's neck, twisted his arms up behind his back, and slipped on the plastic cuffs. Wickett had been blindfolded, pushed up out of the cellar, led to a car trunk, and driven for twenty minutes. Then he'd been dragged out and shoved into this milking shed.

Three hours ago, coarse fingers had lifted the blindfold. And Wickett had felt sick.

The main reason: He'd seen movies. If the abductor is showing you his face, it's because it doesn't matter if you see it, *because he is going to kill you*. Wickett had tried not to look at the broken nose and the close-set eyes, but the thought had sent electrical shards into his spine. Then he'd noticed the holster, and the black revolver. He'd shut his eyes tight.

The man had laughed dryly and gone back to sit on his bucket.

That had been *three hours ago*. Now what could he do? Wickett had done his best to brainstorm. But he'd only gotten a white blizzard. He could see no answers. He could *do nothing*. Just sit here on the concrete. And wait.

Suddenly, the opening bars of Tchaikovsky's violin concerto filled the shed. A digital ring tone. The red-haired man reached for his phone.

A pause, presumably while he listened to someone speak.

"Yeah. I'll be there, I told you. Yeah." Another pause. The cigarette glow cut an arc. The man was checking his watch. "Fifty minutes. Yeah, *I know*. The Nest."

Again Wickett felt nausea rise in his stomach.

The Nest. Fifty minutes. Saxon Webb had told *him* to be there. He had to bring the method for cold fusion. If he didn't, *two thousand people would die*.

Eight miles away, Will was trying to work out exactly what to tell Elke. Andrew and Gaia watched him from the sofa.

"So?" Elke asked.

"Barrington wants me to meet him."

"This Barrington is in Switzerland?" Elke said. "How do you know him? Why does he want to see you? Why have you not told me about him before? If he knows so much, why haven't you been asking him for help, instead of me?"

"Barrington wouldn't help us," Will said at last.

"But now? What has changed?"

"He wants me to meet him," Will said. "He wants me to fill him in on exactly what happened at the Sphere."

Elke's eyes narrowed. "But you just told him."

"You don't know Barrington," Will said, faking mild exasperation. "He isn't happy unless he's had every detail at least three times. Then he thinks he can be certain you aren't making things up."

"He suspects you of lying?"

Andrew came to the rescue: "Does Barrington want to see us too?"

Will shook his head. "He doesn't need all of us."

Andrew nodded. "Right," he said.

Will was relieved. Clearly, Andrew had realized there were things he didn't want to say in front of Elke. Gaia had no doubt gotten the message too. But she wasn't quite as tactful. And she was frowning.

"Barrington says he'll deal with the earthquake threat," Will said. "He says he'll get people sent to the Sphere and the Nest." He looked at Andrew. "Maybe you and Gaia should head to the Nest. Just in case."

"In case what?" Gaia asked.

"In case your friends in MI6 and our Swiss police with all their resources cannot stop InVesta?" Elke said archly. "In case David Wickett turns up? And *we* must intercept him?"

"Actually, yeah," Will said.

"So." Elke folded her arms. "I will drive you to your meeting, yes. I will get a taxi for Andrew and for Gaia. It will be no problem."

Will had to expect this. Of course Elke would want to know exactly what was going on. "No," he said. "Barrington has asked me to go alone."

A pause.

Andrew got up. "Right," he said again. "At least we have a plan."

"So it seems," Gaia said.

Will frowned at her. They trusted him, didn't they?

But he could guess what Gaia was thinking. They were a team. He wouldn't like to be left behind. Again he wished for the tooth phones. If he could get a minute alone, he'd explain everything to them. But there was no point wishing for what he didn't have. What he *did* have was this: a request from Barrington.

Will needed transportation. He looked at Elke. "I saw a Trottibike in the hall."

"You are asking to borrow it?"

"Yeah, if that's all right."

Elke raised an eyebrow. "If you are not used to it, they are not easy to control."

"Oh, Will can drive anything," Gaia said, obviously remembering the Bobcat. "Can't you, Will? He's an *excellent* driver."

Andrew smiled. Will frowned at her.

"Then you can try it outside," Elke said dismissively. "If you do not break your neck, you may take it."

Shute Barrington's neck ached. In the corridor of the Hotel Lindrick, he had his mobile phone wedged between his shoulder and his cheek, and it was quite uncomfortable.

Barrington was absorbed in his task. But not so absorbed that he couldn't appreciate the faint ridiculousness of his situation. Here he was, director of the science and technology unit of one of the world's leading intelligence agencies, fiercely guarding a public telephone while trying to ignore wailing bagpipes.

A dinner with the theme *Music of the Western Isles* had just started in the restaurant. Barrington had been invited to join, but had politely declined. He'd watched guests clad in tourist shop kilts strut in together in pairs. Five minutes ago, he'd even made a quick foray into the merriment—but only because he'd wanted to find the elderly man to whom he'd loaned his phone.

"It worked, you know," the man had said as he'd readily returned it. "I did look for you afterward."

Barrington had nodded. "Thanks." He'd stuffed the phone into the pocket of his black jeans and made a rapid about-face.

"So, you won't be joining us for dinner?" the man had asked.

Barrington had hesitated. "Unfortunately, no. You see, I have to save a brilliant kidnapped scientist from the multitudinous global forces out to steal his astonishing secret, then murder him. Possibly after some rather hideous torture."

The man smiled uncertainly. "Aha . . ." he said. Barrington hadn't been able to resist.

Now Barrington tapped his fingers against the arm of the leather chair. At last, he heard a familiar voice. Oliver Tindle, chief of the MI6 bureau in Switzerland.

"Barrington?"

It was an encrypted line, so in theory, both men could speak freely. If not entirely honestly.

"Tindle, I'm afraid I'm having a bit of trouble with the Eagle. As I think Spicer explained, it *is* experimental, and unfortunately it *is* acting up."

Barrington glanced at his watch. He'd sent Charlie Spicer an encoded e-mail, asking him to cut the Eagle's video signal to MI6 Operations Control at 7:12 P.M. British Summer Time, precisely. Spicer had immediately acknowledged.

"I see." Tindle didn't sound impressed.

"Yes, *sorry* about that. But with all those field officers on the ground, I'm sure you'll have Wickett in no time."

Barrington could almost hear Tindle bridle. But clearly Tindle considered himself too important to have to make any explanation for his field officers' failure.

"The Eagle's video feed has just gone," Tindle said abruptly.

"Ah," Barrington said. *Right on time,* he thought. "Well— yes, that was expected. I'll be in touch if we can bring it back up."

"Right." The line went dead.

Barrington silently thanked Charlie Spicer. He pulled the display screen from his pocket. The camera feeds from the Eagle were still being sent directly to him. Now he had another call to make. He keyed in a number he'd found on MI6's computer network, and was put straight through to the office of Karl Lorenz, police chief in Interlaken.

Quickly, Barrington explained who he was. He told Lorenz he had specific information about an imminent threat to the village of Kleinkirchen. It was vital that Lorenz send men to the Black Sphere and to the Nest, and to find and arrest Mr. Saxon Webb. The Sphere itself should be evacuated, sealed, and guarded.

There was a short silence. "Mr. Webb? You mean Mr. Saxon Webb?"

"Yes, Mr. Saxon Webb."

"The chief executive of InVesta."

"Yes, man!

"But Mr. Webb—"

"But nothing! I have proof of the plot. If two thousand people die because you were afraid of arresting InVesta's chief, the media will crucify you. And they won't be the only ones!"

". . . Very well." Lorenz hung up.

Barrington's heart was pounding. He felt in his other pocket for the Eagle's control pad, then keyed in a map reference and hit ENTER. He checked the robot's present coordinates, and his watch. It would take approximately three minutes for his Eagle to reach Wickett's location.

Now all he could do was wait.

● ● ●

Will kept his head down. Wind blasted into his face, blowing his hair flat against his skull.

He gripped the handlebars tightly, keeping his feet in the center of the scooter platform. The road was straight here, but even around the corners the Trottibike wasn't too difficult to control, once you got the hang of it. Elke had given him a three-minute crash course—literally—on the driveway of her brother's house.

She had let him go without further questions. And Will had managed to snatch a moment alone with Andrew. "Barrington knows where Wickett is. He's asked me to pick him up."

Will glanced at the sky. The sun was well down behind the mountains, and the day was darkening. Perhaps that was a good thing. The night made all kinds of unlikely things seem more reasonable. Even a fourteen-year-old boy trying to rescue a brilliant scientist with an invention that could change the world? Perhaps.

Chocolate brown houses sped past. Will overtook two hikers in neon pink jackets, the reflective stripes bright in his headlight. They were heading toward a tiny gray church. That was the second church. He should see the tunnel soon.

Will had memorized the route from Elke's road map. As he followed it, he thought about Barrington, and why Barrington asked *him* rather than MI6 field officers to get Wickett. Then he thought about Wickett himself, and how he could possibly convince the scientist to go with him: *Don't worry. A robotic eagle has just killed your captor. Now you must come with me. Only I can guarantee your safety.*

Not exactly convincing.

A road sign was approaching. As Will got closer, he read: *Blauweld, 7.5 miles.*

The tunnel was just before Blauweld, and ahead now, Will saw the black mouth in the mountainside open up. He used a trick his father had taught him, closing his right eye to accustom it to the relative darkness he was about to enter. When he sped into the tunnel, his left retina was stunned, but his right eye could see clearly. He raced on, into the dusk.

Will was going downhill. He had to keep an eye out for the first dirt track on the left. He glanced up. Ahead, a ghost-white moon was rising. Will saw a black shape glide across it. He tensed. His eyes strained.

When he looked back at the road, he saw the dirt track— just in time. Will immediately leaned to the left, using his body weight to help steer the Trottibike around the corner. The track was rutted. As Will juddered across it, he lifted his eyes again, and saw the dark shape, closer this time.

His pulse raced.

That was no natural movement.

An armed Frisbee? Or Barrington's Eagle?

He clipped the edge of a mound of dried mud, and the bike skidded. Will crunched the brakes. He regained control, and suddenly the track veered.

There it was.

Six hundred feet away. Two long wooden sheds with tiled roofs.

An old dairy, Barrington had texted him. He'd found it.

Will cut the headlight. He slowed down. At this speed,

there was barely enough momentum to keep the bike upright on the uneven track. But Barrington had been clear: *Stay well back. Wait for my signal. Make sure the guard doesn't see you. I will be watching.*

Will glanced up once more. The dark shape swooped down over the sheds. There was no mistaking it this time. *The Eagle.*

Shute Barrington saw what the Eagle saw. Grass. Trees. A path.

Then the Eagle shifted direction and started to slow.

After a few moments, Barrington made out the roof of a building. Then another. Two sheds. Inside those sheds, the thermal imaging sensors identified two small, dull red outlines. Wickett and his guard. It had to be.

As the Eagle swept on, Barrington saw a burst of color. An exposed human.

Will?

Barrington snatched up the public phone and dialed the familiar number. "Will, it's me. I think I can see you. Are you in position?"

Will had stopped at a hillock about ninety feet from the sheds. He'd slung his bike to the ground, and now he was flat on his stomach. "Yeah."

"Stay down. Understand?"

"*Yeah.*"

Barrington ended the call. He pushed another pound coin into the slot, followed by a second and a third.

Someone would be listening in on every call Wickett's guard made or received. Barrington was sure of that. And that someone would try to identify the location and identity of every person the guard talked to. Which in his case meant "Hotel Lindrick, Scotland," and "the public pay phone."

That wasn't enough to identify Barrington immediately. But would it take long?

He listened to the crackling line.

It'll be fine, he told himself.

35

David Wickett's head throbbed.

Pain leaked from his spine and his temples, spreading through his body. When his guard's mobile phone went off again, Tchaikovsky's violin concerto threatened to split his skull.

The red-haired man had been pacing the milking shed. He stopped. "Yes?"

Wickett held his breath. He could just hear the voice on the other end, but he couldn't make out distinct words.

Clearly, though, this wasn't a call that his guard had been expecting. The uncertainty in his "Yes?" had been unmistakable.

Now the dim light from the screen of his captor's mobile phone showed his face turning pale.

Shute Barrington cleared his throat. Spicer's covert call tapping had revealed that Thatcher—the code name of Wickett's bent MI6 contact—was holding Wickett under the orders of someone by the name of Churchill.

Now, in a fair impersonation of the elderly gent who had pointed out that the Lindrick's pay phone was in fact public, Barrington said: "Thatcher. This is . . . Lloyd-George." There had been only a fraction of a second before Barrington came up with a *possibly* believable code name—another British prime minister.

"Who?"

"I've been sent by Churchill."

Barrington waited for this piece of information to be absorbed. "I'm approaching the milking sheds. But you're being watched. There's an aerial unit out here. A surveillance drone."

A pause. Barrington imagined what was going through Thatcher's mind. This man was an MI6 field officer. If he thought he was being watched by a drone, he'd investigate.

"Your phone number," Thatcher said, "is a *Scottish* number."

Barrington had been prepared for this. "I'm using a Zeta handset!" he lied angrily. "It disguises numbers—it's the latest field issue. And I'm telling you, there's a bloody unit out here and it's watching you! If you don't believe me, just look out the door!"

Wedging the phone back against his shoulder, Barrington used his controls to send the Eagle into a low fly-past of the shed.

"Look out the bloody door," Barrington snapped.

A woman in a tartan shawl and red trousers shot him an uncertain glance as she made her way from the restaurant to the restrooms. Barrington glared at her. She hurried on.

Back in the milking shed, Thatcher crept toward the wooden door. He used the barrel of his Walter P99 pistol to nudge it open. Cautiously, he peered out.

Ninety feet away, lying flat against the hillock, Will saw movement. The Eagle had just swooped, and now the door of one of the sheds had opened.

Very slowly, a red-haired man stepped out. His left hand held a phone to his ear. In his right, he gripped something black.

A gun.

This had to be David Wickett's guard.

Will saw the man glance up—and spot the Eagle. Will watched, stomach knotted, knowing what Barrington was about to do.

In slow motion, the Eagle swerved. And dived.

Thatcher stared. The shape seemed to be racing down out of nowhere. Was that it? That was the *drone*? Thatcher heard wind whistle through its feathers. He saw the beak open. Inanimate eyes dilated. What the hell *was* that? What was that in the beak? Thatcher lifted his gun, but before he could fire he saw two white sparks fly through the air. They hit him full in the stomach, shooting pain like fireworks through every nerve in his body. He dropped his gun, his phone. Staggered. And fell.

In Scotland, Barrington resisted the urge to pump his fist. It had worked! When he'd really needed it, the Eagle's firing beak had worked! He let off two more bullets, aiming right at Thatcher's phone, and watched the plastic casing blast apart.

Then he noticed something else—a chain around Thatcher's neck, with something dangling from it. What was that? A memory stick? The one holding *Wickett's plans*? There was a damn good chance. But he'd just let off electric bullets! Thankfully, the stick looked undamaged. But how stupid! Anxiety was making him careless.

"Take stock," Barrington ordered himself.

Thatcher was down, stunned with an electric shock severe enough to knock him out for a good half hour, and his phone was blasted to pieces. It was too dangerous to try to hit the pistol, Barrington decided. The impact could release bullets.

Now Barrington pushed another coin into the phone and dialed.

A moment later, Will answered. "He's down."

"I can see. I've got the address of a safe house. I'm going to text it to you. Now go to Wickett. And *be careful.*"

Darkness was closing in. Will ran toward the milking shed, careful not to stumble. He had the headlight from the Trottibike, but he didn't want to switch it on unless he had to.

Will could see the guard. He had fallen facedown in front of the shed. As he got closer, Will steeled himself. But he knew the Eagle's weapons spec, and he was sure Barrington would only have stunned the man, not killed him. He'd wake up, but only after Will—and David Wickett—had gone.

Will crept toward the door and listened hard. He could hear breathing. He slipped inside. His foot hit metal. A bucket of water. He'd almost knocked it over. A lamp was glowing dimly. Will jerked his headlight in the direction of the breathing—and he saw Wickett.

Short brown hair. A gaunt face. Wickett's arms were behind his back. He seemed to be tied to a metal hoop in the wall. He was blinking wildly.

Will crossed to him and whispered, "I know you're David Wickett. My name is Will Knight. I'm here to get you out."

"Wh—who?" Wickett stammered. "What happened to the guard?"

"He's been hit with electric stun bullets," Will said. "He'll be out for a while. He won't stop us."

"Hit by who? *Who are you?*"

"I work with MI6. I'm here to take you somewhere safe."

"But how—but—"

Will interrupted: "But what? If I didn't work with MI6, why would I be here? How would I know who you are? I'm taking you to a safe house." Will reached into his backpack for Eye Spy. He flipped the red switch on the base, activating the diamond cutting tool. It sliced effortlessly through the plastic cuffs.

After hours of being fixed in one position, the muscles in Wickett's shoulders and arms had frozen. Moving them was agony. Wickett gritted his teeth. Unsteadily, he started to get up. Will backed away, giving him some room.

"We have to be quick," Will said. "Can you walk all right?"

Wickett took a few uncertain steps. His legs were stiff. They ached. But he nodded.

"Right," Will said. "Follow me."

David Wickett hesitated. The boy was tall, but he had at least a foot on him. It might come in useful, he thought, because time was running out. He couldn't go anywhere with this boy. "I'm grateful to you," he said quietly. "But I'm afraid I can't go with you. Whoever you are."

Will looked back. "I *told you*—"

"You work with MI6, yes, I know." Wickett's gaze

hardened. "Like the man who has been keeping me captive."

Will frowned.

Wickett registered his confusion. "If you really worked with MI6, surely you would know! My contact—Thatcher, or whatever his name really is. He kidnapped me."

Will's frown deepened. What was Wickett talking about? Barrington had asked him to collect Wickett because for some reason he couldn't go to the local field officers. That much Will had worked out for himself. But an MI6 officer had actually *kidnapped* Wickett? Surely not! And if he had, *why*? It made no sense.

"I am sorry," Wickett said. "But there's no time to talk now. There is somewhere I absolutely must be."

"The Nest?"

Wickett's pale face went even whiter. "Then you know."

"You're supposed to be at a meeting with Saxon Webb. He's told you that if you don't make it with your plans for cold fusion, he'll unleash an earthquake that will wipe out Kleinkirchen."

Wickett's lips clamped into a thin line. But from the man's expression, Will could see he was right. He remembered Barrington's assurances on the phone. "MI6 is sending people to the Black Sphere. And to the Nest. They'll arrest Webb. There will be no earthquake. Come with me, and your plans will be safe."

"That's what they told you?" Wickett's eyes were wide. "Then you are not privy to what is actually going on! MI6 will send no one to the Sphere! And the only man MI6 was sending to the meeting at the Nest is the one that I imagine is now lying out there!" Wickett jabbed a finger at the door, toward Thatcher. "He was going to take my invention and *sell* it to InVesta. That's what your precious MI6 have planned! Thatcher talked about it all, because he was planning to *kill me*. As soon as the deal was done. I heard everything!"

Will's thoughts snagged. He stared at Wickett. *MI6* had kidnapped Wickett so they could sell cold fusion to InVesta? This was unbelievable.

And yet . . . if it wasn't true, why weren't MI6 field officers here, rescuing Wickett now? Why had Barrington contacted him? Did Barrington know the truth? Then why hadn't he told Will?

"Who *exactly* was sending Thatcher to the meeting?" Will asked.

"How do I know? He didn't tell me names! I have to get to that meeting. I have to give Webb what he wants."

"You can't! You can't give it to them. And if you go to that meeting, Webb will kill you."

Wickett headed for the door. His face was set. "If he does, so be it. But I am not taking two thousand people with me."

"But I can take you somewhere safe," Will said angrily. "MI6 will be at the Sphere!" But as he spoke, he failed even to convince himself. Would they be there—*really*? Barrington could make requests, but any action on the ground would be down to the local MI6 bureau chief. And if what Wickett was saying was true . . . But Barrington had only said he'd send people. Perhaps he meant the Swiss secret service, or the police.

There was no time to think, because David Wickett was walking out of the shed. Will ran after him, just in time to see Wickett pull something from around Thatcher's neck. Before Wickett rose, he picked up another object that had been lying in the grass.

"*Wickett!*" Will called. "I can't let you go to Webb!"

Wickett looked up. "I'm afraid you can't stop me."

His hand jerked. Will saw the black barrel of a Walther P99. Thatcher's gun. Wickett held it close to his chest. A locket gleamed around his neck. He must have just taken it back from Thatcher, Will realized. The plans for cold fusion. They had to be on it.

"Put that light down and back up," Wickett said, his hand trembling.

Would Wickett really shoot him? Will wondered. He had to hope the answer was no. But he didn't want to stake his life on it. He wasn't sure what to do. Should he raise his hands? Should he tell Wickett he was being a fool?

Wickett waved the gun—and Will obeyed. He put the headlight down and backed up, inside the shed.

"By the wall," Wickett said as he followed Will in. "Now, your phone. Throw it in there." He pointed the gun at the bucket of water by the door.

"Wickett—"

"*Now!*"

Very slowly, his eyes fixed on Wickett's, Will reached into his pocket. He pulled out his phone.

"Wickett—"

"Just *do it*! Or I will shoot!"

Wickett's voice wavered and cracked. Will dropped the phone. Heard the splash.

Wickett nodded. "I don't want to hurt you," he said. "I

don't want to hurt anyone. But I have to get to that meeting."
He suddenly looked panicked.

He had been driven to the milking shed. A few minutes after he'd been tied up, he'd heard his captor go out. A moment later, he'd heard the car start. The engine noise had faded. Later, the guard had come back on foot.

"How did you get here?" Wickett asked now, the gun shaking in his hand.

Will didn't answer. He was still wondering what to do. What would Barrington do? What would Dad have done?

But there was a gun pointing at his chest. *He had no choice.*

If they'd been outside, Barrington would have been able to see what was going on. He could have used the Eagle to stun Wickett. But no point thinking now about what might have been.

"I have a bike," Will said. "It's on its side, ninety feet from here. That way." He pointed.

Wickett's eyes narrowed. "If you're lying—"

Frustration erupted. "Then you can come back and shoot me!" Will said.

Shute Barrington's eyes were glued to the Eagle's monitor. What were they doing? What the hell was going on in there?

Barrington had watched Will enter the milking shed. Four minutes later, a man, presumably David Wickett, had come out. Wickett had bent over Thatcher's body—checking if he was dead?—and Will had emerged. The Eagle had been behind Wickett. It had transmitted grainy images of the man's back.

Then, a minute later, they'd both gone back inside. One and a half minutes after that, Wickett had run out, and now he'd grabbed Will's bike! A red form was moving inside the shed. *Will.*

Barrington dialed Will's number.

"This is Will. Leave a message."

Barrington's blood ran cold. Why wasn't Will with Wickett? Was he injured? "What's happening, Will? Call me! *Are you all right?*"

The first stars were beginning to appear. Up here, more than five thousand feet above sea level, Andrew was closer to the heavens than he had ever been. The moon looked unnaturally big. Pale and glowing.

Down below, he could see artificial lights blinking through the branches of the fir trees—the lights of Kleinkirchen. The reservoir stretched black beside the village. In his mind, Andrew saw the photograph on the tourist information web page. The neat square. The two small girls with their bikes. He shuddered.

Elke grunted. She was beside him, peering through binoculars. Her target was a good deal closer than the village. Through the trees lining the main road, they had a clear view down to the Nest.

Without binoculars, Andrew could make out the driveway that led down from the main road to a parking lot. Beyond was a short path lined with flickering torches. At the end of this path was the entrance to a hexagonal-shaped, low, modern building, with plate glass windows. A rectangular annex, with its own track from the parking lot, was attached to the back—the kitchens, Andrew guessed, or perhaps a store room.

Andrew could see movement inside the restaurant

but couldn't make out individual diners. That's where the binoculars came in. But Elke had them trained not on the main dining room, but on the impressive glass bubble. It was about fifty feet in diameter, and it was perched high above the restaurant on top of a gleaming metal shaft.

"Still the same man," she murmured. "And it does not look like Saxon Webb."

Gaia was on the other side of Elke. She held out her hand. "Can I see?"

Gaia adjusted the gap between the lenses, then zeroed in. In the center of the Bubble, she saw a long, polished table with covered platters of food. A tall man with a gray mustache and a large paunch was standing at one end, looking anxiously out the window. He was holding a pipe.

Gaia recognized him at once. "It's Pritt. We saw him at the Black Sphere. And he saw us. He came after us with a gun."

Andrew tensed. He could still see the fury on Pritt's face as the Frisbee had circled overhead. He could still taste his fear. He looked at his watch. "Twenty minutes until Wickett is due. I wonder where Webb is."

"Maybe MI6 has already got him," Gaia said. "Or maybe Webb's just sent Pritt to do his dirty work."

"If MI6 has Webb, that might explain why we haven't seen any sign of them—or police," Andrew said.

Gaia looked at him. "What makes you think you'd spot MI6? They could be inside the Nest already, *blending in.*"

"*If* Webb and Wickett are still free, I am sure Webb will turn up," Elke whispered. "He would want to get his own hands on those plans." She glanced at Andrew. "So nothing yet from Will? Your friend Barrington has not told us anything useful?"

Andrew shook his head. His phone was in the pocket of his jeans. If Will had called or texted, he'd have felt it. He checked the phone anyway. No messages. "So what now?" Gaia said. She handed the binoculars back to Elke, who once again focused them on the Bubble.

"I don't see we can really do anything but wait," Andrew said, "until we hear from Will. Or we see Webb, or Wickett."

After a moment, Gaia said, "If something does happen, we'll need to be able to protect ourselves."

"*I* am here," Elke put in.

Gaia looked at her. "You said you had kit in your trunk. Maybe you could show us."

"I have a few items. Perhaps some could be useful. In certain circumstances."

"Then perhaps we could take a look," Andrew said. "It's best to be prepared."

Elke dropped the binoculars. "All right," she said irritably. She stood up. The Maserati was behind them, among the trees. Elke pressed a button on her key fob. The trunk sprang open.

Gaia and Andrew hurried over.

Gaia's face fell. "It's empty."

Without a word, Elke pressed a second button. There was a clicking noise. She lifted the false metal floor of the trunk and held it in place with a hook.

Andrew and Gaia stared. Neither of them had seen anything like it.

In the secret compartment, a black metal rack was loaded with weapons.

Elke pointed at a long-barreled gun. "That's the microwave weapon, which you have already seen." Her finger moved on. "This is a U.S military semiautomatic rifle. Here we have a Taser. And here, a Glock single stack .45 pistol. The best-handling pistol Glock has ever made. In my humble opinion."

Elke's voice was low. But there was an undertone of awe. She loved these weapons, Andrew realized. And while ordinarily he would get more excited by technology than perhaps the average person, all this firepower made him nervous.

"So," Elke said. "If we do have to go in, or if we get into trouble, I have more than enough protection. All right?"

Gaia's eyes were fixed on the trunk. "What about me and Andrew?" she said quietly. "What if *we* need protection?"

Elke snorted. "What are you suggesting? That I give you the Glock? You are fourteen years old. What would your mummy say?"

"My *mummy* is dead."

The atmosphere froze. "Perhaps I will give you one thing," Elke said at last. "But I choose it."

Gaia and Andrew watched as Elke rooted around in a plastic crate. Eventually, she produced a canister. It was the size and shape of an aerosol can of deodorant. "Here."

Gaia took it. She read the German on the side. *"Pepper spray?"*

Emerald eyes hardened. "You mean, *thank you.*"

"Thank you," Andrew said, relieved. He had held a gun

once, in Venice, but he had no idea about how to actually handle one, and he was sure that Gaia hadn't either. Pepper spray could still be useful.

Elke faked a smile. "You are so welcome." The smile vanished. Lights had suddenly flashed along the main road.

Elke slammed the trunk shut and they ducked back into the trees. A black limousine slowed. Then it turned down the driveway to the Nest.

At once, Elke picked up the binoculars. She tracked the car to the entrance. After a moment, a stocky man stepped out. The flares lining the path illuminated his face. Andrew didn't need the binoculars to recognize him.

The chief executive of InVesta Corp was gazing up at the Bubble.

Andrew swallowed hard. Saxon Webb *was* here. He was going to meet Pritt. They were waiting for Wickett. But where was he? Where was MI6? Why wasn't Webb being arrested? Andrew knew he shouldn't, but he had to try Will.

He dialed. As Webb's limo turned back up the driveway, Andrew heard Will's voice mail kick in.

"Call me," Andrew whispered urgently. "Webb is here. *He's at the Nest.*"

Diners sipped wine and dabbed their mouths. Their voices were subdued, like the décor. Beige walls, beige carpet. People came here not for the interior design or even the food, but for the views. *Or* they came to meet brilliant scientists who would do exactly as they were told or face the consequences, Saxon Webb reflected as he followed the maitre d' into the Nest.

The maitre d' hit the call button for the elevator. "It won't be a moment, sir."

Webb nodded. He was thinking about Wickett, and about the kids who had somehow gotten into the Sphere. Who were they? How had they gotten in? And who was the woman who had shot down Frisbee Unit 1? Pritt had been charged with finding the answers. So far, he'd found none.

Webb's fingers played with the mobile phone in his pocket. Through the plate glass windows, he could see the lights of Kleinkirchen. If Wickett didn't show, those lights would glint no more. All Webb had to do was call Junior Engineer Schwarz. Ninety seconds later, the earthquake would be initiated.

It would be a terrible accident. An awful tragedy. InVesta would fund a lavish memorial service and half a dozen new schools. The company's lawyers and public relations officers would earn their salaries for once. And Wickett would know that Webb never bluffed. And next time, the stakes would be even higher.

Once Webb had the plans, he would immediately patent the invention in his own name—and take a long vacation while he determined how best to exploit it.

The beige doors slid apart. Webb stepped into the elevator. Like his temper, the journey was extremely short.

When Webb reached the Bubble, he saw Pritt at the window by the table. The fool cleared his throat.

"There is no sign yet of Wickett, Herr Webb. I have placed a disc in a suitable location. Should I deploy it now?"

A disc, Webb thought. "Below us is a restaurant with more than one hundred guests. Do you want them to see?"

"But it is dark, Herr Webb. I—"

"Silence!" Webb strode over to the table. He lifted the lid from a silver dish and recognized *pieds de porc,* a delicacy from Geneva. Webb looked pointedly at Pritt. "Pigs' feet or you—I don't know which is more disgusting. If Wickett doesn't turn up, it will be you on a platter."

David Wickett might be brilliant, but that didn't mean he wasn't ever stupid.

Had Wickett really thought that Thatcher would hide out with him in a milk shed in the middle of nowhere, without a car close at hand, Will thought?

As soon as Wickett had run off to his Trottibike, Will had run to the next shed. The doors were closed but unlocked. Inside, Will found a gold-colored four-liter Ford sedan. The keys were in the ignition, ready for a quick getaway, if Thatcher had needed it.

Will's heart thudded. His palms were slick. He'd never driven a car. But until an hour ago he'd never driven a Trottibike either, and that had worked out all right. He'd been in go-karts before. And this was an automatic. D for drive. R for reverse. What else did he need to know?

Will slipped behind the wheel. He turned the key. The dashboard flashed as the engine caught. He scanned the buttons and levers for lights. At last, he found a dial on the dash and turned it to full beam. What else? Emergency brake. Will tried to lower the lever. It wouldn't budge. Then he noticed a button on the front. He pressed it with his thumb, and the lock released. Will found another lever under the seat and moved it forward. Then he angled the rearview mirror until he could see the open doors of the shed, and the black sky beyond.

Will fastened his seat belt.

R for reverse.

Gingerly, he pressed his foot on what he hoped was the accelerator. First lucky guess. The Ford rolled backward, through the doors, onto grass. The steering wheel felt loose. Will gripped it tight. He turned too far and nearly spun the car. The wheel was more responsive than he'd thought.

His palms damp, Will moved the gearshift into drive. At once, the car rolled forward. Will's first impulse was to slam on the brake. But it was all right. He could make out the road ahead. Gently, he pressed the accelerator. The car started to bounce across the field, picking up speed. When he hit the asphalt, the speedometer read twenty-five miles an hour.

Wickett was out there on a Trottibike. And Will knew the route to the Nest. He'd studied it when he'd used Elke's road map to plot his way to the sheds. It wouldn't take long to catch up. And when he did—

When he did, he'd work out what to do next.

The bagpipe music was still wailing away, but Shute Barrington didn't hear it.

He had David Wickett in his sights, racing downhill on Will's scooter-bike. He nosed the Eagle back in the direction of the sheds—and he saw the lights of a car racing across the grass to the road. It was moving erratically, as though the driver was drunk. Or just couldn't drive. Will! It had to be! What was he doing?

"You're going to bloody well kill yourself!" Barrington shouted aloud.

"Laddie, I've been wearing heels like these for thirty years! I think I'll survive another night!" A woman in black stilettos was stumbling toward the restroom. Barrington stared at her as if she were mad.

He turned back to his screen. Obviously, Wickett was heading to the Nest. Equally obviously, Will was intending to intercept him, or to beat him there. He should call Karl Lorenz at the police station, and find out exactly what was going on. Officers should be at the restaurant already. They could intercept Wickett.

Or perhaps he should use the Eagle to try to take Wickett down? But that locket had to contain the plans for cold fusion, Barrington reasoned. He'd been lucky once. He couldn't risk it again. A bullet could destroy the locket. It would be better to wait and watch.

Was there another option? Was there anyone else who could help?

But he already knew the answer: *No*.

In the corridor of the Hotel Lindrick, Barrington ran an anxious hand through his hair. His eyes were fixed on the Ford.

"Just don't kill yourself," he murmured. "And consider that a bloody order!"

It wasn't a Maserati, but still the Ford was powerful. On straight stretches, it picked up speed almost without Will noticing, and twice at corners he'd had to slam on the brakes as the car had started to skid.

Watch the speedometer, he told himself. But he was also looking out for Wickett. The Nest couldn't be far. Surely he should have seen the bike by now.

And what would he do when he did? He'd swerve in front and force Wickett to stop? Will wasn't sure. But he'd do *something*. More than he'd done back at the shed. He couldn't let Barrington down. He couldn't let himself down. He could not let David Wickett hand cold fusion to Saxon Webb.

Will hunched farther over the steering wheel. A car was approaching from the opposite direction. Will steeled himself. He felt himself lean to the right as it passed. It felt so close!

Then his headlights picked out black arrows marking another corner. This time, he squeezed the brake and took the bend smoothly. Ahead now, he saw the road stretch. Out there, somewhere in the blackness, was the Nest—and David Wickett.

But where?

Will glanced up through the windshield. He couldn't

see the Eagle, but the car's roof obscured most of the sky. Barrington would be watching him. He was sure of that. The Eagle was probably high over the cliff, to his right. On his left, there was only darkness. Valleys. Sheer drops.

Will flinched. Twin bright beams had just ricocheted off his rearview mirror. A moment later, a black Ferrari roared past him. It approached another corner. Will hit the brake. He rolled the wheel, easing the car around the bend.

And he stared. There it was. Down, to the left, a glass bubble gleamed in the moonlight.

The Nest.

Andrew saw him first. Or rather, he saw the Ferrari race down to the Nest. And then he noticed the Ford. Its headlights were on full, and even in the trees, Andrew felt vulnerable. Then the car pulled off the road and the engine cut. The door was flung open and someone jumped out. Andrew couldn't see the face, but he recognized the way this person moved.

"*Will!*" Andrew stood up. "Will, we're over here!" He beckoned.

Will ran to them. "Have you seen Wickett?"

Andrew shook his head. "No. Have you seen him? What's happening?"

Quickly, Will explained. "But I didn't pass Wickett anywhere!"

"He is on a Trottibike," Elke said. "He could have gone cross-country."

"Maybe," Will said.

"What other explanation is there?" she asked. "Where else could he be? Webb is up there with the man called

Pritt." She pointed a red fingernail at the Bubble. "But why has Webb not been arrested? Your MI6 has not appeared. What are they playing at?"

Will shook his head. "I don't know. What about the police? Are they here?"

"No," Gaia said grimly. "Not unless they're undercover and they're waiting for Wickett."

What was Barrington doing? Will trusted him, but it seemed clear by now—MI6 was not going to handle this. And time was running out. He looked at his watch. It was sixteen minutes past nine. His gaze shot back along the main road. Of course, there were no guarantees Wickett would come that way. He might try to find a back entrance. "Somehow we have to get up to the Bubble. We have to try to get Webb out before Wickett gets here."

"And somehow stop him destroying the village . . ." Gaia said.

"But if we go up to the Bubble, Webb will recognize us from the Sphere," Andrew said. "He could kill us before we even got to him!"

"In a restaurant full of people?" Will asked.

Gaia had been thinking. "Maybe we don't have to go up there. We could get a note up to him . . . Pretend it's from Wickett, saying he'll meet Webb, but not in the Bubble. It doesn't have to be far away. It could even be the parking lot. Then Elke can get her guns—"

"Why should he believe a note?" Andrew interrupted.

"Have you got any better ideas?" Gaia demanded.

"Right," Will said. "We get that note to Webb *and* we keep an eye out for Wickett. We have to hurry."

"I'll write it," Gaia said. She was already running to the Maserati. "I'll make sure Webb gets it."

"What guns is she talking about?" Will said to Elke, his eyes on Gaia's back.

"A semiautomatic rifle," Andrew said grimly. "A Taser. And there was a pistol—"

"*Guns,*" Elke interrupted. "What else do you need to know?"

A few moments later, Gaia emerged from the car with a folded sheet of paper. "Webb will be down in five minutes." She jogged toward the driveway. "I *guarantee* it."

It wasn't easy to blend in.

A fourteen-year-old girl in jeans striding into a restaurant that catered to businessmen and middle-aged couples in silk dresses and suits. The only way to carry this off, Gaia decided, was to make it seem as if she didn't notice or care.

She'd quickly spotted the elevator that had to lead up to the Bubble and headed right for it. It was only when she got there that she wondered why no one had approached her. The note felt hot in her hand. She was anxious to deliver it.

Then she saw the maitre d', who earlier had greeted Saxon Webb. He was making his way toward her, smiling. "Mademoiselle? May I help?"

"Yes, you may," Gaia said, hoping her faked upper-class English accent sounded convincing. "My uncle is dining here tonight. Mr. Saxon Webb. I don't want to disturb him, but I do need to get a note to him."

Behind his automatic smile, the maitre d' had been evaluating her. This girl looked bedraggled and downright strange. But then, rich English children were often scruffy, as he knew from his own experience in the restaurant. And this girl did have a confidence about her. If there was even a chance she was Saxon Webb's niece, she had to be treated with the utmost respect. "Perhaps, mademoiselle, if you would leave the note with me, I can see that it is safely delivered."

"It *is* rather urgent."

"Of course, mademoiselle. You would like to take the note up yourself?"

Gaia stiffened. She hadn't actually expected to be invited up. And if Webb saw her, surely he'd recognize her.

"I think not," she said. "It really would be better if I didn't disturb him." She held out the letter. "But perhaps if you could take it now?"

"Certainly, mademoiselle."

The maître d' pressed the call button. He watched as Gaia backed away toward the wall, her bright brown eyes fixed on his face.

As the elevator doors closed behind him, Gaia glanced at her watch. *Rather urgent,* she'd said. That was a bit of an understatement. In more ways than one.

Eight minutes, Saxon Webb thought. David Wickett was cutting it extremely close.

He glared out at the lights of Kleinkirchen, anger surging through his veins. Why wasn't Wickett here already? Didn't he believe the threat?

Suddenly, the elevator pinged. Webb turned on it. *Wickett? At last—*

The doors opened to reveal the maitre d'.

"We *have* food!" Webb roared.

Then he saw that the man was empty-handed, apart from a tightly folded piece of paper.

"Mr. Webb, your niece is downstairs. She asked me to deliver this."

"My *niece?*" Webb strode over, grabbed the note.

By the time Webb had unfolded it, the maitre d' was already back in the elevator.

Webb scanned the black writing. Anger turned to incredulity. He read the words again.

"Sir?"

Pritt. He was watching him like an idiot. Webb read the note out loud, through clenched teeth.

"Flee this restaurant now, for your own good. There are people downstairs who want to kill you. Go to the church in Kleinkirchen. We have the plans for cold fusion and we will bring them to you. STORM.

"PS. This note will self-destruct at 9:25 p.m.

"What is this?" Webb thundered. "Who the hell is STORM?"

"Sir? If I may see?"

Something struck Webb. His eyes shot to his watch. The black minute hand of the Zurich-made, twenty-four-carat-cased chronometer glided almost imperceptibly to 9:25 P.M. Webb hurled the note away from himself. It shot past Pritt's astonished face—

And it exploded.

A split second later, a fracturing crack made Webb cower. He stared as one of the Bubble's picture windows exploded outward into the night.

38

Will flinched. The lenses of his binoculars suddenly burned orange. He had run down to the parking lot with Elke and Andrew, to keep a closer eye on Gaia. They were in the trees. Will was watching the Bubble—and now he was watching glass shatter! Flames billowed into the night.

Andrew jumped up. *"Gaia!"*

"She wasn't up there!" Will said quickly. "She wasn't in the Bubble!"

"Then where was she?"

"I don't know! I was watching Pritt!" Will's head jerked. The door to the Nest had been flung open. People started streaming out. They were shouting. A woman caught her shawl on a torch. It ignited. She screamed. Will lifted the binoculars back to the Bubble, but it was thick with smoke. He could see no one.

"I'm going to find Gaia," Andrew said.

"Andrew, wait!"

But Andrew had already started running toward the torrent of fleeing people. He met them head-on.

Elke had stood up. She was peering at the Bubble.

"Can you wait here?" Will said to her. "No matter what happens. Stay here and watch out for Wickett."

Elke nodded. She took the binoculars. "Who has bombed the Nest? Not MI6?"

"I don't think so," Will said grimly. Gaia had written that note. In *exploding ink*.

The air was shot through with panic. People were stumbling in their rush to get out. As Gaia's ears recovered from the explosion, she heard snatches of shouts.

"Wass?"

"Mon dieu!"

"Bill!"

"Al-Qaida?"

Gaia had been heading for the exit when the letter ignited. She'd gotten halfway across the dining room when she'd heard the glass smash.

For an instant, there had been silence. Then a woman had screamed. Customers started dashing for the door. A man pushing past her knocked over a table. Half-eaten steak and a bottle of red wine slipped to the carpet. Gaia crouched down behind the table. A well-meaning woman tried to grab her shoulder, to drag her up. But Gaia shook her off.

She knew something the diners did not: There would be no more explosions. They had nothing else to flee from.

Here behind the table, she could peer out at the elevator. She could wait, and she could watch for Saxon Webb, who seemed to be taking his time. Why hadn't he come down already?

Her plan had been tidy, Gaia thought—if slightly bigger in the execution than she'd intended. Still, the amount of ink had been relatively small. The explosion had sounded worse than it actually was. *Surely.*

Already, the dining room was almost empty. An old man

and his wife staggered out. The last to leave. The woman was crying. Gaia fixed her eyes on the elevator. *Come on.*

"Gaia!"

Andrew. He'd edged in, past the old lady. He was looking around wildly.

"Here," she hissed.

He ran over to the table. "Are you all right? What were you thinking?"

"I had to get Webb down!"

"You might have killed him! You might have killed yourself!"

"There wasn't enough explosive to kill anyone!" she said. *Hoped.*

A flash caught her eye. The indicator light above the elevator was glowing yellow. It had arrived. Gaia grabbed Andrew's arm. *"Get down."* They shrank back behind the table.

A moment later, a German voice called, "Sir!"

It was Pritt.

There was no response.

But Gaia could hear feet on the carpet, heading away from the elevator. And she could hear someone's heavy breathing. *Webb.* It had to be. He was scanning the room, she guessed.

"My hair . . ." Pritt. Again.

Andrew raised an eyebrow.

"Only hair," Gaia mouthed.

"My face!"

Andrew's eyes widened. Gaia frowned. If she'd hurt him, it was an *accident.* Pritt had tried to *kill* them.

"It is bleeding!" Pritt's voice was shaking. "I cannot touch my face!"

"It is nothing! Shut up!"

So Webb *was* here. And he *was* alive. Gaia had to look. She'd have to move to do it. She rolled forward onto her knees. She was about to peer out, when Andrew grabbed her to stop her. His grip was hard. She didn't cry out, but instinctively she pulled back—and her hand hit wood. There was a sudden *clunk*. She froze. Andrew stared at her, horrified.

"Hey!" Pritt's voice. "*Wer ist hier?* Come out!"

Heavy feet thumped across the carpet. Pritt was heading for the table. Gaia's heart raced. Andrew was still holding her arm. She pushed him away. Then she heard footsteps from the other direction. Someone was coming *into* the restaurant.

An English voice thundered: "You! *Boy!*"

Webb could mean only one boy. Gaia felt sick. The table was no longer any protection. She *had* to see.

When she stood up, she saw Webb, still close to the elevator. Pritt, halfway to the table, pressing a bloodied napkin to his right eye. His face was red, his mustache mostly gone.

And there was Will, between the table and the exit, his back to a beige door.

Guns.

Pritt was the first to pull. He took a black revolver from his jacket. Webb reached for a miniature pistol from a holster strapped to his ankle. He waved it. First at Will. Then Gaia. The mercury barrel flashed.

Will was opening his fists, spreading his fingers, showing he had nothing—that he was unarmed.

Pritt aimed his revolver at Will. His arm was unsteady. Tiny bright red marks crisscrossed his face. Cuts from shards of glass, Gaia guessed. She felt bad, but Pritt had *shot* at them.

"Get over there," Webb said to her. He jerked his gun toward Will. "With the boy."

Gaia's gaze switched to the gun. She could see down the black barrel. For a moment, it transfixed her. Then her legs responded. She edged away from the table over to Will. She wanted to look back at Andrew, but she ordered herself not to. So far, Webb and Pritt didn't know Andrew was even there.

Will's face wore a black expression. His eyes were fixed on Webb. What was he thinking? Gaia wondered. What could they do?

Webb and Pritt were down from the Bubble, but Wickett could turn up at any minute. She cursed her clumsiness. If she hadn't knocked her hand into the wood, Pritt and Webb might have acted on that note. They might have gone to Kleinkirchen. This was her fault. She had to think of a way out.

Then she felt Will's hand grip hers and his breath hot on her ear. "We're getting out of here. Backward. *Now.*"

Crack.

Will had just yanked her back so hard, she'd almost fallen. Something had smacked into the door frame, inches from her left shoulder. A bullet!

Will still had hold of her hand. As she ran, Gaia glimpsed

white tiles. Ovens. Sinks. Pans, steaming. The chefs had all fled. Will was heading toward an open door. She could see *Fire Exit* stamped on the glass. They were almost there. Then she heard a shout:

"Stop!"

Will was pulling her on, but she glanced back.

Saw a bald head. Pug face. Webb. He was aiming his gun right at them.

Andrew wiped his palms on his trousers.

From behind the table, he'd seen Gaia go to Will. He'd watched them suddenly vanish backward—and he'd seen the bullet hit the door frame! Now Webb and Pritt had run after them.

Think, Andrew ordered himself. He had a decision to make, and he had to make it now: Go after Will and Gaia and two men with guns, with nothing, or get Elke—*get help*.

39

Tiles shattered. Fragments of ceramic blasted into the kitchen. Webb's shot had been wild, but he'd wanted to scare the kids, not kill them—not yet.

"Stop. *Now*," he yelled.

They skidded. They stopped and turned. The boy pushed the girl behind him.

The exit at the far end of the kitchen was a good five strides behind them, and Webb had that boy in his sights. He was going nowhere.

Behind Webb, Pritt was breathing heavily. He sounded like a pig, Webb thought. It was revolting. But he had more pressing matters to deal with.

"Who are you?" Webb demanded, his voice sharp as ice. "What are you doing here? What do you think you know? Speak now. If you are convincing, perhaps I won't kill both of you."

There was a pause. Then Will said, "My name is Will Knight. I know why you're here. I know about Project FIREball. Edmund Pope—did you ever meet him? I met his niece in London."

He talked on, buying time, Gaia guessed, while he tried to come up with a plan. She thought furiously. Webb and Pritt had guns. What did they have? Or what could they use?

Her eyes scanned the kitchen. On the stove, she could see two commercial-sized stainless steel pans. They were bubbling. The liquid was dense and spitting violently. Oil.

"We looked around the Black Sphere," Will was saying. "We know what you're planning."

"Keep talking," Gaia breathed. "I have an idea."

Concealed behind Will, she reached into the pocket of her jacket. She'd pushed the pen in there after she'd written the note. The reservoir had to be half-full still. Her fingers touched something else. It was cold and hard. Then she remembered: Elke's can of pepper spray.

"We know about the report," Will was saying. "Hudson warned you about the risky drilling, and you're using it to try to blackmail Wickett. What have you done with Hudson? Where did you take him? Did you kill him?"

Gaia took a deep breath. She moved the can to her left pocket. In her right hand, she held the pen.

Will had finished his story—or as much of it as he was prepared to tell. He glanced back at Gaia. She didn't look at him, but she nodded slightly. Gaia had her eyes on Webb. His face was reddening.

"Then you know nothing that I don't," Webb said, "which makes you useless to me." A pause. "But not to others."

Webb closed his right eye. He was actually going to shoot!

"Wait," Gaia shouted. "I have what you want!"

Her voice had sounded shrill, and she was angry with herself. She had to appear confident.

The gun didn't waver, but Webb's right eye opened. He looked at her.

Gaia's heart pounded. With each beat, the anticipation spread through her body. Yes, she had a plan. But it was extremely risky. And Pritt's gun, as well as Webb's, was pointing right at her.

Very slowly, Gaia stepped out in front of Will. She saw Pritt tense. His hands clasped tighter around that revolver. Blood was still running from his chin. It pooled on the kitchen floor.

Ordering her hand not to shake, Gaia held up the fountain pen. "I have what you want right here," she said. "There's a miniature hard drive hidden inside. We got to Wickett first. We have his plans. Just like I told you in that note. If you'd come to Kleinkirchen, we'd have given them to you. *We are STORM.* And *we* have the key to cold fusion."

"You—" Webb started. But he stopped.

Gaia had just moved forward. She was at the stove. She was holding the pen close to the pan of bubbling oil. "Now put your guns down," she said defiantly. "Or I *will* drop it."

Webb stared. His tanned face turned blotchy, then pale. "Don't be a fool!"

Gaia hid her relief. He believed her. He actually believed her.

"I have the gun!" Webb spat, his eyes blazing. "You think I won't shoot you?" He jabbed the pistol in her direction. "Now, you put that pen on the floor. And get over by the sinks. Or I will kill you both!"

Gaia didn't move. She could not back down. She had to try to bluff Webb. She couldn't see Will's face, but surely he'd have worked out what she was planning. He'd be ready if Webb didn't obey.

Gaia took a deep breath. "No," she said slowly. "You put your guns down."

"You think I'm joking?" Webb's hand was shaking now with fury. "When I kill your friend, you will see I am not! Now, since you are children, we will play the little children's game. I will count to three. If in that time you do not do what I say, your friend suffers the consequences with a bullet through his head! *One . . .*"

Gaia's blood ran cold. She could see that Webb meant it. He'd shoot Will.

Webb had won.

She'd have to go with Plan B.

"Two . . ."

Gaia suddenly reached her left hand into her pocket and pulled out the can of pepper spray. Before Webb could say *three*, she threw first the pen and then the can into the boiling fat. The ink ignited at once, setting fire to the oil. Flames burst into the kitchen. But Gaia was already running—right behind Will.

The physics of what she'd just done raced through her head. The pepper spray was in a pressurized can. Heat the can to about 140 degrees Fahrenheit and the contents would expand to such an extent that the thin metal container wouldn't be able to take the pressure.

The cooking oil probably boiled at about 570 degrees Fahrenheit. So how long would it take the can to get to that critical 140 degrees—to explode?

As Gaia watched Will slam the fire exit shut behind them, she got her answer.

There was a bang. Then a scream. Gray smoke billowed against the glass of the door.

"What was in that can?" Will demanded.

"Pepper spray," Gaia said. "Elke gave it to me. It was all I could think of. I gave them a chance . . ." She looked up at him.

Will nodded.

If Webb and Pritt had survived the burning fat, they'd be in agony right now, he thought. Their eyes would be streaming and closing up. Pepper spray contained an extract of chili peppers that made mucous membranes swell. They'd feel like they were choking.

Gaia was still staring through the glass door, which was keeping the smoke and the flames inside the kitchen. Will took in their new surroundings. He was surprised.

He'd expected to be outside, but they'd emerged into another room. It was rectangular. Long. Large double doors were at the far end. Will saw four vast stainless steel fridges. A pile of sacks. Cardboard boxes, flattened. This had to be the storage room.

"Gaia, we need to get out of here," Will said.

She didn't move.

Vanya's cigar box was still slung on Will's belt. Quickly, he opened it up and flipped the insects onto their backs, until he found the roach marked with a 4.

Will held it to his mouth. "Elke, we're round the back, in a store room. We're coming out now. Meet us—" And he stopped.

Gaia was backing away from the kitchen. The fire door was *opening*.

From behind him, there was another noise. A creaking from the double doors. Will saw a slash of black sky as they were pulled back.

Elke, he thought, with a surge of relief. That was quick! But as the figure stepped inside, the surge turned to stone.

"No," he whispered. "Not you."

Gaia's head swiveled. She wasn't sure who to look at.

Saxon Webb, who was stumbling from the kitchen, retching and coughing as he pushed the fire door closed.

Or David Wickett.

A photograph on Wickett's old Kings College web page had showed a gaunt face, sunken eyes, thinning brown hair. Now it was even thinner, and those eyes looked fearful. Wickett was breathing hard.

Gaia heard Will hissing into the roach: "Elke, the back doors. Now! Wickett's turned up. Webb's here!"

Webb coughed again. His eyes were almost swollen shut. Blood and phlegm were spattered across his face. There was no sign of the pistol—or of Pritt.

Webb suddenly plunged his hand into his pocket.

"Wickett, get out of here!" Will cried.

But Wickett didn't move. He was staring at Will, confusion plain on his face. "I—I have the plans," he said, his eyes flicking to Webb. "I came, as you asked."

Webb thumped himself hard in the chest. He was clutching something in his other hand. Now Gaia saw that it was a phone. "The plans?" he croaked. The capsaicin must have been burning. "This girl told me *she* had the plans!"

"She was lying! I have them here, around my neck. I brought them to you." Wickett touched the memory stick.

Gaia's thoughts raced. If Webb believed the plans had gone up in burning fat, they had nothing left to bargain with.

"It's true," she said. "I was lying. I was trying to get you to put down your gun."

Webb wiped sweat and blood from his eyes. "Wickett, put the chain on the ground," he spat. "Then get out. All of you. Or I speed-dial my colleague back at the Sphere—and you know what will happen then."

Wickett nodded. Without hesitation, he lifted the chain from his neck. For a moment, he held it. The locket swung like a hypnotist's pendulum. Gaia stared. They had to do something. But if they tried anything, Webb might dial Schwarz and set the quake in motion. Where was Elke, she thought. *What was Elke doing?*

Will was thinking exactly the same thing. Could Pritt have escaped back through the kitchen and somehow gotten to her—and to Andrew? He doubted it. Elke was a professional spy and a professional killer. She was highly trained and she was armed and—

The wooden doors behind him opened. Will swung around.

Andrew. He dashed in, his face pale.

Then Will saw the barrel of a gun. It was black and long. Will recognized it—Elke's microwave weapon. It was poking into the storeroom. Then he saw the large hand that gripped it, and the red scales of the Snake. Elke was here! She could stop Webb. She could force Wickett to give them the plans.

So why did he have the sudden feeling that something was terribly wrong?

40

"What the hell is going on?" Shute Barrington paced the corridor, talking to himself. The Eagle was circling, but at that moment, it was about as useful as a piece of space junk. It was telling him *nothing*.

Three minutes ago, the thermal cameras had picked up one adult running into the Nest from the rear. Barrington had been using the robot to watch the front entrance, where Andrew had been standing with a woman. He'd only just caught the running figure. And he'd been too late to glimpse the face. Wickett? It was possible.

But where were the police? And who was this woman? Barrington had seen her before—at the top of the driveway, when Will had arrived in the car. He had a decent face shot. But he didn't recognize her.

Barrington ran up to his room. He dialed the number for Karl Lorenz and got through to an assistant, who explained that the officer was unavailable. "Get him to call me! Shute Barrington! *Now!*"

Barrington downloaded the shot of the woman onto the laptop and he connected to the STASIS network. The photo databases should be accessible, so long as he had the right password—which he did. Barrington submitted the picture.

Thirty seconds later, he got a result.

Elke Hahn

Age: 47

Nationality: Swiss

History: Trained by the Swiss secret service. Resigned in 1982. Became a mercenary. Charged in 1988 with the murder of two smugglers involved in transporting arms across the Alps. Acquitted. Suspected of involvement in a European people-smuggling racket in the late 1990s, and the related killings of three policemen in Berlin in January 2000. No recorded activity since February 2002. Retired?

A retired mercenary! What was Andrew doing with a woman like that? Barrington thought. Was she threatening him? It hadn't looked like it. Was she helping him? It was possible.

But where were Will and Gaia?

Where was Webb?

What was Lorenz doing?

What was going *on*?

Barrington sent the Eagle back to the parking lot. It was empty now, apart from two people crouching in the trees. Just as this thought crossed his mind, they started to move.

Barrington auto-adjusted the focus of the low-light camera. He saw zips. Outdoor trousers. *Andrew.* And Elke Hahn. They were heading for that rear entrance. Elke was carrying two guns. One looked like a shotgun—but not one that Barrington had ever seen before. The other seemed to be a pistol.

Barrington tried Will's number again.

Voice mail.

He punched in Andrew's number and ran a hand through his hair.

The phone was ringing.

And ringing . . .

At last, Barrington heard: "Hi, this is Andrew. I'm busy right now. Leave a message and I will get back to you."

"Busy!" Barrington exclaimed. "Something of an *understatement,* I suspect."

41

"Everybody, stay exactly where you are."

Elke's voice was dead calm.

With her right hand, she held the microwave weapon. In her left was the Glock.

Wickett looked at her uncertainly. He slipped the chain back over his neck and backed up to the wall.

Webb took a step forward. "Who are you?" Spittle gleamed on his lips.

"It does not matter who I am," Elke said calmly. "What matters is what I want."

Webb's eyes narrowed. He held up his phone. "I warn you, if I press this button, it will set off a chain of events that will destroy the village of Kleinkirchen and kill more than two thousand people. Put your guns down. Back up. Or I will press it."

Elke said: "You think I care?"

Webb's expression faltered.

Elke snorted. "Do not deceive yourself, Saxon Webb. I am not secret service. I work for no one. Except myself."

There was something chilling in Elke's tone. Her face was set. She looked poised, in control. She was just doing her job, Gaia told herself. But she felt uncomfortable. Something wasn't quite right. Andrew had backed up toward Wickett, his face white.

"Elke works with us," Gaia said suddenly.

There was a pause. Her eyes still fixed on Webb, Elke said, "Gaia has the wrong tense. I *worked*. In fact, she has the wrong verb. I *used*."

Gaia stared at her. No. *No.*

"But Elke—" Andrew started.

"Shut up!" Elke's right arm swung so that the Glock was pointing at Andrew. "Shut up—and get away from Wickett. Over there, with Will. Gaia, you too."

Gaia couldn't believe what she was seeing. Elke had *used them*? Elke was betraying them? It was impossible. This had to be a trick. She was Vanya's friend. She'd saved their lives.

"*Now!*" Elke barked.

The shout made Gaia jump. She did as she was told. Andrew ran to Will's other side.

Will's face was black. "Elke, what are you doing?"

"What does it look like I am doing!"

"But Vanya—"

"Vanya should know better! He was strong once, but he has become a soft old man. What does he think—that I will help children out of the goodness of my heart?"

"No, because you owe him," Will said. "You said he saved your life!"

"And I saved his. Twice also. And I went to meet you because I was curious, and then—"

"And then you found out about the plans for cold fusion and you've been *using* us to get them ever since?"

Again Elke snorted. "You are children, and yet still your naivety surprises me. You should be thanking me! I have taught you a valuable lesson: *Trust no one.*"

She turned her attention back to Webb, who had been watching in disbelief. Then she swung the pistol to Wickett. His hand was around the memory stick.

"You—the locket on that chain—it holds the plans for cold fusion?"

Wickett looked stunned.

Elke shook the gun. "I said—"

"Yes!" Wickett said. "Yes, it holds the plans."

"Which he is going to give to me!" Webb raised the phone. His thumb was over the number 1. His eyes burned. Perhaps he should have brought backup. He should have hired bodyguards. But it was too late now. "I press this button and Kleinkirchen is destroyed!"

Elke tossed her head in irritation. "Are you senile, old man? You already told us that!"

Webb spluttered: "Put down your guns or . . ."

Will saw a split second of hesitation on Elke's face. Was she thinking about those innocent people? Was she wondering whether to shoot Webb?

A moment later, Webb yelped as the microwave beam caught his hand. It burned his flesh. And Will heard a hiss as the electronics inside the phone were destroyed.

Will felt a faint wash of relief.

Kleinkirchen was safe.

So, Will thought, Elke *did* have a heart—of a sort. She'd stopped Webb from pressing that button—saving more than two thousand lives. And she hadn't killed him in the process.

Clearly Webb didn't feel the same way. He was trembling with anger. Now he shouted: "Are you mad? Who do you think you are? You think you can come here and interfere with my business. Do you know who I am? *Do you know what I will do to you!*"

He started to run at her.

Will's eyes shot to Elke. He saw her drop the microwave weapon. She closed both her hands around the Glock. And she fired.

Beside Will, Andrew leaped back. He moved so violently, he smacked his shoulder against the wall. Gaia's hands flew to her head. She was gripping her temples. Will felt nausea rise. David Wickett was shaking. His knuckles were white around the memory stick. Saxon Webb . . .

Will forced himself to look. Saxon Webb was on his back. *Dead.*

Why hadn't he listened to Barrington? He shouldn't have told Elke anything. But she was *Vanya's friend* and they'd needed help. Now she'd betrayed them—and she'd killed Webb.

Then Will heard a new sound. It was in the distance, but it was unmistakable. The Nest was half an hour's drive from the nearest village, Elke had said. And that was a siren. The police were coming. *At last.*

Elke heard it too. She swerved to face David Wickett. "That locket: It holds the plans for cold fusion—you swear *on your life?*"

"Yes, yes, I swear, on my life!"

"Then give it to me before I shoot you!"

Wickett's arm was shaking. The chain trembled as, once more, he lifted the memory stick from his neck, and held it out. Elke took two quick steps forward and grabbed it, slipping it over her own head.

Gaia's face was close to Will's shoulder. She whispered, "What do we do?"

"Don't move," he whispered back. "Don't speak." Will tensed. Elke was aiming the pistol at Wickett's head.

Wickett shrank back. He looked confused. "I have given you the plans. Take them. Run now. The police are coming."

Elke tut-tutted. "So brilliant, and yet you do not understand. When I said give me the locket before I shoot you, the statement was not contingent, it was temporal! You understand? Give first, then I shoot. This is business. Pure and simple. You also have these plans in your head. If I let you live, you can write them out, you can release them tonight, and the value of this memory stick becomes zero. This locket is valuable only if you are dead."

"*No!*" Wickett's hand started to move for his pocket. "No, I can come with you. I can explain the plans. You need me to—" And his fingers clasped around the butt of his guard's gun.

Will watched. What else could he do? He knew what was going to happen. Gaia looked up at him, her face stricken.

"What is that? A *gun*?" Elke's voice was laden with disbelief.

A shot rang out.

Gaia's face crumpled. Will held her arm. He watched Elke pick up the gun that Wickett had dropped. Wickett was slumped on the ground. He wasn't moving. Will's heart thudded so hard he could barely breathe. Andrew was crouching in a ball, his arms around his legs.

The sirens were getting louder now.

If she would shoot Webb, Will thought . . . If she would shoot Wickett . . .

But Will wasn't going to cower. And he wasn't going to beg. He stood up.

Elke met his gaze. He saw a moment's hesitation on her face. What was she thinking? That if she killed him and Andrew and Gaia, MI6 would hunt her down? They'd do that anyway, Will thought. But Vanya would come after her too. And he would never give up.

Elke swallowed. "If you want to live, tell the police the killer was masked," she rasped. "I need twenty-four hours. Then you can tell the truth, if you like. I will be gone, and it will not matter to me. But for now, stay here. *If you try to follow me, you will die.*"

Seconds ticked.

Five since Elke had fled the storeroom with the plans for cold fusion.

Six. Seven.

The microwave weapon was on the ground, where Elke had left it. She had the Glock, and Wickett's gun. She'd wanted to travel light, Will guessed.

He ran to the weapon. It was heavier than he'd imagined.

"What are you doing?" Andrew asked. He was still crouched with Gaia by the wall.

"I'm going after her," Will said.

Andrew's blue eyes blinked furiously. "She'll kill you, Will. You heard her. Let her go!"

Will shook his head. He had to follow her. He had to do

what he could. Barrington had the Eagle. Between them, they had a chance.

"I'll go with you," Gaia said.

"No—"

"There's no time to argue, Will! I'm going with you." She looked at Andrew. His face was white.

"Andrew, one of us has to stay here and call Barrington," Will said. "Tell him what's happened. Then hide before the police get here. We'll come back for you." He held the microwave weapon against his chest. He was trying not to look at Webb and Wickett.

Eleven seconds.

Andrew didn't want to stay behind. But someone had to. And he couldn't help it if part of him felt relieved. He nodded.

Twelve.

Gaia ran to Will. "Come on!"

42

"Why!" Barrington thundered. "Why didn't you call me earlier!"

Hiding in the trees beside the parking lot, Andrew tried to explain. Things had happened so fast.

"You're sure they're dead?" Barrington asked.

Andrew swallowed. "Yes."

"Charlie Spicer called me from Interlaken airport forty minutes ago. He's on his way. Find somewhere secure to wait until he gets there. He'll triangulate your position from your phone signal."

"What are you going to do?"

"I've got the Eagle," Barrington said grimly. "I'm going to stop her."

"Will and Gaia—"

"Are fools for going after her, but they'll be all right," Barrington said. "I'll make sure of it."

"But why weren't the police here earlier?" Andrew asked. "Why didn't they stop Webb? Where are the MI6 field officers? They didn't come!"

There was a short silence. "Later," Barrington said. "We'll talk about it all later."

Andrew shoved his phone back inside his pocket. The sirens were loud now. He could see the flash of colored lights from the main road. Another few seconds, and the police would be streaming down to the Nest.

He was about to head deeper into the woods when he heard another sound. A twig snapping.

Through the trees, he could see a man moving from behind the rear wall of the Nest. He was staggering. Limping. He stepped into the moonlight and Andrew's pulse rocketed. It was *Pritt*.

It was obvious the man was injured. He stumbled into the woods, reached into his pocket, pulled something out.

Three seconds later, Andrew saw movement in the shrubs on the other side of the parking lot. A shadow. It rose into the air. A black disc.

Running helped clear Will's head. As his blood pumped harder, his thoughts stopped seething.

Elke had a good lead. She was almost back up at the main road. He and Gaia were racing through the fir trees lining the driveway. The ground was littered with branches. But this was no time to tread carefully. Will held the microwave weapon tightly. And he glanced up as suddenly, the Eagle swooped above their heads. It reached Elke in a second, then just . . . hovered.

"What's Barrington waiting for?" Gaia panted.

Perhaps Barrington was waiting to get a clear shot, Will thought. Or perhaps he was worried that if he hit Elke with an electric bullet, he'd also fry the memory stick. But if he just hit her in the leg, at least it would bring her down.

"Just shoot," Will whispered. "Barrington, *you have to shoot.*"

"Dammit, *shoot!*"

Barrington was hitting the FIRE icon, but nothing was happening.

"Not now!" Barrington said through clenched teeth. "Don't you bloody jam up now!"

To get rid of the software gremlins, and to get the beak working, his only option was to try rebooting the system. It would take a good thirty seconds.

Barrington cursed. He had no choice. Elke Hahn was firmly in his sights. She was on the road, and she was running toward the Maserati.

Two fire engines. Three police cars. They came thundering down the driveway before screeching to a halt outside the Nest. Within seconds, a dozen police officers were staring up at the devastated Bubble. Smoke was pouring through the roof of the dining room, Andrew noticed. Obviously a fire was still burning in there somewhere.

Andrew backed farther into the woods, his eyes still fixed on Pritt. The man was sitting down, with his back against a trunk. His head was bent over what had to be the control pad for the Frisbee. What was he planning? Whatever it was, Andrew thought, it would be dangerous for Gaia and Will.

Andrew decided he had two options: Either he could try to use physical force to overcome Pritt and wrench away the control pad, or he could see whether it might be possible to intercept the wireless data stream, and hijack the Frisbee remotely.

Andrew knew where his skills lay.

⊙ ⊙ ⊙

"Go on!" Will breathed. *"Fire,* Barrington!"

They were at the main road. Fire engines and police cars had just raced down beside them. Ahead, they could see moonlight glinting off a wing mirror of Elke's Maserati.

She was almost there. Soon she'd be behind the wheel. The Eagle was still just hovering. If Barrington didn't want to shoot her, why didn't he at least blast the tires?

Will stopped running. Gaia shot past him, then turned and looked back.

"Something's wrong with the Eagle," Will said. "We have to do something."

"Like what?"

His eyes went to the microwave weapon.

"It's too dangerous. She's got a gun, Will!"

"Someone has to stop her from getting away."

He glanced up again. The Eagle was doing absolutely nothing. Then Will saw something else moving above the trees. A black disc. He stiffened. No. *No.* It couldn't be.

He looked back at Gaia. Her eyes widened. Will saw the whites gleam in the darkness.

"How?" she said. "Pritt?" Was it possible?

What if he'd escaped from the kitchen the way they'd gone in? she thought. He might have run to safety. He might be controlling the Frisbee. She stared as it flipped on its side, started to spin, and headed right for Elke. "What if it hits the memory stick!" she hissed, then winced as a flash of white light whizzed through the air. *White* light. But the Frisbee shot *red*! Then she realized what was happening. The Eagle! It was firing!

270

Another flash. Tarmac smoked. And the Eagle swept on, toward Elke. The Frisbee hovered, then shifted. It started to spin, hot on the bird's carbon-fiber tail.

Will and Gaia threw themselves down among the trees. Elke had seen the flash too. She was running backward now, facing them, her eyes fixed on the Eagle. She lifted her pistol.

"Now, Barrington!" Will urged quietly. *"Do it now!"* He squeezed his eyes shut. A red beam had just lit up the sky. *The Frisbee was firing!* When Will opened his eyes, he saw Elke crouching by the Maserati. She was still gripping the pistol. The Frisbee circled, and it started to arc back—not toward her, but right at the Eagle.

Another red beam flashed. A flurry of sparks exploded. The Eagle juddered, then it swept high before swerving and dropping like a stone. It fired as it fell. A hail of electric bullets filled the night air. The Frisbee fled. The Eagle raced after it.

Will could hardly believe it. Elke had her hand on the car door—*she was about to get in*—and the Eagle and the Frisbee were locked in combat!

The microwave weapon was fitted with sights. But in these conditions they were useless. The Frisbee was moving far too fast. It was impossible to track it, let alone hit it. If Will did fire, he'd risk catching the Eagle by mistake.

"Can you get it? *Will?*"

"No!" Angrily, he lowered the weapon.

Down the road, Elke had stopped watching the robots, which were still absorbed in each other. She was yanking open the car door, about to drive away with the plans for cold fusion. Will couldn't let her. He stepped out into the road. He was exposed, but he'd need a clear shot. He heard Gaia yell out behind him. A red laser beam flashed.

"Will!"

He didn't respond. He had to concentrate. The moonlight was dim. But he'd shot an air rifle hundreds of times. In the garden of his old home in Dorset, he'd regularly hit a bull's-eye just a hundredth of an inch across. All he had to do was breathe out, line up the target, and—

Fire!

He staggered backward. The kick had been stronger than he'd expected. Then he dashed sideways, back to Gaia among the trees.

Will's eyes flicked over to Elke. She seemed to be staring at the car. *But had he hit it?* If he had, the microwave beam would have turned the Maserati's high-tech insides to mush. Elke wouldn't even be able to start the engine.

Elke was getting in now. She slammed the door shut. Overhead, the Frisbee rocketed past, the Eagle right behind it. Will could only wait.

And wait . . .

The engine wasn't starting.

Two seconds later, Elke jumped out. She stood on the road, gun raised. She was squinting in their direction. Suddenly, she flinched as the Eagle dived from nowhere, a red beam slicing above its tail. As soon as the robots had passed, Elke turned and began to run.

Barrington's jaws were clenched, his muscles like rocks. But he felt nothing. Heard nothing. The *Music of the Western*

Isles was still echoing from the restaurant, but for Barrington it might as well have been playing on the moon. Every atom of his body was focused on the Eagle's controls and on the video screen.

The Eagle's cameras had picked up the red flash. Then the on-board impact sensors had fired. The laser had clipped the tip of the Eagle's right wing. Enough to unsettle the bird. Barrington had to learn to compensate for the loss. It didn't take long.

Now he caught glimpses of the countryside as the Eagle swooped and dived. He saw the Maserati, and Will and Gaia. And *Elke*. He had to stop that woman, but he was engaged in aerial combat. Barrington had no idea who was controlling the Frisbee, but he'd read the patent months ago. This was *InVesta* technology.

Suddenly he saw the Frisbee slicing back toward the Eagle. It was skimming the tops of the trees and turning fast, preparing to fire. Barrington waited until the last moment, then he sent the bird racing sideways.

Moves from World War II movies—it was all he had to go on. But when it came to agility, the old fighter planes had nothing on these robots. The Eagle could hover, stationary, upside down. She could spiral with ease. She could—*yes*, she could shoot electric bullets at the enemy! Barrington almost whooped as he saw the white bursts. *But the Frisbee was still coming.* He had missed!

Barrington sent the bird soaring. Her cameras showed stars. Then he folded her wings and brought her back. She was diving faster than a peregrine falcon, the quickest animal ever clocked in the air. Two hundred twenty miles per hour.

The Eagle was a blur. She was closing in fast. She was right on target. The Frisbee was in range. *FIRE!* Barrington's heart skipped.

Then the camera feed went dark.

The on-board impact sensors had registered *nothing.* But Barrington caught a glimpse of a branch. The Eagle was still flying! She'd entered the woods. Dead ahead was a black disc. The Frisbee. Still moving. Dammit. He tried to fix it in the Eagle's high-tech sights.

Barrington urged the Eagle back to top speed. She was catching up. She was closing in! The Frisbee ducked east. It flipped on one side and slipped between two trunks. The Eagle followed. Barrington's reflexes were lightning. His brain had a hotline to his hand. He fired! And he cursed. The Frisbee had unexpectedly right-angled.

It was burning up the air. Now it was cartwheeling, lasers shooting. Branches burned. A trunk was sliced in two. Barrington saw the tree start to topple. His hand jerked. He pulled the Eagle back. He flinched as another laser shot grazed the feathers on her head. Then the Frisbee vanished. It had swerved up behind a tree. Was it hiding in the branches?

This was turning into a dogfight. Though his bird was fast, she was being outmaneuvered. He *had* to give her a fighting chance. He had to lure that Frisbee back out of the woods.

Barrington sent the Eagle soaring high above the trees. He could see stars again. The silver moon.

He nudged the low-light camera down—and saw the Frisbee. Now Barrington cut the Eagle's speed. She hovered.

Ahead, the Frisbee started to rise from the fir trees. It was preparing to spin. It was going to take a shot. Then Barrington let her loose. She was fast as a catapult. He opened the beak. He was ready. *FIRE!*

A second. Longer. The cameras showed trees. Sky.

Barrington's heart pounded. What had happened? Where was the Frisbee? The faintest trace of bagpipe music entered his consciousness.

"Where are you?" he said out loud. "Where the hell are you?"

Barrington panned the Eagle's cameras. Infrared showed nothing. Then the low-light cameras picked out a black shape. It was circular. And it was on the ground. The Frisbee. It was shuddering. It was down. *"Yes!"*

Gently now, Barrington pushed the controls, sending the Eagle in for a closer look. He'd do a quick fly-by, then he'd bring her right out—

Barrington's spine seized. The cameras had just detected a red flash. The Frisbee was stirring. It was starting to rise. Had it been *faking*?

The Frisbee suddenly spun upward, faster than the Eagle's cameras could track it. Barrington jerked the Eagle's head and saw a rush of forest. Then the cameras shook violently. The impact sensors screamed. It was the strangest sensation—as though he himself were falling.

A split second later, the video feed went black.

43

Andrew gritted his teeth. He'd just tapped into the Frisbee's video feed. In about another twenty seconds he'd have physical control over the robot. *Nineteen. Eighteen—*

Then on the screen of his smart phone, he saw the Eagle blown apart! Fragments of carbon fiber burst through the sky.

"Damn!"

Andrew could still see Pritt. The man hadn't moved. But now that the Eagle was down, the Frisbee was free to go after Elke.

Or Will and Gaia.

Come on, Andrew urged himself. Almost there. Come on!

Elke was fast. She veered away from the road and down the mountainside. Will and Gaia followed.

They were in the trees. The firs were dense, blotting out the moonlight. Ahead, Will could just make out Elke's red T-shirt darting through the trunks. He and Gaia were making a lot of noise. Surely Elke could hear them. Will glanced up through the branches. No sign of either the Frisbee or the Eagle. But the Eagle would come. He was sure of it.

Will stumbled. He nearly dropped the microwave

weapon. It was heavy. Perhaps he should leave it. Will knew he wouldn't use it on Elke. Wickett was dead. The secret to cold fusion existed only on that memory stick. Will didn't want Elke to have it, but he knew he wouldn't destroy it just to stop her.

Suddenly he ducked. He'd heard the crack of a pistol shot! Saw a flash of white. Elke's face. She had heard them! She was shooting! But she didn't stop. The red of her T-shirt raced on through the trees. Will glanced back at Gaia.

"*Go on*," she panted. "The Eagle will come."

Will looked up and saw only stars. He ran on. They were coming to the edge of the woods. He could see grass ahead. The slope was flattening out.

Then Elke was out of the trees. She was on open ground. She was turning! *Crack!*

Will ducked. Gaia ran into him. They fell. As Will's injured hand hit the ground, he smothered a shout. He scrambled up. And stared. A shadow had just swept past overhead.

A disc-shaped shadow. *The Frisbee.*

"Where's the Eagle?" Gaia whispered.

Will looked back. It was nowhere to be seen.

No, he thought. *No!* There was no way Barrington could have been beaten. *Surely.*

The Frisbee was cutting an arc through the sky. Was it coming for them? Gaia crouched. Will lifted the microwave weapon to his shoulder. *Concentrate*, he told himself. *Take aim—*

No! He'd missed his chance! The Frisbee had suddenly veered to the west. Red flashed. The laser was firing. The robot started to spin. It ducked, then it soared, blasting red through the sky.

Will hunched back over the weapon. But he couldn't get a fix. The Frisbee was zigzagging, shooting all over the place, as if out of control. It spun faster and faster, a deadly Catherine Wheel.

Then suddenly, the Frisbee froze. The beams stopped. Elke raised her pistol. And the robot rocketed up, until Will could barely see it.

"What's it doing?" Gaia whispered.

Will looked at her. "I have no idea."

Back in the parking lot of the Nest, Andrew's heart was thudding wildly.

At last, he had control of the Frisbee! He heard a low curse through the trees. *Pritt.* The man wouldn't have a clue what had happened, Andrew thought. He'd just assume the wireless connection had dropped.

Now Andrew had to follow through. This was just like playing a computer game.

His smart phone showed Elke raising her pistol. She'd been firing at Will and at Gaia. Andrew couldn't let her do that.

He'd aim carefully. He'd try to hit her in the leg. Spicer would be here any minute. He'd go after the memory stick. He'd get Elke to the hospital.

Andrew's jaws were clenched tight. Every nerve in his body was rebelling. *Shooting at someone?* How could he do it? He *had* to, he told himself. He had to help Will and Gaia.

Quickly, he sent the Frisbee into a spiraling retreat. The robot's camera showed Elke, still aiming—with two guns, now, one clasped in each hand. Andrew's fingers trembled. He knew what he had to do. Using the arrow keys, he nudged the primary laser toward her legs. He couldn't look. He squeezed his eyes shut. And he fired.

Gaia jumped up. A single laser beam had just blasted from the Frisbee—and Elke had fallen.

She was lying on her back. She wasn't moving. Now the Frisbee dove. It was coming down far too fast. *Smash.* It collided with the ground and shattered into pieces. Jagged black shards sprang up and fell back into the grass.

"Will—"

He thrust the microwave weapon into her hands. Elke was down. He had to take his chance. "Point it at Elke. Cover me."

"Will! No. Wait!"

But Will was already moving. He stepped over a broken branch and picked it up. If Elke was still able to fight, it would be better than nothing. His breathing was fast. He could feel his pulse throbbing hard in his neck.

Gaia yelled, "Elke!" If she was alive, Gaia wanted to know *now*, before Will got close.

No response. Elke didn't move.

"*Elke!*" she shouted again.

Nothing.

Gaia lifted the barrel of the microwave weapon. She took aim.

Will was closing in.

He saw Elke's pistol. It was lying in the grass, a few inches from her outstretched hand. She was spread-eagled. Her eyes were closed. Blood seeped down her side. The wound ran from the top of her rib cage, down across her stomach.

The memory stick was resting on her chest. It didn't seem to be damaged.

"Elke," he said.

No reaction. Will glanced back. Gaia was aiming the weapon. Will swallowed hard.

Gripping tight to the branch, he took two steps closer. Now he saw that her chest was moving. She was still breathing. Quickly, he kicked at the butt of the pistol, sending it skidding away across the ground. Wickett's gun was resting on the grass, just out of her reach.

Will crouched. The titanium chain gleaming. He had to hold his nerve.

Very slowly, he reached out. His sweating fingers touched her hair. Carefully, he reached under her head, to lift it. And he froze. Elke's face had twitched.

She grimaced. Will was about to drop her head, when her left eyelid flickered. Will stared as her lips parted. Then both eyes opened. She blinked up at him. Every muscle in his body was taut, ready to spring back. His eyes shot to Wickett's gun. His right hand gripped the stick.

Elke whispered hoarsely: "It hit me."

"Yeah," Will said.

She blinked at him. "I can't move. How bad is it?"

Will wasn't sure what to say. This woman had just killed two men. She'd been sliced across her stomach by a laser beam. And she was still alive. She was still talking. Had the laser cut through to her spine? Was she paralyzed? Or was she about to grab him?

"If you're wondering, when I say I can't move, I mean it. Now, how bad is it?"

"As soon as I get out of here, I'll call an ambulance," Will said.

Elke swallowed. "When you get out of here with the memory stick, you mean?"

Will didn't reply. Very gently, he lifted her head. His nerves were frayed, waiting for her to reach out, to throw him off. But she didn't. His hand trembling, Will pulled the chain clear. Quickly, he slipped it around his own neck. Then he backed away.

Blood still oozed from her wound. It gleamed red. *But he had it.* He had the memory stick. The realization pumped through his body.

"I'm going to get an ambulance," Will said, his chest tight. "Hold on."

"Wait." Elke paused, licked her lips. "You beat me. There aren't many people who can say that. Consider it an honor."

"I'll try to," Will said.

Then he dashed back to Gaia. She lowered the weapon. She was watching him closely, her face strained. She hadn't heard a word of the conversation. She'd only seen Will take forever to get the chain.

As he reached her, he lifted up the locket. It glinted in the moonlight.

"We've got it," he said.

Charlie Spicer jammed his foot on the accelerator.

He was driving fast, and talking even faster. "Yes, I have them. They're with me. Yes, we have the memory stick."

There was a long silence, evidently while Shute Barrington spoke.

"Yes. Yes, I'll tell them."

In the backseat of the black BMW, Will, Andrew, and Gaia were watching Spicer's face in the rearview mirror. They saw him throw down his phone. "Barrington wants to tell you well done."

"Well done?" Will said. "That's it?"

"For now. Of course, there'll be a lot more he'll want to say when you're safely back in London."

Through the windshield, Will could see the lights of Interlaken. Spicer was taking them straight to the airport. It would be best, he'd said, if they left Switzerland immediately, before official questions could be asked.

After picking up Andrew, and then Will and Gaia, Spicer had called an ambulance. Then he'd phoned the Swiss secret service, and left a brief message—including a request to look out for Gustav Pritt, who seemed to have fled the Nest on foot. There would be plenty of time for detailed discussions with other security agencies later, Spicer had said.

While Spicer had talked, Andrew had told Will and Gaia about the Frisbee. He hadn't been able to keep his voice from shaking.

"It's all right," Gaia had said. "Elke's alive. And you stopped her. Andrew, you did it."

Will had touched the memory stick, which was safe around his neck. He'd smiled grimly—but it had still been a smile.

Spicer hurled the BMW around a corner. Will gripped the back of his seat. "I have some questions. First, why was *MI6* holding Wickett? And Barrington said he'd get Webb arrested. What happened? Why weren't there field officers at the Nest?"

Spicer glanced into the rearview mirror. He looked uncomfortable. "Will, I'm afraid Barrington will have to explain."

Gaia glanced at Will. "Why can't *you* tell us?"

A sixty-degree, right-hand bend. Brakes screeched.

"Wickett's dead," Gaia said. "Webb's dead. We saw them killed. And we risked our lives to get those plans. And you can't even tell us why MI6 had Wickett?"

"I really am sorry. But Barrington will have to explain."

"What about the police?" Will asked. "If MI6 wouldn't arrest Webb, why didn't the police? Why weren't they at the Nest? Barrington said he'd handle it!"

A pause. "Will, I *am* sorry. But I'll have to refer that—"

"To *Barrington*," Gaia finished, shaking her head. "Right. So when's he going to talk to us?"

"When we get back to London. Once he's sorted a few things out."

"What *things*?" Andrew asked.

Spicer was silent.

Will flopped back against the seat.

"Look," Spicer said. "You did an excellent job. Better than anyone could have possibly expected. Barrington will tell you what he can, when he can. I've found out things today—" He stopped. "The real story is bigger than Project FIREball. But Barrington is the one who has to tell you. It's not up to me."

45

Fortnum and Mason, London. July 19

The music was classical. Something uplifting, with violins. Will strode into the elegant restaurant, and it struck him as surreal. Two old ladies were sipping tea. A table of Spanish tourists tucked into cake.

For two days they'd heard nothing from Barrington, and they'd had just one call from Spicer. He'd informed them, to Andrew's relief, that Elke was expected to make a full recovery.

Then, an hour ago, they'd each received this:

Afternoon tea. It's on me. Café at Fortnum and Mason, Piccadilly. One hour. SB.

They'd walked together from Andrew's house in Bloomsbury. Then, just as they'd reached the restaurant, Will's phone had vibrated. He'd checked the name of the caller. Surprises. They kept coming.

The first had been Abigail Pope's reaction when Andrew had phoned to say they were back in London. Charlie Spicer had asked them not to tell anyone anything about events in Switzerland until Barrington had debriefed them. But Andrew had felt that the least they could do was inform Abigail they were home, and that in due course, information should be coming her way.

Andrew hit speakerphone. He wanted Will and Gaia to share in Abigail's praise.

"Hello, Abigail Pope."

"Abigail, it's Andrew." He smiled. "Just to let you know we're back. It's a bit tricky for us to tell you much at the moment, but we found out a great deal. Very soon, we should be able to explain in a bit more detail."

The silence lasted five seconds. "Ah, thank you. I'm so glad you've called . . . It's just, we've had a visit. I'm not supposed to talk about my uncle anymore."

"What do you mean?" Andrew asked, surprised. "A visit from whom?"

"Some men," Abigail said vaguely. "They explained what happened to my uncle. I should have let you know, I'm sorry, but it's all happened so quickly."

"Ask her what happened to her uncle," Will whispered.

"Abigail, what did they tell you happened to your uncle?"

A pause. "I'm so sorry, but I have signed the official secrets act. I really do appreciate all your efforts. If you have expenses—"

Andrew was astonished. "No, thank you, Abigail. That's quite all right." The line went dead.

"What's going on?" Gaia said.

Will had shook his head.

Next, Andrew had called Greta. "I'm sorry I can't tell you exactly what happened. But it's safe to go back to the village." He hesitated. "And you should know—if you hadn't told us what you did, the situation might be very different. You really did help save Kleinkirchen."

Then Will had gone home, and his mother had insisted on taking him to St. Thomas's hospital. The cut in his hand needed stitches. His ribs would be sore for a few weeks.

The following morning, Will called Vanya. Will couldn't give him details, but he could tell Vanya that Elke Hahn had turned traitor.

"The Snake betrayed you!" Vanya's voice quivered with anger. "Did she threaten you? I'll find her, I'll—"

"It's all right," Will said. "She's in the hospital. She was injured."

"She will survive?"

"That's what we've heard."

"*Chert!* I will kick her out of the association. The Snake will—"

"Be locked up for a very long time," Will interrupted. "You don't need to do anything."

He heard Vanya whistle. "I knew she was an odd one, but I didn't think she was rotten. I saved her life! Well, I'm sorry. I don't know what else to say. And you're all right?"

"Yeah," Will said.

"Yes. Good. Well, perhaps there is no need to mention all this to your mother and grandmother? Eh?"

After putting down the phone, Will walked straight back to Andrew's house. Andrew shouted from the kitchen that Will should go down to the basement. He'd be along in a moment.

Gaia was at the dining table with a laptop. She looked different. It took Will a moment to realize it was just that she was clean and dry.

Bright brown eyes smiled. "You're looking a lot better," she said.

"I was thinking the same about you."

The smile broadened.

Then Andrew appeared with cookies and coffee.

For the next two hours, they scoured Internet news sites. Will didn't exactly expect front page headlines heralding the arrival of cold fusion thanks to STORM. But he'd expected *something*.

All they found was a short article in the business pages of the *Times,* noting that Saxon Webb, CEO of InVesta Corp, had been found dead of a heart attack in the multinational's Swiss R&D base. InVesta's share price dropped at the news, but quickly recovered.

And they also found this, in the Swiss newspaper *Tages-Anzeiger.* Gaia translated:

Mystery explosion bursts Nest's Bubble.

Diners fled the world-famous restaurant last night, after an explosion destroyed the private dining room. No one was injured. Accident investigators say a fire in the kitchen was the likely cause.

"A fire in the kitchen!" Gaia was incredulous. "There's nothing else—just background stuff on the restaurant, and who was eating there. *No one was injured.* I can't believe it. What about the dead bodies?"

Andrew regarded her grimly through his new frameless glasses: "Barrington will have to explain."

Gaia and Andrew were now sitting at a table inside Fortnum and Mason. Andrew was polishing his glasses. Gaia was watching trays of scones, sandwiches, and pastries being ferried around the dining room. She noticed Will. Waved.

"Everything all right?" Andrew asked as Will sat down heavily.

He hesitated. Nodded.

Andrew looked around for the restroom. "I'll just be a minute. If Barrington arrives, make him wait for me."

Will watched Andrew weave his way through the tables.

He hadn't expected that phone call. It left him feeling odd. In one sense, he was glad. But it stoked up old emotions.

Will made a decision. He fixed his eyes on Gaia.

Will was looking at her strangely, she thought. Intently. Gaia tensed.

One evening, the week before they'd gone to Switzerland, Andrew had asked her how she felt about Will. She'd been caught off guard, and she'd blushed and changed the subject. But the question had lingered in the back of her mind. Had Andrew asked Will the same thing about her, she'd wondered. If so, what had Will said?

"I want to ask you something," Will said. "You don't have to say yes. You can think about if you want."

Gaia's mouth felt dry. She waited.

"That call was from David Allott."

Gaia was momentarily disappointed. Then she recovered. She knew the name. David Allott—the MI6 field officer they'd met in Venice. The one who'd told Will he had things to tell him about his father's death.

"He's in London. He can see me tonight. I wanted to ask you—" Will stopped. He didn't know how she'd react. "Will you come with me?"

Gaia stared at him. She'd thought—no point in pretending otherwise—she'd thought he was going to ask her out. Then he'd talked about Allott, and she'd tried to put the thought out of her mind.

But this was *Will*, asking her to go with him to see someone who had information about his father's death. He wanted her there, in the part of his life he didn't talk to anyone about. A movie was nothing in comparison. She nodded slowly. "Yeah. Of course."

"Still no Shute?"

Will's head jerked up. Andrew was back. He sat down. "By the way, I've been trying to come up with a new meaning for STORM. How about Society To Once-again Rescue Mankind."

Gaia smiled. "The sentiment's right. And this was the toughest STORM job yet. But I think you'll find *once* and *again* are separate words."

"Gaia, I didn't think you'd be one to be so quibbly about English."

"*Quibbly?*" she said.

Will smiled. "How about this: Society to Take Out Retired Mercenaries."

Gaia's grin broadened. Andrew blinked at him. "But I didn't actually *want* to hurt her, you know. I was only trying to stop her—I—"

"It's all right, Andrew," Will said. "Spicer said she's going to be all right. You didn't kill anyone."

"You just saved the secret of cold fusion for the world," Gaia said, and patted his shoulder.

"Well, if you put it that way . . ." Andrew smiled. He pretended it was reluctant. Then he picked up the menu. "Shall we wait for Shute, do you think, or should we order?"

At that moment, a voice from the other side of the restaurant boomed, "So, what are three self-respecting teenagers doing in a nice place like this?"

Barrington sat down and waved at a waiter. "Sandwiches. Cakes. Coffee. Forget the tea." He slapped an envelope on the table. Dark circles rimmed his eyes. His hair was all over the place, his black T-shirt creased.

"You look like you haven't slept in days," Andrew said.

"That'll be because I haven't." Barrington looked around, annoyed. He bellowed: "What do you need to do to get served round here!"

"Give them a chance?" Gaia said. "Talk nicely?"

"Take after your example, you mean?" He sighed. "Look, I haven't got long." He jabbed a finger at the envelope. "Before I leave, I need your signatures on the papers inside. It's the official secrets act, in case you're wondering."

"Okay," Will said. He watched Barrington closely. He hadn't seen the man so jumpy before.

"First things first," Barrington said. "You did very well. You all know that. I didn't think for a moment I'd actually be relying on you again."

"Maybe you should just get rid of everyone else and hire us," Gaia said, unsure whether Barrington's comment was a compliment or not.

"Hmm," Barrington said. "I think there are laws against children working—only you don't do it for money, I hear, which might help us get around those pesky legal issues."

Andrew stared. How on earth did Barrington know about that? He must have talked to Abigail!

"So, what can you tell us?" Will said impatiently. "What's happened to the memory stick?"

Barrington took a deep breath. "The memory stick . . . yes, well, that's with our people. They're poring over it as we speak."

"So it's really got the plans on it?" Gaia asked.

"It's got *plans* on it," Barrington said. "But you have to remember that the six world leaders in the field of cold fusion all recently met an untimely death. We're scrambling to get people we can trust to decipher it."

"So you haven't deciphered it?" Andrew asked.

"Not entirely," Barrington admitted.

Gaia couldn't believe what she was hearing. "So you don't even know if the plans can be used?"

"I didn't say that. Wickett seemed sure he'd succeeded. If he did, we'll work through it soon enough."

Andrew adjusted his glasses. "Then there will be cheap energy for all."

Barrington caught the insistence in Andrew's tone. "Well . . . as you can appreciate, the invention of cold fusion doesn't only have scientific implications."

"It has political ones," Andrew said quietly.

"Yes. And before you get all teen-green on me, those implications cannot be dismissed. We're talking about an invention that could destabilize relations between dozens of countries. It would have to be handled extremely delicately. Or we could find ourselves with cheap energy but at war."

A waitress arrived with a laden tray. As soon as the girl had gone, Barrington took a swig of black coffee. "I will keep you updated on our progress. But now I suggest we move on. I have one question: The woman in a secure unit of the hospital in Zurich—I checked her out. She's got a checkered background, to put it mildly. How on earth did you come to team up with her?"

"Vanya," Will said. "He knows her."

Barrington raised an eyebrow. "Well, that explains everything."

"We only went to her because you wouldn't help us. I mean, couldn't help us," Gaia said.

"Hmm," Barrington said. "At the risk of repeating myself, let's move on. Other questions?"

"What about Pritt?" Andrew asked. "By the time Charlie got to me, he'd vanished."

"Gustav Pritt is in custody," Barrington said. "He's helping the Swiss intelligence agencies with their inquiries. And InVesta has been forced to open up its arms labs for inspection. If nothing else, I think the Swiss would rather like to get their hands on some of those Frisbees."

Will wasn't interested in Pritt. "Who exactly was Thatcher?" he said. "Why was MI6 holding Wickett? And why wasn't Webb arrested? I told you about the earthquake—you said you'd handle it."

Barrington thought for a moment. "I'm not sure how much you already know, so let's backtrack a moment. MI6 was keeping tabs on Project FIREball. Bailey—one of the scientists on that project—was being paid by InVesta. He was supposed to tell them if one of the team actually cracked cold fusion. Which he duly did. But InVesta screwed up. They'd intended to kidnap Wickett and kill the others—but then the explosives obviously went off too early, and Wickett escaped with the plans. He hid out for a while. Then he made a phone call to his housekeeper. And he received a phone call—from Saxon Webb, telling Wickett that if he didn't bring the memory stick to the Nest, Kleinkirchen would be history.

"Thatcher, Wickett's MI6 contact, was the only security officer with clearance to intercept Wickett's phone calls, using ECHELON," Barrington continued. "And as soon as Wickett made a call to his housekeeper, he effectively gave his location away. Thatcher used the signal to pinpoint his location, and he went straight to him. By the time he actually grabbed Wickett, he'd already overheard Webb and Wickett talk, so he knew about the meeting they'd set up at the Nest. So Thatcher had Wickett, with his plans—and Webb was lined up as the perfect buyer.

"Acting under orders, Thatcher took Wickett to a secret location—the old dairy—where he planned to keep Wickett nicely out of the way, until the meeting. Which he would go to, in Wickett's place. He intended to demand *vast* amounts of money from Saxon Webb in return for the memory stick."

"But what about the other MI6 field officers in Switzerland?" Will said. "Why didn't they work out what was going on? And surely they'd have been onto InVesta. Didn't they know about the meeting in the Nest? What about the police?"

Barrington swilled his coffee around the cup and downed it. "This is where the situation, for want of a better word, *deteriorates*. From the word go, the other MI6 field officers were fed seriously believable but false information. That misinformation was designed to keep them well away from

Wickett, Saxon Webb, and the Nest. The misinformation was shared with the Swiss secret service and the CIA, which also had operatives on the ground. When you told me about the earthquake threat, I knew I couldn't go to our field officers— or anyone else's. So I called the local chief of police."

"Who did nothing," Will said.

"Who, it seems, had already been contacted by the person distributing the false information. After our conversation, the police chief made a call—and he was told my facts were wrong, and Webb should be left well alone. More false information."

"So who was supplying all this false information?" Gaia asked. "Thatcher?"

"No. Thatcher wouldn't have had the power to do that."

"Then who?" Will asked.

Barrington looked at him. "You remember I told you Project FIREball was so secret that in theory only three people in Britain even have clearance to access the full detail."

Will stared. "The defense minister was behind all this?"

"No."

"The prime minister?"

"No, the other one!"

"What other one?" Andrew asked.

Will could hardly say it. "C."

46

"*C*?" Gaia was staring at Barrington. "You mean the head of MI6?"

Will and Gaia had met C in Venice. Will remembered a nondescript, moon-faced man. Gray hair. Gray clothes. "Are you sure?" Will said.

"What do *you* think? Of course I'm bloody sure! And Switzerland was only the tip of the iceberg. It looks as though C has had his fingers in other rather unpleasant pies. Like Sir James Parramore, the British businessman—you remember him from St. Petersburg? MI6 has been after him for some time. Now it looks as though C might have helped Parramore evade our officers in return for quite substantial sums of cash. Then there have been other instances when MI5 has blamed us for bad information. It seems they were right. But that bad information was *mis*information originating from C."

Will shook his head. This was a lot to take in. "How did you find all this out?"

"I'm one of the few people on this planet who could have found out," Barrington said. "STASIS runs the MI6 computer networks. *We*—or to be more specific, Charlie Spicer—accessed Thatcher's communications and worked out exactly who he was talking to. That 'who' was using top-level encryption. It's supposed to be utterly uncrackable. But our department designed it. It was Spicer who found out that Thatcher was talking to 'Churchill'—talking to C.

"The CIA had a clue something was wrong," Barrington continued. "Two agents were onto Thatcher, but they were found dead in their apartment yesterday morning. That visit by the U.S. vice president to London this week—part of the reason was to talk to the prime minister about FIREball." Barrington's blue eyes shot to Will. "Speaking of Vice President Dillane, I'm supposed to slap your wrist severely."

"Why?" Will asked.

"A postcard. Big Ben. *Hope you're enjoying your stay. MI5.* Ring any bells? The chief of MI5 is furious. I'm supposed to tell you that your actions showed an abysmal lapse of judgment, even for a fourteen-year-old." Barrington paused. "I'm also supposed to ask you how the hell you did it, and to tell you that it showed even the CIA aren't perfect. So, well done. *Unofficially.*" Barrington put his cup down.

"And well done in Switzerland," he said. "It sounds trite, I know. But I don't know what else to say. Once I knew C was feeding false information to the MI6 officers on the ground, I couldn't ask any of them for help—not without risking C finding out and stopping me. I thought the local police might be able to help, but I was wrong. I had to rely on you. And you came through."

"Again," Gaia said.

Barrington nodded. "Yes. Again. Now, I'm probably supposed to reward you. Perhaps you'd like something. A holiday, perhaps. On us."

"A *holiday*?" Gaia said.

Barrington bit his lip. "Yes, it doesn't really sound much, does it? The new head of MI6—it was his idea."

"Well, I think that's very . . . nice," Andrew put in. "Maybe somewhere a long way away."

"The Antarctic, then? Or maybe Australia?" Barrington nodded. "I'll get my people to call your people." He picked up a sandwich. Looked at it warily. "By the way," he said to Will. "I hear from Charlie Spicer that the invisibility glove is missing from Sutton Hall. That wouldn't have anything to do with you, now, would it?"

Will hesitated. He could say no. But it would be better to go with the truth. Or at least a version of it. "I thought it could do with some more testing," he said slowly. "And it does seem to have some . . . robustness issues."

"Robustness issues?" Barrington raised an eyebrow.

"Yeah . . . So, the new head of MI6," Will said, trying to change the subject. "Who is it?"

Suddenly Barrington's frown vanished. Will was amazed—his ploy seemed to have worked.

"Ah," Barrington said as he munched on a cucumber sandwich. "The new head of MI6, you say? The man with access to more top secrets than STORM seems to have lives?" Barrington beamed. "That would be me."

"*You?*" Gaia said.

Barrington pretended to be put out. "If I were you, I wouldn't go around insulting friends in high places."

"I didn't mean—"

"I know exactly what you meant," Barrington said. "And fair's fair. I'm not sure which is more surprising—a techie becoming head of MI6 or three kids securing the secret to cold fusion." He raised a china cup. "Apparently you're old enough to risk your lives for your country, but not old enough for champagne, so coffee will have to do. My very first toast as C: Here's to you."

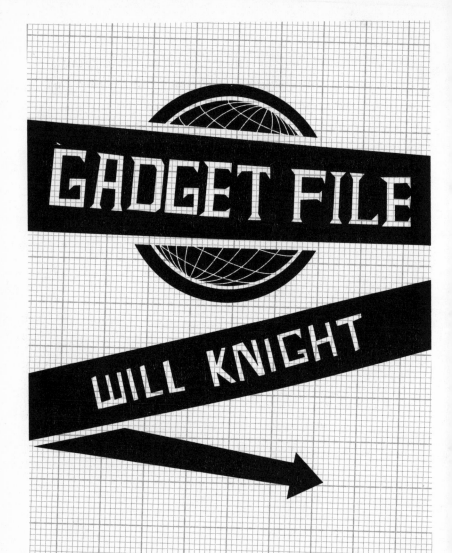

NAME

BRAIN SPRAIN

INTENTION:

To make someone more relaxed and trusting

SPECS:

Contains oxytocin, the natural human "trust hormone." Delivered using a modified asthma inhaler, which blasts a fine spray.

TESTED:

In the cafeteria at Sutton Hall (subjects were told the food was actually cooked by a top chef — and they believed it!) Also tested on CIA officer at Bushell House

CREATED: Sutton Hall

POTENTIAL MODIFICATIONS:

Ability to tailor dose according to size of target and desired duration of effect.

(Perhaps a better name would be Brain Drain — that's what it did to me . . . — Andrew)

HARD WEAR

INTENTION:
To provide armored protection but allow normal movement

SPECS:
Seven thin layers of Kevlar (bulletproof fabric) impregnated with silicon dioxide in a mix of ethylene glycol and ethanol. In normal circumstances, liquid acts like a lubricant. On impact, it hardens — turning the fabric into a shield.

CREATED:
Bedroom, London, and Sutton Hall

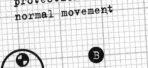

TESTED:
In the weapons testing lab at Sutton Hall (first with forks, then ice picks, air rifles, and semiautomatic pistols)

● POTENTIAL MODIFICATIONS:
Make impervious to beams from laser weapons??

(Make it quick-drying? So uncomfortable searching secret laboratories when you're wet ☺ — Andrew)

NAME

EYE SPY

INTENTION:

To provide wraparound visual surveillance

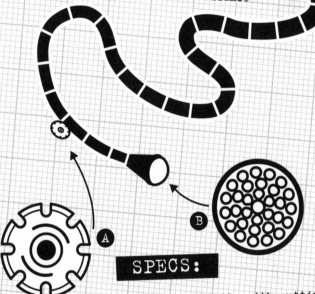

SPECS:

CREATED:

Bedroom and
Sutton Hall

Titanium-jointed tendril, with cutting
tool (tip is made of diamond, 500 microns
thick) and video camera, with wide-field
lens. Lens is a molded plastic dome,
one-tenth of an inch across. Surface
contains thousands of miniature
micro-lenses. Each channels light
to the center of the "eye."

POTENTIAL MODIFICATIONS: Make waterproof?

("Eye of the Storm" is much better! — Andrew)

NAME

???

CREATED:
Sutton Hall
(Shute Barrington's
personal lab)

INTENTION:
To render the wearer
(or at least the wearer's arm)
invisible

SPECS:

Constructed from a
meta-material with
nano-fibers. Length
of fibers match the
wavelengths of visible
light. Light striking
the fabric is pushed
around it — so it
appears invisible.

● POTENTIAL MODIFICATIONS:

It has to be more robust . . .

*(Why hasn't Barrington
made an invisibility
cloak? I've read about
them in books, so it must
be possible ;) — Andrew)*

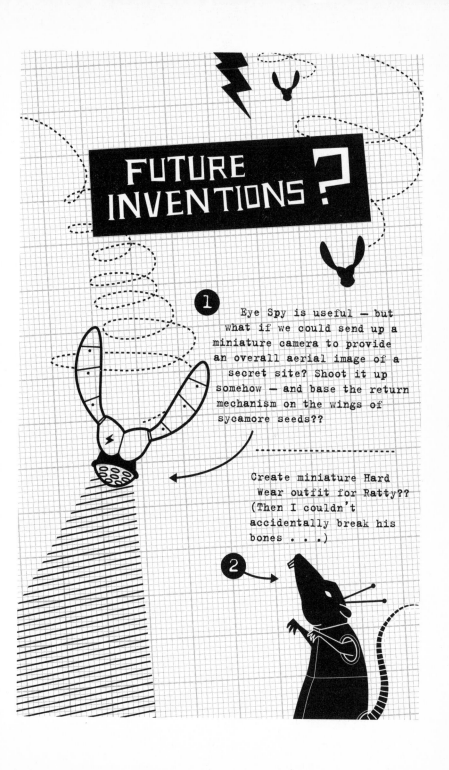

FUTURE INVENTIONS ?

1 Eye Spy is useful — but what if we could send up a miniature camera to provide an overall aerial image of a secret site? Shoot it up somehow — and base the return mechanism on the wings of sycamore seeds??

Create miniature Hard Wear outfit for Ratty?? (Then I couldn't accidentally break his bones . . .)

2

The Gadgets

1. The invisibility glove is based on research by a team at Imperial College, London, and Duke University, U.S. They have used meta-materials to make a shield that is invisible to certain wavelengths of light—but not yet to visible light.

2. Will's spray is based on research at the University of Zurich, Switzerland, which has found that men who inhale a nasal spray containing the hormone oxytocin become more trusting. (I've increased the extent to which they become more trusting in this book.)

3. A paper by Ajai Vyas of Stanford University, U.S., and colleagues, showing that the parasite *Toxoplasma gondii* can "brainwash" a rat into liking the scent of cats, was publishing in the Proceedings of the National Academy of Sciences in April 2007.

4. The U.S. Defense Advanced Research Projects Agency has plans to create an army of cyber-insects. The idea is to insert micro-engineered parts at the pupa stage. These parts would later allow the insect to be remote-controlled or to sense chemicals, such as explosives. This was the inspiration for the cockroaches.

5. Will's self-hardening armor is a genuine invention by researchers at the U.S. Army's Research Laboratories in Maryland. They've tested it with bullets fired from a gas gun and have stabbed it with an ice pick, and found that it offers better protection than Kevlar (the standard bulletproof fabric) alone.

6. Eye Spy's camera is based on an artificial insect eye

created at the University of California, Berkeley. The "compound lens" is made up of thousands of tiny components that each point in a different direction to give the insect a very wide field of vision. The diamond cutting tool is standard technology.

7. Gaia's exploding ink is based on a patent by British company QinetiQ. They have developed a printer cartridge filled with an ink that contains particles of aluminum, copper oxide, epoxy varnish, and alcohol. This ink is stable in liquid form, but becomes explosive when dry (though it does not use a sodium-based trigger).

8. A covert iris scanner (of the sort that lets Saxon Webb into the Black Sphere) has been patented by Sarnoff Labs in New Jersey, U.S. The system uses an array of cameras and an infrared strobe light, which lights up a person's face.

9. The Eagle's wings are based on a technology developed at the University of Missouri-Rolla. Guns that fire electric bullets (which also featured in *The Infinity Code*) are being developed in the U.S., under a Homeland Security Advanced Research Projects Agency program.

10. High-powered microwave weapons have been developed by the U.S. military, among others. They are usually mounted on vehicles.

11. InVesta's armed robotic Frisbees are based on a concept from U.S. company Triton Systems for a Frisbee-UAV (unmanned aerial vehicle). The UAVs would be able to fire armor-piercing explosives.

Notes on the Science

Cold fusion

I intended the information on cold fusion to reflect mainstream thinking. Most researchers do think it's crank science, and those claiming to have conducted successful experiments have become academic outcasts. But cold fusion experiments are still going on, and are being published, with some interesting results. Some highly regarded scientists are also receptive to the idea. The interview with Brian Josephson in *New Scientist* was published on December 9, 2006.

Earthquake induction

Some geologists think Taiwan's skyscraper Taipei 101 has reopened an ancient earthquake fault, and is triggering tiny "micro-quakes." British experts who studied the Indonesian mud volcano concluded that it was most probably caused by drilling for gas. Scientists in America have also published articles about earthquakes caused by underground mining in Utah.

So inducing an earthquake is thought to be possible, though it certainly wouldn't be easy.

Printer hacking

Some printers really are vulnerable to hacking. This discovery was made by a researcher at a company called Sec-1, and reported on the website of *New Scientist* magazine.

Acknowledgments

Thank you to James, to Harriet Wilson, my editor at Macmillan, and to Sarah Molloy, my agent. Special thanks to Jessica and Regina at Dial for another great job. If only I could run everything I write past you two.

Thanks also to Bruce at Clark Equipment in Sydney, who showed me around a Bobcat. And to David Cohen for the Russian.

New Scientist magazine (www.newscientist.com) was an important source of information about new gadgets, cold fusion, earthquake induction, and more.